MURDER ON THE DAY OF JUDGMENT

VIRGINIA RATH

MURDER ON THE DAY OF JUDGMENT

VIRGINIA RATH

COACHWHIP PUBLICATIONS
Greenville, Ohio

Murder on the Day of Judgment, by Virginia Rath
© 2019 Coachwhip Publications

Published 1936
No claims made on public domain material.
Cover image: Lightning / US Forest Service (PNW)

CoachwhipBooks.com

ISBN 1-61646-471-2
ISBN-13 978-1-61646-471-4

MURDER ON THE
DAY OF JUDGMENT

To My Mother

CHAPTER ONE
"LEAVE ELEANOR AT HOME"

The car slid into a deep rut, seemed about to settle there permanently and finally crawled protestingly out of it. Rocky Allan set his brakes; said:

"I wouldn't be surprised if we hadn't bust a spring that time," and got out to look under the back of the car.

Eleanor winked tears out of her eyes and touched her tongue where her teeth had just met on it. "Oh," she said, "has this car got springs? I wouldn't know."

Rocky grinned: his wife's occasional sweet sarcasm amused him. "They was sold to me for springs, honey, and they look like springs. And they ain't busted—yet."

He got into the second-hand coupé that only he loved and only he could drive successfully.

"Yet is the right word. I should be used to mountain roads by now but I've never seen one like this. How long has it taken us to come thirty miles?"

"I don't think that speedometer is awful acc'rate," Rocky said. "We've come nearer thirty-five—in about three hours. That ain't so bad, considerin' all these grades we've had to take in low."

"Darling, I wouldn't think of casting aspersions on your precious car. I'm sure it's done all that could be expected of any car. But have they never repaired this road? Most of the ruts look as if they had been made when the road was muddy."

"An' that would have been quite some time ago," Rocky agreed. "No, they don't bother to work this road. It ain't been used much for years. Oh sure, I've always heard about it. We started in such a hurry I didn't have time to tell you."

Eleanor produced the remains of lunch: four rather crushed and soggy ham sandwiches and a dilapidated piece of cake. "Suppose you tell me while we eat these."

"There's two grades: Placenta and Oso. This is the Oso. Both over the same summit and not very far apart on a straight line. The Placenta is easier; got more hotels on it and it's mostly paved or oiled, now. Since they did that hardly anybody ever uses this one."

"I believe you. We've only passed three cars—a good thing, considering how many places there were where we would have had to back down to pass. And we're going—where?"

"He said Coon Hollow."

"So named, I suppose, because there aren't any coons there?"

"Most likely. I've heard of it though. Remember Ferrier, that little station down the canyon from Merton? There's a trail there, up and down across two or three canyons, that brings you in somewhere near this Coon Hollow place."

Eleanor said: "No, you eat the cake. I don't want it. Rocky, what on earth do you suppose Mr. Pope wants with us?"

"He didn't," Rocky reminded her, "want you. He distinc'ly said not to bring you."

"He knew perfectly well that I would come. Let me see that wire again."

Rocky produced the telegram and they studied it together. Theophilus Pope had been rather lavish with words:

IF POSSIBLE, JOIN ME ON THE 24TH AT PLACE CALLED COON HOLLOW, ON OSO GRADE, FIVE MILES PAST MANZANITA. TURN OFF AT SIGN; GO FOUR MILES TO LARGE CABIN. BRING CAMPING EQUIPMENT. WOULD LIKE VERY MUCH HAVE YOUR HELP. LEAVE ELEANOR AT HOME.

"He is the most exasperating man! This is from San Francisco and he didn't send it until the twenty-third. . . ."

"Day before yesterday. It was too bad, us being out of town that day."

Rocky crushed out his cigarette, carefully, on the floor of the car. As the self-starter was a rather uncertain affair he had not turned off the ignition. He released the brakes and they bumped on along the narrow road.

"We're only a day behind and he could only have got there yesterday himself. Doesn't matter what he wants: we had to come."

"Oh, of course. But we haven't heard from him since he left us in Texas, and that was six months ago. He may have been halfway around the world and back in that time. I wonder how he knew we were in Merton?"

"Well, I told him we'd be goin' back there sometime. He could find out from the treasurer's office in the city if I was on the railroad pay roll."

"I suppose," Eleanor said, "that he is *not* minding his own business again. He— Is this Manzanita? Thank heaven for that!"

Manzanita was not a town, only a small wooden hotel and a little shack with "Store" painted across its front in crooked red letters. Both store and hotel had an appearance of disuse, and there was no human being to be seen outside. But a big dog dashed out and ran barking beside the car for fifty yards, and a battered Model T Ford was parked in front of the hotel.

"People live here all right," Rocky said in answer to Eleanor's question. "None of these places we've passed have anybody stayin' in them unless someone happens to break down in front of the door." He kept his eyes on the inaccurate speedometer as they rattled along the dusty, rutted road. "It's about five miles now," he said finally. "We'd ought to be—"

"There it is; the sign," Eleanor said, leaning over the side of the car. "See? On that tree. . . ."

A crude hand had been fashioned from a piece of bark, with the words "Coon Hollow" pointing down what an optimist might call a road. It was a narrow track that humanely did not disturb rocks, trees or fallen logs, but wound around them. Rocky grinned and tightened his big hands on the steering wheel.

"You'd better hold on, honey. I don't know about this."

"People have been over it, though, and not very long ago," Eleanor said. "You can see fresh marks of tires."

They narrowly escaped hitting a tree, took a nearly right-angled turn and came onto a large, flat clearing. But there was no cabin to be seen here and the road climbed up; up and over a thickly wooded hill where small trees and underbrush scraped the sides of the car. Then from the summit of that hill down to a riotous mountain river.

"Now what?" Eleanor said, stretching her fingers, cramped from gripping the door of the car.

"He said a large cabin, so we must be supposed to ford the crick." Rocky chuckled at Eleanor's dubious expression. "If we get stuck in the middle of it I'll carry you out, sugar, so you won't get your feet wet. It wouldn't be the first time we got stuck in a crick."

"Yes, and that is why I know this car hates water like a cat—"

But they were already safely through the shallow water with no more protest from the car than a wheezing cough or two. The road was unexpectedly wider and more level now, until suddenly it turned again, depositing them in a small gully with a wrenching jar.

Rocky said: "Well, I guess that did it," but Eleanor was staring wide-eyed, straight ahead.

They had come to another clearing, and nailed on each side of a tall pine was an enormous white board. Blackly, its inscription urged:

REPENT! FOR THE DAY OF JUDGMENT IS AT HAND!

CHAPTER TWO
THE ANIMALS AND THE ARK

After an instant Rocky said pensively: "I must be gettin' so I can't carry my liquor. I only had one drink all day. . . ."

"But this must be the place. See, there's the cabin. . . ."

"Yeah. The question is, where's Pope? I hope he's all right in his mind," Rocky said, eyeing the sign uneasily.

He looked at the clearing beyond; a pleasant camping ground, for groups of trees seemed conveniently arranged to give privacy to individual camps, of which there were four to be seen. Rocky looked at them critically and decided that only one person there knew the right way to put up a tent.

The stream they had forded was close to the clearing. There was an indistinct murmur of water not far away and a heavy growth of willows near the right side of the camp ground.

The cabin on the far edge of the clearing had obviously been built many years ago; a long, low building, probably with only two rooms. Smoke curled out of an enormous stone chimney, so there was somebody living there.

"Are we stuck?" Eleanor said abruptly.

"Hunh? Oh, I wouldn't be surprised if there was a spring sure 'nough broke this time."

Rocky got out of the car, then reached back and pulled the lever controlling a horn that sounded like a choice collection of cowbells. He had time only to see that one back spring was broken before Eleanor said:

"Here he comes!" She added: "He walks more like a Thin Man of Oz than ever."

Rocky helped her climb over the rolled blankets tied to the running board. He thought, going to meet him, that Theophilus Pope seemed thinner, taller, more angular than ever; but that might be only because he hadn't had time to get used to Pope's appearance again. They met him halfway across the clearing, and Rocky grinned to see Pope blush when Eleanor stood on tiptoe and kissed him. Eleanor was a tall girl, but she had to stretch to reach Pope's leathery, brown cheek. He said:

"Child, it's good to see you. But I told Rocky to leave you at home."

"And you knew I wouldn't stay, didn't you?"

"I was afraid you wouldn't." Pope looked at her thoughtfully for an instant. His most ordinary expression was rather like that of a sad bloodhound, so it was very difficult to tell if he was really worried about something. He went on politely: "Did you have a pleasant trip?"

Rocky snorted. "You've been over that road, I take it? An' we busted a spring just now. We'll have to push the car out of that ditch to get it in here. We was in Reno the night of the twenty-third, so we didn't get your telegram until yesterday. Started soon's we could and drove like hell, but we couldn't make it in one day, startin' in the afternoon. Now that we've observed all the social what-you-call-'ems, what's it all about? What's this day-of-judgment business?"

"It is quite a shock to be suddenly confronted by a sign like that, you know; especially when you feel as if your spine had just been driven six inches into the car seat," Eleanor said.

"If I'd known that sign was to be here I would have warned you. . . ."

"You don't take any stock in this day-of-judgment business, do you?" Rocky said rather apprehensively. "Because if you've dragged us all the way here just for that . . ."

The corners of Pope's mouth twitched a little. "I don't anticipate the world will come to an end,

Rocky, so set your mind at ease. As to the day of judgment—that I'm not so sure of."

"Is tomorrow the appointed day?" Eleanor said casually. She knew, as Rocky did, that impatience was wasted on Pope.

"Yes, tomorrow morning at quarter of four. Don't you children ever read the newspapers? Not that this particular expedition has attracted much attention."

"I read the sportin' section and Eleanor looks over the woman's page. Editorials make me mad. Which one of these camps is yours?"

"You can't see my modest establishment. It's off the clearing, hidden in the trees at one side of the cabin. It's inconvenient so far as carrying water is concerned, but I had the best of reasons for choosing that place. You can drive in to it, Rocky, if you go very slowly and carefully. You'll have to turn off the clearing and go through the trees to do it. Can we get your car out of that rut?"

"Rut? It's a small canyon. I'll drive and you two can push," Eleanor said. "But where are all the people who belong to these camps?"

"They are attending services— No, that isn't the word. Séance is a better one, though still not very exact."

Rocky said without heat: "Damn your soul. In that cabin, I suppose. Well, put your shoulder to the car an' when you get good and damn ready to tell us something, I reckon you will. Better let me drive when we get her out of this rut, Eleanor."

Pope's camp was a very simple affair; a bed of pine boughs, a small circle of blackened rocks, a skillet, coffee pot, dutch oven, a box of provisions, a battered suitcase. Rocky looked about for a car, saw none and asked:

"How did you get here?"

"I intended renting a car in Oroville. You know how little I like to drive and what dangerous business my driving is apt to be. But in Oroville I ran into Doyle—Warren Doyle. Supposedly a reporter on a vacation."

"Isn't he?" Rocky said, pulling a small tent from the car.

"He does work for a Los Angeles newspaper. But he's a sports writer, so his activity in this affair seems a bit extra-curricular. At any rate I saw no reason why I shouldn't accept his offer of a seat in his car. I counted on you being here with yours, and meanwhile Doyle certainly had a great deal of very useful and interesting information. I think this space is level enough for your tent, Rocky."

Eleanor shivered and put on her sweater. The sun was dropping toward the rim of the tall mountains and already chill was in the air.

"Didn't you freeze to death last night out in the open?" she said.

"I didn't undress, or sleep a great deal. I thought Rocky could help me put up some sort of shelter with a large piece of canvas I have. And—" He stopped, listening; then said quietly: "They're leaving the cabin. Look out between those two trees and you can see them. No, you'll have to come farther down this path. Here. . . ."

Rocky murmured: "'The animals came out of the Ark, two by two,'" and Eleanor giggled, muffling the sound against his arm.

"'The elephant and the kangaroo,'" she whispered. Pope frowned at them, and said cautiously:

"Your kangaroo is the Reverend—so called— Saul Cheney. The lady trotting at his heels is his wife, Naomi. It would be unbecoming for me to cast aspersions upon Mr. Cheney for his kangaroo-like qualities but at least I can truthfully say that my chest has never fallen to the place where my waist should be."

The Reverend Saul was indeed nearly as thin as Theophilus Pope, and the belt of his black trousers did bisect a neat little watermelon of stomach. A very long and scrawny neck rising from a stiff white collar made him appear taller than he was. His head was long and pointed, and his hair had wearied of the climb up its sides and stopped short of its top.

Eleanor said: "He should have 'sacred to the memory of' written on his face. I don't like him. His wife doesn't look so bad."

Mrs. Cheney, walking heavily along behind her husband's long black coattails, was dressed in purple bedroom slippers, a faded blue bungalow apron and a lace boudoir cap. The face below the lace frill was broad and placid; her mouth was curved in a half-smile amiable and habitual.

The stout man who followed Mrs. Cheney was smiling too, but as if he were genuinely amused. He had a round pink face, an unfashionably long and reddish mustache, and even from that distance it was obvious that he wore a toupee; a most exactly waved and very bright brown toupee.

"Either he knows anyone could tell it's a toupee and doesn't give a damn or else he has a very touching faith in the credulity of his acquaintances," Eleanor murmured.

Rocky looked at the man's wrinkled khaki trousers and the fishing jacket with sagging, wide pockets, and said that he imagined "he just don't give a damn." Pope said:

"Mr. and Mrs. Thomas Greer. The lady's name is Eva."

By nature Eva Greer would have been as comfortably plump as her husband. She was expensively corseted, uncomfortably rigid in fawn-colored

riding trousers and an orange sweater. Her too
blonde hair was severely waved; she was carefully
made-up, her face suggestive of expensive facial
creams, wrinkle eradicators and chin straps worn
at night. Her expression was a nice blend of melancholy and sweet resignation, but without looking at him she suddenly jerked a reproving elbow
into her husband's ribs.

Rocky chuckled. "I'll bet she breathes a sigh of
relief when she gets those pants off. Who are the
others, Pope?"

"The older woman is Minna Leroy; the younger her niece, Margaret Corwin. The young man is
Henry Powell."

Minna Leroy was probably not a great deal
younger than Eva Greer, but she accepted her years
without protest. Her dark hair was brushed straight
back from her forehead; her face was pale, except
for a slash of scarlet lipstick. She was beautiful in
a worn and haggard fashion. She wore stout, flat-
heeled shoes and a plain dress that Rocky thought
was very sensible and Eleanor knew was probably
an import that had cost at least fifty dollars.

Margaret Corwin resembled her in many ways,
though her dark hair was curly, her face rounder
and she was not so tall. She had the same pale
olive skin and dark-brown eyes. But she wore beach

shoes that showed toenails painted a brilliant red, white linen shorts and a dark-green sweater. Eleanor looked at Rocky severely.

"You will kindly remember that you are my lawfully wedded husband, Mr. Allan!"

"She ain't got as good a figure as you have. And those shorts always look funny in back, to me. Her legs will get plenty scratched up the first time she goes through some underbrush. As far as that's concerned, you'll please not gaze so long on that handsome young fellow that's with them."

Eleanor looked at the slim, dark young man with the correct profile and rather long, curling dark hair, then at Rocky's tanned blondness; his slender, powerful figure. She shook her head, smiling, but said only:

"He may be poetical—he looks a bit like young Byron—but more than likely the melancholy is due to a bad digestion. I suppose you notice the lovelorn look in his eyes? Now, Mr. Pope, we've seen your animals come out of the Ark, so won't you explain them?"

Rocky said: "We'd better sneak back to camp. Here's another one, comin' here. Is this the reporter?" Pope nodded as Mr. Doyle came toward them through the trees, thrusting a small notebook into his pocket. He was a thick-set young man with very pale-yellow hair that persisted in falling over his forehead with the effect of square-cut bangs. He said:

"What the— I thought I heard a car a while ago. Are these friends of yours, Pope, or have they come to join the faithful?"

"They're friends of mine. I sent for them."

"So I suspected. They don't look like any of Sapphira's satellites. Not bad, is it—'Sapphira's satellites?' I like your taste, Pope," Doyle said, looking at Eleanor. "Lord, how I love red-headed women!"

Pope was polishing his glasses; his vivid blue eyes twinkled. "Mr. and Mrs. Allan," he said casually.

"Well, I still like red-heads. Just my luck though." Doyle looked at Rocky, frowning. "Say, where have I seen you before? You didn't happen to be an All-American fullback, did you? No? Just the same—"

Rocky said: "I cert'nly never saw you before," and hoped that Doyle did not have too good a memory for newspaper photographs. His own had been pretty well splashed over the city papers last January and Eleanor's had been in one or two, but somehow Pope had escaped publicity. Probably Doyle wouldn't remember. . . .

"Got it!" Doyle said. "You were the railroader deputy sheriff in that case at Dayton's Folly. And Mrs. Allan was the old lady's nurse. And there was a mysterious Mr. Pope present. . . ."

Rocky, scowled at him. Eleanor didn't like to talk about what had happened at Dayton's Folly. "We were lucky in one way; we weren't bothered any with reporters till afterwards," he said.

"Brother, I accept your reproof. But I almost weep when I think of a story like that breaking with no one to know about it till it was over— All right, all right. Has Mr. Pope put you wise to things here?"

"He has not," Eleanor said with an exasperated glance toward Pope.

Pope put on his glasses. "I won't need to now. Mr. Doyle is so well acquainted with the necessary history and he will be very glad to—"

"What he means is that Mr. Doyle likes to talk," the young man said cheerfully. He sat down on an empty box. "Mean to say you've never heard about Sapphira Barlow? Well, well! it's a small world. Make yourselves comfortable, children, and listen to old Uncle Warren relate the saga of Sapphira."

CHAPTER THREE
THE SAGA OF SAPPHIRA

When and where Sapphira Barlow was born, Doyle said, was a matter of conjecture. Certainly she was now near seventy, and as certainly she was not a native Californian. Her own statement that she had once been a kootch dancer in a sideshow that had been stranded in California seemed reasonable enough.

She had at one time, the police discovered, graced the very pretentious establishment of a certain Madam Sophie. "But she was smarter than most prostitutes," Doyle said. "She got out of there about 1894, when she was still young and good-looking, and with some money. Money's always had a way of sticking to her fingers."

Where Sapphira was for the next ten years no one knew. Not in California; probably somewhere in the East or Middle West. But if she had ever married, Doyle argued, it must have been sometime during those ten years. Perhaps she had tried to settle down to respectability and had failed. At any rate no one had ever seen the daughter she claimed to have had. She was alone when she returned to Los Angeles in the year 1904.

"I don't know," Doyle said, "what she did for the next eight or nine years. She managed to keep out of the police courts. She finally took to fortunetelling. She called it a lot of other names, but that one will do. She kept clear of trouble, and no one realized how much money she had or they'd have known you couldn't get that kind of dough running a third-rate fortune-telling joint.

"The thing that finally got Sapphira in the spotlight was that some movie star had her fortune told and then told all her friends about it. Sapphira got to be the rage for a while. This was about ten years ago. After a while the rush died down, but by that time she'd taken a good house; put in soft lights, rugs; hired attendants and burned incense. . . ."

Doyle held his nose expressively. "Damned incense— She's gotten so she can't breathe air. I sat next to Greer this afternoon and that fishy jacket of his smelled good to me. However— Sapphira took to crystal-gazing. Then she began going in for table-tipping and got psychic, but she paid her hush money and no one bothered her. Until lately—

"Before I come to that, though, there's this grandson of hers. He's about eleven or twelve. He appeared about five years ago, out of a clear sky. Sapphira was pretty good copy by that time and when she was interviewed she says calmly: yes, she'd had a daughter one time but she was dead and the boy had nowhere else to go. And no, she didn't care to tell what her daughter's name had been, but the kid—David Leon—was to inherit everything she had. She'd made her will to that effect.

"Well, her lawyer is a shyster who talks too much and the boys were beginning to be curious how much money Sapphira had. They didn't get figures out of him but after three or four drinks he did admit that his client was a very wealthy woman. I guess she gave him hell for it. He denied having said it. But the boys were real curious now and they poked around, and by fair means and more foul ones they found out Sapphira had plenty of dough and about fifty-grand worth of rubies. She likes rubies."

"Has she got 'em with her?" Rocky said.

"You think of everything, don't you? I wish I knew, brother. I do know she's never stuck her money in a teapot; good, sound banks for Sapphira. And she's left it all to the kid. I guess she's been good enough to him but it did go against the grain with me to see her dress that little peanut in a turban and robe with moons and stars all over it. Well, he still wears it, so maybe you'll see for yourself.

"Anyway she had him for her assistant. He's quite a drawing card, just too, too cute! It was his turning up and this will that brought out how rich Sapphira was, and of course we began to wonder where she got it all. Not much happened for a long time, but a fellow I know on the police force was digging quietly around for the last five years.

"He came to the conclusion Sapphira combined blackmailing with fortunetelling. Nothing new in that; they go well together. He couldn't get any proof; still hasn't any. Just putting two and two together—two or three suicides and a divorce or two among people who went to her place for a while. In the divorce cases the injured parties never explained where they got the written evidence they had.

"Then this fellow—Blake—checked up still more and began to believe Sapphira's biggest income might come from passing out dope. That's how I came to attend her séances. Blake couldn't go without being spotted for what he was, but Sapphira never banned the press. I think," Doyle said with sudden grimness, "that Blake was right.

No proof, but—I had a brother died in a sanitarium. This dope proposition is one weak point in an otherwise tough skin. . . .

"Well, there was finally enough suspicion against her that Sapphira began to be watched pretty closely, and she got the wind up. Trust her to know when to quit. About three weeks ago she announces that she is old and tired and is going to seek quiet and seclusion for the rest of her days.

"She'd acquired quite a retinue by that time: a secretary—a good-looking dame hard as nails—and a kind of major-domo. He was a slick, oily guy. There were some others not so important. They must have been pretty well scared, because they cleared out of the state and she hired some strange girl—Lisa Wood—to come up here with her.

"She didn't say at first where she was going, but she slipped up on that one. The way I see it, the old girl wanted to save her face. I was at the last séance she gave. She went into a trance and began to groan and mumble a lot of stuff, mostly quotations from the Bible. I can't give them word for word."

"If the newspaper report was correct she said, among other things: *There were voices and thunderings and lightnings and an earthquake . . .*'" Pope said.

"That must've made a big hit with the Los Angeles Chamber of Commerce," Rocky remarked. "Anything else?"

"'*Woe, woe, woe, to the inhabiters of the earth by reason of the other voices of the trumpets of the three angels, which are yet to sound.*' She found that Revelation suited her purpose admirably, I imagine."

Doyle nodded. "Yes, she said that, and things about trees and grass burning up and people being destroyed. Made it sound quite convincing. Well, that was good for a story and on the follow-up she didn't deny she believed the world was to end. She wouldn't come right out and say she did or didn't, or set a date for the big event. It was Cheney who did that."

Cheney's earlier life was as obscure as much of Sapphira Barlow's, though he was younger by twelve or thirteen years. Like Sapphira, he was not a native Californian and had once been connected with a sideshow, as a barker. He had never been an ordained minister but had gone into partnership with a husky tenor and had had some success as an evangelist.

"Only fashions change, and Saul's fire and brimstone style finally didn't go over so good," Doyle said: "And a lot of his meetings ended in a big stink. He got too friendly with some of the fair repentants. One girl's father and another woman's husband chased him out of town with shotguns. I dug those cases up from old newspapers. And two or three times people wanted to know where all the collections went to. So his reputation may truthfully be said to smell.

"He hadn't done anything along that line for quite a while and I guess he was pretty much on his uppers when he landed in L.A. about four years ago. He hadn't been there long before he took up spiritualism, and pretty soon he and Sapphira were regular pals. I guess he was useful to her."

"But it must have been more than that. Or you think so, don't you?" Eleanor said. "One's tempted to guess right away that he had some hold on her. Their paths might have crossed during those ten years that no one knows anything about."

"That would be my guess," Doyle admitted. "But you can't get him to say he doesn't really think Sapphira's revelations are divinely inspired. If you ask him, the world ends at fifteen minutes to four tomorrow morning, Pacific Standard Time, courtesy Western Union. He says she set the time but didn't know it, being in a trance. He really interpreted all her utterances. He loves publicity and he couldn't resist the chance to get some. And maybe he has some plan this is a part of. I don't know.

"Of course this is nothing new. It happens every year or two. The police weren't worrying as long as Sapphira got out of town. Saul refused to desert her and it was easy enough to trace his movements. He had his own car, and they hired another one and sent it back after they got here.

"This place belongs to an admirer of Sapphira's talents and he donated it to her. I don't know if it was her idea or Saul's, though she might have thought it would be a good place to hole in for a while. The owner's father built it but he's never seen it. He's too busy trying to sell real estate to stop for a day of judgment."

"What about these other people?" Rocky asked. "Did you expect them to be here?"

"Brother, I did not! Blake put me wise to what was happening and I had a vacation coming. Sapphira had gotten to be a hobby with me and I thought I wouldn't mind coming up here. A day of judgment that doesn't come off is always good for a line or two. I'd no idea it was such an out-of-the-way place when we started."

"We?" Eleanor said.

"Hank Powell came with me. Hank," Doyle said slowly, "is a friend of mine—I guess. Only I really don't know much about him. He came to L.A. about three years ago to try to break into the movies. He does a few movie articles for papers and magazines now and then, and works as an extra quite a bit. He has a pretty good singing voice.

"I mentioned to him I was going to make this trip; didn't tell him why. But he'd heard me talk about Sapphira and maybe he guessed. Anyway, one night he showed up and asked to come with me, and I didn't mind having company.

"Sapphira, Saul and Company left the twenty-first, took it easy and got here the night of the twenty-third. Hank and I left the day after they did. I guess Pope did too?"

Pope nodded.

"Well, we ran into him in Oroville and that was the first idea I had that anyone but us would be here. Halfway up the Oso grade we ran into Minna and Margie trying to change a tire. That was surprise number one, but then I began to see why Hank wanted to come with me and where he might have gotten his information.

"Hank has known Margie about two years." Doyle stopped to light a cigarette; went on: "I've known her most of my life. Margie's got nothing to do with this, except through Minna. She brought Margie up and they're very fond of each other. Leroy is well-to-do and an ultra-respectable lawyer, quite a bit older than Minna. I'll bet my bottom dollar he doesn't have any idea where the two of them are.

"The way I figure it out, Margie told Hank where they were coming. As for Minna—well, it's always seemed to me she had too much sense to believe in Sapphira's flapdoodle. I can see why she'd go there a time or two just to say she'd been, but she wouldn't keep going unless— Well, damn it all, I like Minna, but—"

"Blackmail or dope," Eleanor said. "I don't think she's an addict now."

"Neither do I. I've watched her. But she was sick for quite a while about four months ago. She was out of town and came back two weeks ago. I think she may have had guts enough to break off. But no one knows what may have happened before she did. I never told either her or Margie that this trip was anything more than a vacation.

"The Greers are harmless. Thomas used to make shoes in Indiana, retired and came out here. Eva is one of these middle-aged women who run to fads. Sapphira was her latest one and she doesn't want to miss anything. If the world is going to end Eva wants to see it out in style.

"Greer says he's been trying to get a fishing trip for ten years, so he took her up on it when she suggested coming up here. Oh yes, their destination was in the papers. Mrs. Cheney's all right. She's rather numb and dumb after living so long with Cheney. She just says: 'Yes, Saul,' to everything.

"And that's that," Doyle ended, tossing his cigarette in the general direction of Pope's crude fireplace. Rocky sprang to his feet; ground the smoldering stub to ashes with the heel of his boot.

"I hope," he said disgustedly, "that the rest of these folks have more sense than you. Did anyone ever tell you about forest fires?"

"Oh! I'm sorry; I didn't think—"

"You would if you ever fought fire for three days and nights without any rest to speak of." Rocky began to pull the rest of their camping equipment from the car. "You'll have to 'scuse me but the sun's already behind the hills and I've got to cut some pine boughs before it gets too dark."

Doyle lighted another cigarette, extinguished the match very carefully and watched Rocky and Pope pitch the tent.

"I wish you'd come over and tighten ours up tomorrow," he said. "It sags like the dickens. The only time I slept on pine boughs I carried the marks for months. Hank and I brought cots, but we nearly froze to death last night."

"You'd be warmer sleepin' on the ground," Rocky said pityingly. "On a cot you need more cover underneath than over you. Pine boughs are all right if you don't cut 'em too big. You didn't need to get that wood, honey. If I build a fire will you start supper?"

"Mountain stew? Of course. That," Eleanor explained, "is our name for a haphazard concoction of anything that comes to hand."

"We're living on beans, and I think all Minna and Margie eat is tea and crackers. But I'm not hinting for an invitation—tonight," Doyle said.

Rocky's method of starting a fire by building a tepee of very small pitchy splinters seemed to fascinate him. "Distribution without waste," he murmured. "By golly, it burns!"

"Of course it does," Eleanor said proudly, feeding the tiny blaze with larger pieces of wood.

Doyle got up, hesitated and said finally: "See here, Pope, I know you can't quite trust me and I don't know, yet, why you're here. But you might at least think things over and count me in if you need any help. I don't like the situation."

"Neither do I," Pope said sadly. "Certainly I will count on you, Mr. Doyle, but I haven't any plan of campaign."

"Neither have I. Well, I guess I'll get back—" Doyle stopped and looked at the .38 special that Rocky had just taken from the car. "Can you shoot that thing?"

Rocky grinned. "No, I carry it to scare folks with. One time that Pope remembers I'd have felt a lot better to 've had a gun, so I brought this along."

"But can you shoot anything when you fire it; hit what you aim at, I mean?"

Rocky looked doubtfully at Pope, received a half-nod and stooped to pick up an empty tomato can. "I'm out of practice," he said, tossing the can into the air. The gun barked three times before the battered can came to ground again.

"My dad would say that ain't so good. He gave Eleanor a pretty little gun and taught her how to shoot it, down in Texas."

"Great state, Texas," Doyle said, staring thoughtfully at the three holes in the can. "Well, I'll go and assure the others that the world is not beginning to end before schedule."

"Now what," Rocky said to Pope, "was the reason for me showin' off like that?"

"I thought it might be a very good thing if all present knew there is someone in camp who can shoot straight when necessary," Pope said. "We'll go for pine boughs now and talk after supper."

CHAPTER FOUR
"WOMEN ARE FOOLS"

Eleanor's mountain stew and three cups of very strong coffee apparently put Pope in a humor for talking. He sat before the campfire, his back to a tree, and filled his odorous old pipe.

"You might tell me first what you've been doing all these months," he said.

Eleanor and Rocky, supremely satisfied with life together, were only too selfishly ready to tell their story. Rocky said:

"Oh, we stayed down in Texas till the middle of May; three months ago. Dad seemed lots older to me and he was crazy about Eleanor. Well, you saw him, so you know."

"He's a darling, and he and Rocky wouldn't think of admitting how fond they are of each other. Of course they are both very stubborn," Eleanor said. "But Mr. Allan was really quite proud of Rocky because he hadn't ever come running home or wired him for money."

"I came damn near it once. I was stony broke and my belly was stickin' to my backbone. Know what? We never made much out of the ranch, but Dad sold a piece that turned out to have oil on it four or five years ago. Never said a word about it till he up an' offered us five grand for a weddin' present."

"Did you take it?" Pope said.

"Of course not. It's safe in his hands and we've already more money than we need. What Rocky's railroader uncle left him and what—Mr. Leale of Dayton's Folly left me," Eleanor said. "You'd be surprised how little money two vagabonds need. Or perhaps you wouldn't."

"I wouldn't. I know."

"Well, I'd intended stayin' with Dad. But he told us to clear out for a while; said he could see my feet was itchin' to go places. Anyhow I had to work at least one trip to hold my seniority on the railroad," Rocky said. "No use losin' what few whiskers I have. Things've been so tight I wouldn't have been workin' much anyway. If I hadn't been cut off it I'd have been hangin' onto the extra board by the skin of my teeth. I got a fair amount of work when we went back to Merton in May, but I took thirty days lay-off when we got your wire. I reckon you found out in San Francisco that I was back on the pay roll?"

"Yes. You had told me you would be going back to Merton sometime in the spring."

"It don't look as good to me as it used to. They got an airport now and I been takin' flying lessons there and in Reno. I can get my private pilot's license in a little while more, but I'm startin' in too late to get anywhere in that game." He added, putting his arm about Eleanor as she leaned against him: "It's kind of tough on Eleanor, though, being married to a guy like me."

"But we have such a nice time together. When you carry passengers I'll go up with you. Oh, we'll have to settle down sometime. We know that."

Rocky grinned down at her. "Sure, I know. You can't raise kids in airplanes or auto camps. Now you've heard about us, Pope. What've you been doin'?"

Pope said: "I was in South America for a few months," and seemed to feel that this was a quite adequate explanation of his recent activities.

Before he spoke again Eleanor had time to recall a conversation she had had with Paul Taylor, a San Francisco lawyer who had known Pope's grandfather.

"Theo's father was a handsome swashbuckling Irishman," the old man had said. "The boy adored him, though I don't believe he has any illusions about him. His mother was pretty and gentle, but

a soldier's daughter nevertheless. She died when
Theo was twelve. His father sent him to school in
England and I think he was thoroughly miserable
there. Even then he was very tall and awkward and
serious. Then his grandfather sent him to a military academy in this country and that experiment
was not any more successful.

"He'd have done well in college, I think. But his
father was killed in '14 and his grandfather died
that same year. He left him a small income. I've
heard Theo was finally in the intelligence service
during the war. I don't know. He comes to see me
when he's in the city but he doesn't tell me what
he has been doing or where he's been and what
information I gather by chance he never explains.

"I'm very fond of the boy. Yes, I know he is
nearly thirty-nine. I suppose his father in him
keeps him wandering, but he is too much like his
mother to be satisfied with his life. I'm afraid he
must often be very lonely. . . ."

He looked lonely, Eleanor thought. She had
seen in his eyes when she quite naturally kissed
him, an almost piteous gratitude for affection.
Perhaps he had been too much laughed at because
he was so long and lean and melancholy? There
was something ludicrous about his face; all long
lines carven on tanned, weather-beaten skin. If
he wouldn't wear those tinted glasses, so that you

could always see the blue eyes that must be like those of his Irish father . . .

"This month I landed in Los Angeles," Pope said abruptly. "I have an old friend there, really a cousin of sorts. He was very kind to me when I was a boy. He is a wealthy man, widowed, with one daughter. He brought her up unaided—and very badly. But she is the center of his existence. As he always gave her everything she could think of wanting, she doesn't know what to wish for. Any new sensation is—was a thing to be sought after."

"Sapphira?" Eleanor said, as Pope paused.

"Sapphira. It was too interesting to attend séances or have her fortune read privately. It was only a passing fad, of course, but her own foolishness conspired against her. She has been married for a year to a fine young fellow who is also something of a prig. I should imagine he is a younger edition of what we've been told Mrs. Leroy's husband is. Well, they quarrel of course. Herbert has neither her father's money nor his inclination to indulge all Rose's whims.

"Herbert had to be out of town for several days. They quarreled and didn't make up before he left. Rose was in a humor to 'show him.' He has always objected to her going to Sapphira's, so there she went, struck up an acquaintance with a very charming young man who said this was his first visit to Sapphira's and referred to a number of people whom she knew slightly. She went to dinner and the theater with him; later they danced. They met again; she went to his apartment for cocktails. . . ."

Eleanor said: "There is no denying women are inclined to be fools."

"I must agree with you, so far as Rose's type is concerned. It was fun, she thought, to play with fire. Yet she never intended to tell Herbert about it. I gathered that the whole affair would have been merely a secret satisfaction to her. She was not doing anything really wrong, she said, but one has to remember that she is married to Herbert."

"But was that all?" Rocky asked.

"Oh, by no means. The charming young man became too amorous and she became frightened, not being half so sophisticated as she likes to believe. She was ready to break off with him. But he had written her such charming notes and she had answered them—Rose would."

Rocky groaned. "The 'letters'?"

"Exactly. While it seems an overdone device of melodrama to you, the fact still remains that women will write letters that appear to mean more than is true in actual fact. Rose has an allowance from her father, but that did not go very far and she was not able to redeem the prize letter of the collection.

"Meanwhile she discovered that she was to have a child. That made her still more frantic; the possibility that Herbert might possibly question the paternity of his own child if he ever found out about her little escapade. At last she lost her nerve and told the whole story to her father.

"By that time Sapphira's establishment was on its way to being broken up. She had one last interview with the man, whose connection with Sapphira seems not to have been generally known. He seemed, on the whole, to be rather sorry for her. He told her that there was nothing he could do about the business; that all of them had orders to—"

"Take it on the lam?" Rocky suggested.

"Yes. He said that she would have to go to Sapphira for the last letter, and that he doubted if Rose could get to see her, and had no idea what Sapphira would do with certain important documents like the one in question. He also admitted that he would not put it past the 'old devil' to hold on to anything that might mean money to her and to return to her usual activities whenever she thought it safe.

"Rose's father tried to get in touch with Sapphira and failed, partly because he wanted to avoid

publicity and because Sapphira evidently was being very careful what she did just then. I advised
them to wait and deal with her later, if it was
ever necessary, but it seems that won't do. The
child is hysterical with fear. For her father's sake I
consented to follow Sapphira when I'd discovered
where she was going.

"After all, the business could be more quietly
and safely finished here. I am carrying," Pope said
with a grimace, "an uncomfortably large roll of
bills on me. So far Sapphira has been inaccessible,
unless I wanted literally to force her to see me—
and I don't."

"She ought to come out of seclusion when she
finds the world continues right on," Rocky said.

"Yes, of course, if— I hadn't counted on the
presence of these other people, you see. I particularly detest," Pope said, "chasing what are commonly called 'the documents' more than half the
length of a very long state. In addition to that I
find that I am not the only one who wants to talk
to Sapphira, and I, at least, have no idea of killing
her."

"Then you do think that— We have visitors,"
Eleanor said. "There is a light coming this way."

A woman's voice, unpleasantly shrill and pene-
trating, was heard saying: "You should be ashamed
of yourself, Thomas Greer! You just want to be

aggravating. The idea of saying you won't get up for—for—*it*. We're to go to the top of that hill back of the cabin, where you can see the sun rise."

"According to what the old lady says, the sun isn't going to rise tomorrow," Mr. Greer said mildly.

"Well, where you could see it if it did. Of course you're going to get up!"

"I never had any great ambition to die with my boots on, and if it was left to me to set a time for the world to end, I wouldn't pick an ungodly time like 4 a.m. At that, I may get up. Sometimes the fish bite better real early in the morning."

"Fish! Can't you ever think of anything but fish?"

"Well, Toots, I've been wanting to come fishing—real mountain fishing—for ten years, but you always insisted on going to fashionable places for vacations. And I guess you'll eat a nice trout or two if anybody's around to eat any breakfast."

"Don't call me Toots! Haven't you any—any sense of the fitness of things?" Mrs. Greer's tone changed abruptly; she said in her best lady-come-to-call voice: "I do hope we aren't disturbing you? But I really thought we should get acquainted. Of course we are only ships that pass in the night—"

Rocky whispered: "If she tries to set on the ground she'll sure as hell split those pants," and got up to draw a box to the fire for Mrs. Greer.

Eleanor buried her face in her handkerchief and coughed convulsively.

"Dear me, you haven't caught cold, have you?" Mrs. Greer said. "Do you think aspirin or quinine is better? Or both? I have some very good gargle—"

"If she's caught cold, it's one cold that won't ever get any worse, according to you and Sapphira. I thought maybe we had some more blamed fools in camp," Greer said candidly, squatting down by the fire and puffing away at a shiny corncob pipe. "But Doyle said not, and you both look like you had some sense. You don't want to mind Eva," he added stolidly, meeting his wife's outraged glance. "She's just kidding herself along because it's no fun unless she does. When she gets back to L.A. she'll have conversation enough for two weeks of hen parties."

"Thomas Gre-er! Don't," Mrs. Greer said, turning to Eleanor, "ever marry a widower. You'll soon find out that his first wife was perfect!"

Eleanor said hastily: "Have you had good fishing, Mr. Greer?"

Greer smiled at her understandingly. "Pretty fair, Mrs.—Allan, is it? I got a dandy mess of Eastern Brook and Rainbows yesterday. If I have good luck tomorrow I'll bring you some."

"Do you use bait or flies?" Rocky asked politely.

Greer said: "Flies!" in a way to make it plain he considered bait fishing a cardinal sin. Rocky grinned and said that he preferred fly fishing himself, and had Greer had any luck with the red ant?

Greer had found that a gray hackle was the best thing in this stream and wished he had brought more of them with him. Pope had, unexpectedly, a word to say for the royal coachman.

Mrs. Greer did not return to the subject of her predecessor's perfections, but asked Eleanor if she didn't thing that it was absolutely essential for the "modren" woman to have some interest in life beyond housekeeping. Eleanor said gravely that she supposed it was and gathered that during the past two years Mrs. Greer's outside interests had ranged from classic dancing to spiritualism, with courses in psychology, French conversation and landscape gardening scattered in between.

What, Mrs. Greer inquired, did Eleanor think about nudism? Was there really something to it or was it just—well—*just?* Rocky snorted but Eleanor was spared the necessity of an answer when Greer said suddenly:

"This is a funny business. No, Eva, I don't mean it the way you think I do—this time. What're some of these people doing here? Us you can account for, and young Doyle. I take it Powell is here because he's in love with little Miss Corwin. But her aunt—there's a woman who looks like she had some sense."

"And very good-looking—you say," Mrs. Greer remarked acidly.

"Well, isn't she? What's she here for, though? She doesn't talk to anyone," Greer said, pushing his toupee farther back on his head. "Of course Cheney accounts for himself if you can believe anything he says. I can't."

"Mr. Cheney is a very spiritual man," Mrs. Greer began, but Rocky said softly:

"Speak of the devil! By the len'th of his shadow that'd ought to be Cheney now."

CHAPTER FIVE
FAT SPIDER

The Reverend Saul Cheney, materializing finally from the black, shadowed trees into the circle of light about the campfire, looked rebukingly at Mrs. Greer and ignored her husband. He said in a peculiarly hollow voice that had, at times, an odd, sing-songing quality:

"It is later than you think."

Eleanor shivered. The man was putting on an act, of course. But those words, that she had seen carven on sundials and old clocks, were always disturbing. Even when you were young and very happy you found them so; always it is later than you think. . . .

Mrs. Greer was flutteringly saying good night and murmuring something about meditation. Thomas Greer said:

"Meditation, hell! I'll try to bring you some fish in the morning, Mrs. Allan."

He lumbered away behind his wife's indignant back, turning to grin at them before the trees hid him from sight. Rocky said:

"Have a drink, Brother Cheney?"

Eleanor returned Pope's quizzical look with a smile and shake of her head. Rocky's jeering question was a sure sign that he had taken an instinctive and violent dislike to Saul Cheney. Well, she didn't like him either; didn't like his narrow eyes and thick eyelids and the sidewise glance he gave her. It was perfectly true that some men never looked at a woman without wondering how she would look with her clothes off. She said:

"Yes, do give Mr. Cheney a drink, Rocky. I'm sure he needs to be fortified for his labors, past and present."

"'*Wine,*'" Cheney said automatically, "'*is a mocker, strong drink is raging . . .*' I have come to take you to Madam Sapphira. She wishes to see you."

"What about? We ain't trespassin'," Rocky said. "I found out before we came up here that nothing but the land it sets on goes with that cabin. So if we want to camp here—"

"No, you are not trespassing," Cheney admitted. "But Madam Sapphira has seen all the others and would like to see you before we meet tomorrow, at dawn, to await judgment."

Pope said: "If you were really awaiting judgment, Cheney, I should pity you, I think—because you must wait, not because you could be unjustly judged."

Cheney's sallow face flushed briefly and Eleanor thought suddenly of a line from a favorite poem: *"And his face is as a fungus of a leprous white and gray . . ."* but Pope was tapping his pipe gently on a blackened stone.

"However, I am anxious to see Mrs. Barlow and I prefer my friends to be with me, so we will obey the summons. If you don't mind . . ."

"Not a bit," Rocky said, helping Eleanor to her feet. "It had ought to be right amusin'."

The cabin smelled of rotting wood; the heavy, sweet fumes of burning incense only intensified that odor. No one had bothered to brush down the spiderwebs in the corners of the long room; in spite of the dim lights, Eleanor thought she saw a fat black spider peering at them from an intricate design of silver web. About the whole place was an air of sickening decay that seemed to emanate less from the moldering house than from the tiny figure in a big chair in front of the fireplace.

Knowing the woman's history you were not being clever but only rather trite when you thought she looked like that spider in the corner. But she did have a small, plump body and a head rather too large for her height, and long curved fingers with pointed nails. Her thumbnails were at least an inch long, red-lacquered and not too clean.

Rocky's eyes were fixed on them in fascinated disgust; unconsciously he held Eleanor's arm more tightly. She saw a muscle tighten in his cheek as Sapphira Barlow looked at her appraisingly; he, too, must have thought that the old woman's glance was reminiscent of Saul Cheney's.

"Wonderful hair," Sapphira murmured. "Yes, very good. . . ."

Then she seemed to forget that they were there and sat staring unwinkingly into a small crystal ball that sat on the table in front of her. Her eyes, small and slightly protruding, were a pale and filmy blue. Her hair was hidden under a red silk turban, fastened in front with a pin of brilliants. She wore a shapeless robe of some sort of changeable silk, and the chair in which she sat was untidy with bright-colored scarves and shawls.

The only light in the room came from the fire and a lantern hanging on a hook in the wall. The girl who sat in a corner near one of the windows was staring at the floor. There was a tangle of brown hair about her face. Eleanor saw only that she was young and angular and that face and eyes were sullen. But the boy who had been sitting cross-legged at one side of the fireplace got to his feet and said politely:

"How do you do? It's very cold this evening, isn't it?"

"Yes, it is; very cold," Eleanor said inanely.

This, then, was the grandson whom Sapphira had made her assistant and dressed for the part. He also wore a turban, but he had pushed it off his forehead to show his curling yellow hair. He had his grandmother's pale blue eyes but they were not incongruous to his child's face. Underneath a dirty white robe sprinkled with signs of the zodiac he wore a purple-velvet jacket with green turkish trousers bagging over pointed red shoes. He went on:

"I've never been in the mountains before and it's very int'resting but a little frightening. Of course there's the fishing. I've never fished. Mr. Greer said he would take me with him, but I don't suppose I'd do very well at it in these clothes and Saul says that we should not be thinking of such things."

Cheney said, not unkindly: "No, David, you should not. If I were you I'd go to bed."

Sapphira was still staring at the crystal ball, muttering to herself. The mutter grew to words:

"*'Breathing out threatenings and slaughter . . .'*" then: "*'Suddenly there shined round him a light from heaven,'"* and, as inexplicably: *"'When his eyes were opened he saw no man. . . .'"*

Rocky stirred restively beside her and Eleanor knew that he was going to speak, perhaps unwisely, and that it would be useless to try to stop him. He said:

"Did you bring us here just to stage a show, Cheney? Because it ain't worth the price of admission. I'm tired and it's gettin' late."

"I must agree with Mr. Allan," Pope said from where he stood behind them. "Mrs. Barlow, I am sorry to have to say that none of us are impressed by the performance. Would it ease your mind if I told you that I am very well acquainted with Scripture?"

Sapphira's head jerked up and she looked at Pope fixedly. At last she smiled, showing two rows of shining white—and false—teeth.

"Sir, I am . . . impressed." It was the first time she had spoken naturally and her voice was surprisingly clear and sweet. "You were the one who wanted to see me? Of course a great many people have wanted that, but I know the others who have. Well, Mr. Pope, if it is possible I will talk to you tomorrow."

"Why not tonight?"

The old lady shook her head. "Not tonight. Tomorrow I will know—"

"If I insisted—"

"Insist and be damned to you," Sapphira said languidly. "It won't do you any good to try to use force. You wouldn't get what you—what I suppose you want. Shall we say good night?"

"You won't tell me your real reason for wanting to see us tonight?"

"I hadn't any other reason than that I wanted to see—what kind of people you are. Well, I've seen, so you might as well go. I suppose"—the wrinkled old face was impassive, but for an instant there was a faint spark of amusement in Sapphira's eyes—"I suppose we will not see you on the hill tomorrow morning?"

"I think not." Eleanor had never seen Theophilus Pope angry but she guessed that he was at this moment. He turned toward the door. Sapphira said:

"Show them out, David. Saul, too. . . . No, Saul, I wish to be alone. We have only a few hours left for meditation."

Cheney appeared not to catch the derision in her voice, but his narrow eyes grew more narrow. He bowed stiffly, turned and collided with Rocky, who seemed suddenly in a hurry to leave the cabin. David, waiting at the door, smiled at them wistfully.

"You sleep in tents, don't you? I should think that would be rather nice. I don't like this house very much, do you? It smells so—old. I guess it is old too, because I never saw any doors like these before." He pointed to the heavy, sliding bar of wood that secured the door from the inside.

"Most old cabins are made like that," Rocky said absently. "Would you like to go fishing with me, kid?"

"Oh yes! Well, I mean . . . I would, but—"

"Oh, I get it. Do you believe all this cr—rot?" Rocky said bluntly.

The boy frowned and looked from Saul back to his grandmother. "Well, it's often very hard to know what to believe, isn't it?" Then, childishly: "But Grandma and Saul are almost always right about everything, so I guess they are about this. I mostly don't think about it. Only I do think I'd like to smoke a cigarette while I have a chance."

Cheney said: "David! I'm disappointed in you."

"You," Rocky said, "can go— Oh, skip it! Use your imagination. Here you are, kid; two cigarettes. Is that enough?"

"Oh yes, thank you. I really don't see what difference it makes if I take time from meditation to smoke one cigarette or smoke while I meditate. You see, if I'm not going to do any more growing it doesn't matter about the smoking. You're both very tall, aren't you? Did you smoke when you were young? Saul says he never did."

Sapphira said from her nest of shawls: "The room is getting cold with the door open, David. I've no objection to your smoking those cigarettes, but don't expect any sympathy if they make you sick." Her voice sounded as if she were laughing at Cheney again. "Lisa, you'd better help him with that door. It's too heavy for him."

Thus dismissed, they stepped out into the sharp air of the mountain night. Cheney muttered indistinctly and left them. After an instant Pope said:

"That damned old—" and stopped.

"Always the gentleman. Don't mind me," Eleanor said. "I know a word or two for her."

"Cheney was right in calling her madam—omittin' the Sapphira," Rocky said. "If she ain't been a procuress I'll eat my hat. She looked Eleanor over just like a horse trader does a horse. As for Cheney, he's a—"

"Yes?" Eleanor said encouragingly.

"No'th end of a horse headed south. I respect really religious people. Makin' your living working on feelings like that is pretty low."

Eleanor spread her hands to the fire as Rocky threw wood on the coals. "What makes me boil is thinking of a youngster being brought up in such an atmosphere. She doesn't believe in her own prophecies, so why can't she tell him so? At least I don't think she believes in her own pet and personal day of judgment."

"She smelled of gin," Rocky said irrelevantly. "Both her and the kid need washin' too. He stinks."

"She probably has a bottle of gin concealed among her many robes and draperies," Pope said. "I'm quite certain she doesn't believe in her own prophecies. She has evidently always been just a good actress. Doyle said as much and his idea of her motive for starting this whole foolish business seems reasonable enough. That is, to save her face by making it appear that she was not running away from the police. Of course there is always the possibility that the idea was Cheney's and not hers." He added apologetically: "I'm going to need Rocky's help tonight, Eleanor."

"I was afraid of that. Well, pick out a nice flat stone and heat it in those coals. But don't get it hot enough to burn the blankets. I can take a hint: I'm going to bed."

"Uh—what is the rock for?" Pope said diffidently.

"Subst'ute for a hot-water bottle. Eleanor has a warm heart—an' very cold feet. Cheney," Rocky said, raking coals over a flat stone, "packs a gun."

"Oh? I wondered. You are not very often clumsy, and it was entirely your fault that he bumped into you."

"It's an old trick. What is it you want me to do?"

"After your long trip I don't like to ask you. . . ."

"If one of us has got to stay awake it'd better be me. You look like the mornin' after. Didn't you sleep at all last night? I didn't think so. What were you doing?"

"Guarding Sapphira Barlow." Pope made a gesture of distaste. "I must say I have no enthusiasm for that task, but I want her to be alive tomorrow to bargain with me. After that we will leave here as quickly as possible. Yes, I mean that!" he said, at Rocky's doubting smile. "For once I am determined to mind my own business. I don't care if someone kills Sapphira after I have what I came here for."

"Oh yes, you do. I reckon you don't pity Sapphira as much as whoever it might be who'd kill her. It ain't very often abs'lutely necessary to kill a person. Even when you'd say it was almost justified, lots of times it was just the easiest way out. Some people kill because they haven't guts to face a damn unpleasant situation. An' they're . . . what you call egoists to think they've got a right to say when someone else should stop livin'. Well—can you see through the two windows in that front room?"

"Fairly well. The other rooms are a kitchen and bedroom—so called. The bedroom has no outside door and only one small window; a very small one set high up in the wall. The kitchen window is the same kind, and according to Doyle its outside door fastens inside with a wooden bar. The boy and Lisa Wood sleep in the bedroom, but fortunately Sapphira sits up most of the night. At least she did last night; sat before the fire and appeared to be looking into that crystal.

"You can see the top of her head over the back of her chair. From the way it—her head—tilted now and then, I think she took several drinks. I imagine she likes that room because it is warm. The fire never went entirely out, but she did finally lie down on a couch at the side of the fireplace."

"You stayed there all night and nothing happened but that?"

"I think someone tried to get into the cabin," Pope said.

"You do? And I suppose there wasn't any way to get in, except through the windows you was watching?"

"So far as I've been able to determine, one would have to enter by way of those windows. However, though they have no locks they are very heavy and probably haven't been raised for years. As you will find, trees and brush grow close to the cabin on three sides, except for a small open space at the back door. There is a trail there that leads down to the stream. As there is a path along the stream, that is the best way for anyone in the other camps to approach the house without being seen."

"What do I do; go through these trees?"

"Yes. Go straight back for about a hundred yards, then turn to your right. That will bring you through the trees to the side of the cabin where the windows are. About these camps—I suppose you have noticed that they are all on one side of the clearing; the side nearest the stream. They are in a line: Cheney quite close to the cabin, then the Greers, Doyle and Powell, Mrs. Leroy and her niece. Perhaps it would have been better if we had been nearer them but I preferred to be off the clearing and as close as possible to the cabin."

"You ain't said yet why you think someone tried to get into the cabin," Rocky reminded him.

"Instinct, I suppose. There were . . . noises," Pope said unsatisfactorily. "Someone was prowling around the house, but it was useless to try to catch him. It might only have been Cheney. However I am quite certain that someone did investigate the kitchen window and door. Perhaps the bedroom window too, but that is on the other side of the house. I saw a light flash back there and moved as silently and quickly as I could, but I must have been heard; it was easy enough for the prowler to get away down the path to the stream."

"Well, I'll get going. Are you going to stay here or are you figurin' on doing some investigatin' on your own account?"

"I thought I would sleep, for a while at least. I'll relieve you about one o'clock. It's ten now."

"Well, I'd prefer you'd stay here till I get back," Rocky said. "I don't suppose there's any danger, but I don't want to leave Eleanor alone here. Have you got a gun?"

"I have one but I hope to God I don't have to use it," Pope said devoutly. "You know what my shooting is."

Rocky grinned. They had done some target shooting down in Texas and he knew Pope's marksmanship to be marvelously erratic. On the other hand Pope could bisect a playing card with a knife from a distance of fifteen feet.

"You'd better stick to knife throwin'," he said.

"It is certainly more practical in my case. But I always have a sense of guilt, thinking of my grandfather. 'A grandson of mine handling a knife like a dirty greaser!'" Pope said in a gruff military voice. Then, in his own accent: "I'll stay in camp unless there is an alarm. If you need me you'd better fire two shots."

CHAPTER SIX
TWO SHOTS AT MIDNIGHT

The tent was so small that when a bed was put in it there was very little space left for anything else. Rocky found his feet tangled up in suitcases and then bumped into the box Eleanor had set by one side of the bed. She switched on an electric lantern and blinked up at him sleepily.

"Precious, you'd better either sit down or stand right in the middle of this structure if you don't want to knock it down," she said.

"I can't stand in the middle when the bed's there. Lift up your feet." Rocky slid the heated stone, wrapped in old woolen rags, between the covers. "That better? Some women are funny. They'd rather freeze to death than wear flannel nightgowns. What you need for nights like these is a pair of those kid's sleepers that have closed feet."

"I don't need them when you're so nice and warm blooded."

Her habit of wearing low-cut silk nightgowns even in zero weather was certainly not a very sensible one, but you couldn't deny the things were darned becoming. And she looked sweet snuggled down in bed with her red hair curling all over the pillow. Rocky said thoughtfully:

"If Pope was married to you he'd think twice before he spent the night guarding that dame."

"Is that what you're going to do? I was afraid of that," Eleanor said, her arms tight about his neck. "Of course I have to let you do it and I know you can take care of yourself—but I don't have to like it. Why can't I stand guard with you?"

"I b'lieve you would, at that. In fact I know it. But you can't," Rocky said definitely. He kissed her and pulled the covers up about her shoulders. "I want a bottle of whisky to take off the chill, and my gun an' a flashlight . . ."

He found what he wanted in a suitcase, pulled on a heavy mackinaw and then loaded Eleanor's little .25 automatic and put it on the box beside her.

"There ain't many women I'd trust with a loaded gun, but I'll take a chance you won't up and shoot me by mistake when I come back. Pope said he'd relieve me about one. He's right outside."

"For heaven's sake, don't worry about me," Eleanor said crossly. "I'm just one of those who 'also serve.' I might as well have stayed in Merton for all the use I'm going to be."

"I wouldn't say that. You're a swell cook. Go to sleep, honey—I mean it."

Pope had retired behind the small lean-to they had rigged up for him with poles and a piece of canvas. Rocky stopped to bank the fire with ashes and plunged into the woods backing the camp. Pope had broken something of a path through the underbrush—manzanita, gooseberry and chaparral—so that it was easy enough to see where he should turn to swing in to the cabin.

The twelve paned windows had not been washed for years and light shone through them dimly, but Rocky found that two panes were broken and that he could get a clear view of the room through one of these. The lantern that hung on the wall was not lighted now, but the fire had been replenished recently and was blazing high enough to bathe half the room with flickering light.

Rocky leaned his elbows on the window sill and studied the room. He had been too busy watching Sapphira when they had been inside to look about him very carefully. But there was nothing much to see. There were cushions scattered about the floor; he remembered that both David and Lisa Wood seemed to be used to sitting cross-legged on the floor. Sapphira's chair, with its back to the windows, the table to one side of her and the couch Pope had spoken of, were the only furniture in the room.

The old lady was still burning incense; he could see the thick gray curl of smoke from the little cone beside the crystal. Only Sapphira's turbaned head was visible and she sat very still. But presently she stirred and her head tilted unmistakably backward. Rocky's mouth twisted disgustedly. Pope had been right: the old girl sat there half the night drinking gin. More than likely she was usually half soused when she gave her séances, though he'd admit that—if she'd been drinking all through the day—she knew how to carry her liquor.

He yawned soundlessly and looked wistfully at the fire. He wouldn't have minded a little of its warmth; even in summer night was cold in the high Sierras, and this was late August. Sapphira Barlow leaned forward and threw another stick of wood on the fire. Sparks danced upward and the crystal ball, reflecting them, was for an instant a swirl of gold.

Sapphira's white hand reached toward the globe, pulling it to the edge of the table out of Rocky's sight. So that she could look into it, he thought. Well, maybe she really did see things in it—or thought she did, which was just as good.

She didn't move again until more than half an hour had passed. He had just risked looking at his watch, bending down close to the ground and shielding his light with his coat, when one of the two doors toward the back of the house opened and Lisa Wood came in.

She carried a candle stuck on a saucer and a plate of sandwiches. She put them on the table, left the room again and came back with a cup and coffee pot.

Rocky wished he could hear what they were saying, but the cabin walls were thick and the voices very low. At least he could take a good look at the girl. She could not have been more than eighteen and she looked as if she had never had quite enough to eat. Her face was all eyes: a white thin face with a beautifully shaped mouth and a chin that was too small and pointed. She stood before Sapphira for an instant as if awaiting orders; then nodded, picked up the candle and left the old lady alone once more.

Sapphira seemed to be in no hurry to eat her late meal. Rocky wondered what she would say if he tapped on the window and asked her for a cup of coffee. He had half a mind to do it; if the old girl had to be guarded, her guard might at least do his work in comfort. He was getting stiff and cramped from standing so still.

If he were Pope he'd charge into the place and tear it to pieces to find what he wanted. At least he felt as if he would—right now. He supposed that if he were in Pope's place he'd think twice before he raised such a hell of a row. And there was no telling where the old girl kept her—what would you call them? Valuables? She might have those rubies with her for all any of them knew.

Rocky sank abruptly to the ground so that the top of his head was underneath the window sill. The other door had opened to show David Leon, sleepy-eyed, tousle-headed. For an instant he was facing the windows, but Rocky thought that the boy hadn't seen him.

Cautiously he raised himself until he could look through one of the broken panes, thankful that it was one of the lower four. Again he wished they would talk more loudly. It was hard to tell what was going on when you had only gestures and facial expressions to go by.

But he thought that David acted as if something might have frightened him. He was talking to his grandmother and glancing back toward the door he had come through. Finally the old lady got up, spoke to him in a soothing murmur, and with her arm about his shoulders led him back toward the bedroom.

That is, you'd naturally suppose it was the bedroom they went into, if you took for granted Lisa

Wood had come from the kitchen. Rocky decided to take a look at the rest of the cabin while Sapphira was getting the kid back to sleep. He edged his way cautiously around the outside wall until his groping fingers found the corner of the house.

As Pope had said, there was a small cleared space here at the back. A little light fell on it from a window high in the wall; a window too high for anyone to reach easily and far too small to squeeze through if one did. The kitchen had evidently been built as an afterthought; built of lumber instead of logs. It was as wide across as the big front room but very narrow in length.

At the same time they must have built the bedroom onto the right side of the cabin and cut a door into it from that side of the living room. There was a faint light in its high window too, but Rocky was satisfied that no one could get into that room.

He returned quietly to the back of the house, flashed his torch for an instant on the beginning of the path to the river, looked at his watch. He wondered what Lisa Wood had to do in the kitchen at ten minutes after eleven. Did people eat an early breakfast before they went out to wait for the day of judgment?

But the light went out and it was quiet; as quiet as woods could ever be. The mountain river murmured drowsily; red pine, sugar pine, spruce and redwood talked the language that trees speak at night; a rustling, softly sighing speech to which Rocky had always liked to listen. But tonight the sound was expressive of hostility. Toward Sapphira? Yes, that would be it. . . .

Rocky smiled sheepishly, establishing himself once more at the window. It beat hell, the effect a dark night and a little wind in the trees had on your imagination. Sapphira was back in her chair drinking her coffee. You could tell that from the way her head moved. Rocky could just see the plate of sandwiches. As Sapphira ate he mentally located bread and cheese among their provisions. Pope had promised to relieve him at one o'clock and it must be at least midnight by now. Funny noise, like a rock falling somewhere. When he got back to camp he'd make himself a sandwich and—

He thought: "It's happened! But how could it," and crashed toward the back of the house, through the brush. He felt as if the dark night still quivered from the harsh explosions that had torn through it; from those sounds of shots and the shrill, high scream that followed.

There was a dim light in the kitchen. It shone through the open door where Saul Cheney lay very still across the threshold and Lisa Wood stood staring down at him.

CHAPTER SEVEN
"A SMALL, SQUARE-TOED SHOE"

She was getting ready to scream again. Her brown, hard hands went up to her tangled hair and clenched there. Rocky looked for water but the tin bucket on the floor was empty. He said:

"Stop looking at him, sister. If you get hysterical I'll have to slap you 'cross the jaw."

So many questions to be asked, so many things to be done crowded in on him that afterward he wondered how so much could have happened in such a short time. Instinctively he bent down and tugged at Cheney's shoulders. But the man was dead; you didn't go on living with two bullets in your back.

It had been good shooting, for it didn't take an expert to see that Cheney had not been shot from close range. As he stood in the door with the light in front of him he would have been a long, black silhouette to someone waiting in the dark outside. And his murderer must have stood outside; on that trail that led to the stream.

Rocky hesitated. Should he chase down that path? No, he didn't dare leave here until Pope came. Pope had said to signal him, but surely he'd have heard those shots if he was awake. He should be here in an instant. Rocky looked at his watch again; it had been five minutes after twelve when he burst into the kitchen; exactly three minutes had passed since then.

Sapphira Barlow said: "Saul?" Then: "Why did you kill him, Lisa?"

Lisa backed against a rough pine table, her thin body trembling. She said hoarsely: "I didn't—kill him."

"No? What was he doing here then? You let him in? I suppose that's why you wanted to sleep in the kitchen tonight?"

The girl flinched as if each question were a blow. She muttered: "It was warmer in here."

"Oh!" Sapphira laughed. "I thought perhaps Saul was up to his old tricks."

"I'll gamble you know plenty about his—tricks, ma'am," Rocky drawled. "S'pose you wait and let Mr. Pope carry on this examination." He said to Lisa, pushing a chair toward her: "Set down." And to Sapphira: "Seems to me you take this mighty calm. You don't seem much surprised."

"I'm greatly relieved," Sapphira said coolly. "I expected him to try to kill me. I was— Don't come in here, David."

"But I woke up again. I don't like this place, Grandma. I heard—" David looked across his grandmother's shoulders at Cheney's body. He said: "Oh!" with frank and unhorrified curiosity. "It's Saul, isn't it? Is he dead?"

"He appears to be kind of that way," Rocky said dryly. "It'd be a good idea if you ran back to bed, sonny. You might tell me, though, if something frightened you before. You said you woke up again."

"I had bad dreams. Nothing happened really. I can't even remember what it was I dreamed, now. Must I go back to bed, Grandma?"

"You'd better. Light your candle if you want to." Sapphira was looking at Cheney with narrowed eyes. After an instant she said: "Hadn't you better go after your Mr. Pope?"

Rocky thought: *She'd like to get me away from here for a few minutes.* He fingered his gun tentatively. He'd better step outside and signal, but two more shots might bring everyone in the place running to see what was the matter. At that, it was funny that they hadn't already been roused.

Pope had been. He made plenty of noise coming around the house, swinging a powerful flashlight in one hand. He said:

"Rocky—you're all right? I didn't know—" and fumbled in a breast pocket for his glasses. "Tell me what happened."

"I stood guard at the windows and nothing at all happened till I heard two shots. Sprinted around here and found the door open, Cheney like he is now, and Miss Wood standin' here looking at him. There ain't any gun, 'less she has it on her."

Lisa Wood whispered: "I haven't. None of you ask me what happened, except Mrs. Barlow and she seems to think— Well, it's not so! That Mr. Cheney came here to see me. I wanted to sleep in here because it's warmer and I had to get up early tomorrow—today—to make the coffee. That's the only reason I came in here to sleep. I wasn't asleep because I'd made some coffee for Mrs. Barlow. I was lying there."

She jerked her head in the direction of a pile of blankets on the floor. "I hadn't undressed. It didn't seem worth while. Then there was this knock on the door and Mr. Cheney spoke to me and I opened the door for him. How did I know I shouldn't let him in? Mrs. Barlow says he wanted to kill her, but I thought they were friends and maybe he had something important to talk to her about. I opened the door—I'd lighted the candle first—and then there were two shots and he fell over, and I thought I heard someone running away down that path."

"You didn't hear Cheney at this door, Rocky? No? Didn't Mr. Cheney have to speak rather loud-ly for you to hear him, child?"

"Yes— Oh, I don't know! But I did hear him. He said: 'It's Mr. Cheney. I must see Mrs. Barlow.' That's all. And I did think I heard someone on the path."

Rocky looked questioningly at Pope and then stepped outside and started down the path to the stream. The ground in the center of the trail was soft and moist, crisscrossed with footprints. Cheney, Rocky had just noticed, had worn old-fashioned high shoes with rounded toes, so it was easy enough to pick out his tracks in several places.

There were a number of prints of a small foot, long and narrow. Those might have been made by Lisa Wood. They looked, Rocky thought, as if their maker had been carrying something; a pail of water, perhaps. He wished he remembered more of the things he'd been told about footprints by that old guide who usually wintered in Merton.

But he thought these tracks had been made at least two or three hours ago. They had had time to dry a little around the edges. The murmur of the river came closer; he was approximately fifty feet from the back door when he picked out a third set of prints.

These had been made by someone wearing a small, square-toed shoe, flat-heeled. Where they ended, the impressions were broken as if someone had whirled about to run down the path, but in

other places they were distinct enough. He made
them out, going toward the cabin and coming back
toward the stream. But now two tall pines shed
their needles on the path and feet left no definite
mark on it. Rocky started back to the cabin whist-
ling softly.

"Somebody was out there all right," he reported, purposely indefinite. "Miss Wood couldn't've
seen anyone, I suppose. You was holdin' the candle in front of you? What kind of shoes do you
wear?"

Lisa produced a pair of worn, black slippers
with narrow toes and run-over Cuban heels.

"These are all the shoes I've got, except for the
bedroom slippers I've got on now. I go for water,
if you mean my footprints are on the path."

Pope glanced briefly at the cheap, too-large felt
slippers on the foot she stretched out for inspec-
tion. Sapphira, smiling obscurely, showed an embroidered Chinese slipper of black silk and David
stood wriggling his bare toes on the rough floor.
Pope said:

"Young man, you've no business here."

"I like it better here than all alone in the bedroom," David said stubbornly.

"Then lie down on the couch in the front room.
Perhaps," Sapphira said, "you'll want the bedroom
for him." Although she said "him," she might as
well have referred to Cheney as "that." "I suppose

he has to be put somewhere. So you'd better stay in the front room, David. If you're still awake when Mr. Pope is through in here Lisa can make you some chocolate."

"I'll make the choc'late—but I won't stay another night in this place!" Lisa said violently. "It—chokes me! I'd rather sleep under a tree, or anywhere."

You couldn't say that there was really anything definitely threatening about the way Sapphira looked at the girl, but the glance made Rocky uneasy. The old lady's vague smile was as evil as that of some oriental god. He said:

"We'll find somewheres for you to sleep, if Pope says it's all right. My wife— Say, Pope, what about Eleanor? If she heard those shots—"

"She didn't. I spoke to her softly, but she would have heard me if she had been awake. So I thought it best not to disturb her. David," Pope said; "please go into the front room and go to sleep if you can."

David looked at him mutinously for an instant, but he turned to go, only delaying to ask: "Then we don't have to get up so early in the morning, Grandma? I mean—it—you really didn't mean it about the judgment day?"

"I didn't mean it," Sapphira said calmly. "That was Saul's idea. He wasn't a nice man and he wanted to kill me. Remember that, David."

"But why—"

Sapphira said: "David!" and the boy backed hastily out of the room. "He's an impressionable child, brought up the way he's been, and Saul had too much influence over him. Appealed to his imagination. I suppose you want to know why I say Saul would have liked to kill me? Well, I had to make him David's guardian and trustee."

"Had to?" Pope said suggestively. He turned Cheney's body over and began to go through the man's pockets.

"Yes. Never mind why. You're shrewd enough to know I wouldn't have put up with Saul if I hadn't thought it was absolutely necessary. He was often very useful, though I never let him know too much. He might have squealed. It was easier to satisfy him in other ways. He'd have liked to have had the handling of my money for David for nine years. He'd have made a pretty penny out of that."

"Then you appointed only one trustee?"

"Saul chose the other one. But by himself, though he's a rascal, he won't do much damage. And I expect, now, to live a few years longer."

"You didn't expect Cheney to come here to-night?" Pope looked thoughtfully at Cheney's gun and put it in his own pocket.

"I wouldn't have been surprised if he had, on some excuse or other. But as long as he didn't sneak up on me I wasn't afraid. You showing up here put a crimp in his plans, I imagine. He hadn't counted on the others either, but he always talked too much. And the fool halfway hypnotized himself into believing that the world might end tomorrow. I said that was his idea. Well, he carried it farther than I would have. I only wanted an excuse for getting out of Los Angeles. And it was funny, scaring some of the half-wits that took my mumblings seriously. Saul made me do it up in style; picked out this place and I had to come here."

"Where does Miss Wood come in?" Pope asked.

"I had to have someone with me to do the work and I'd gotten rid of the old gang," Sapphira said carelessly. "She's an orphan. Too old to stay at the asylum and couldn't find work. I thought she'd do."

She looked covetously at a thick brown wallet that Pope had just taken from an inside pocket of Cheney's coat. "You haven't any authority here, Mr. Pope," she said finally. "You're not a police officer. You can suppress evidence, especially when it hasn't any bearing on this murder. I'll give you whatever it is you came up here for, for that wallet."

If he were Pope, Rocky thought, he'd make the trade. It would save a lot of trouble. But he

didn't think Pope would take her up on the proposition. Pope turned the wallet over in his long
brown hands and then put it in an already over-
laden pocket.

"I would be singularly lacking in the shrewdness with which you credit me if it didn't occur to
me that when I have looked over the contents of
this, I may be in a very good position for bargain-
ing with you," he said gently.

Rocky chuckled and Sapphira said: "Damn you!"
Rocky waited interestedly for more of the same,
suspecting that even he could learn a few words
from Sapphira if she let herself go. But she didn't.
She said, shrugging: "I should have thought of
that."

"Did it ever occur to you," Pope said mildly,
"that Cheney's death would make things easier for
you?"

"It occurred to me on the average of a dozen
times a day, but murder is a hard rap to beat.
And he was pretty careful. If you mean, did I kill
him—no. You might ask your young man here
about that."

"I don't see how she could have," Rocky said.
"She was setting in front of the fire when I heard
the shots."

"Inconvenient, isn't it, Mr. Pope?" Sapphira
said mockingly. "Pardon my curiosity, but what
are the authorities in this God-forsaken place?"

"I reckon I'll do until someone else gets here," Rocky said. "I'm a dep'ty sheriff in this county." He enjoyed seeing the old woman's half-smile vanish abruptly. "Cheney wouldn't have known that. I can show you a badge if you like. Cheney probably counted on the authorities being hard to get in touch with, here. And he was right. We're just out of Butte County, so we'll have to get in touch with Brookdale when Oroville'd been a lot easier."

Pope said: "Yes, it would have been. Rocky, will you help me carry Cheney into that bedroom? It seems the only place to put him. I suppose that if we had chalk we should draw an outline of the position in which he fell. But we haven't."

Lisa Wood muttered: "I'll build up the fire and make that choc'late," but Sapphira followed them into the living room. David's head bobbed up from the couch where he was lying and he complained:

"I can't seem to go to sleep at all. I keep seeing funny things when I close my eyes."

"Imagination," Sapphira said absently. "You'll go to sleep when you've had something hot to drink." She sat down in her big chair and draped an embroidered shawl about her shoulders.

Pope pulled a blanket over Cheney's face and stood erect. There were no bunks in the bedroom; David's bed was a thin mattress covered with soiled blankets. Lisa had evidently slept on another such mattress, stripped now of its covers. Four suitcases and a wooden box on which were set out candles and matches were the only other things in the small, airless room.

"It don't look like the old girl could hide anything in here," Rocky said. "Dismal sort of place. About those footprints on the path. There was Cheney's and the girl's, I think, and someone else's; made by a flat-heeled shoe, square-toed. A woman's, of course. They didn't come any nearer the house than about forty-five or fifty feet. Looked to me like someone stopped there and then whirled aroun' and ran back down the path. I didn't go quite down to the crick. You can tell more about it in the daytime."

"I can't," Pope said flatly. "I don't like to pore over footprints. But of course we should try to keep people away from that path until we can examine it. You said a small, square-toed shoe? Well, Mrs. Leroy is the only one who wears that type of shoe—I think."

"I know it. Her niece wears sandals without much toe, and her feet are pretty large considerin' she's a small girl. Mrs. Greer was wearin' riding boots and her feet are plenty big. So are Mrs. Cheney's and she had on bedroom slippers. An' those things Sapphira and the boy wears have padded soles."

"I'm quite certain your facts will be proved to be perfectly correct. Fifty feet, you said?"

"Fifty— Oh, you mean the distance from the door that this person stood? Well, that's just guessin'. If he was shot from that distance it was damn good shooting, no matter what kind of gun was used. Of course Cheney's standin' right in front of a light made it easier. Was Cheney's gun loaded?"

"No. I doubt if he was the type to use a gun with any assurance. Except for that wallet there was nothing of interest in his pockets. What," Pope said frowning, "are we to do with that girl? I want to keep her away from Sapphira until we've had time to talk to her. She'll never talk coherently with Sapphira present."

"If you're suggestin' I tuck her in with Eleanor for the rest of the night you can go sit on a tack. I aim to get a little sleep sometime before long."

"I want you to. If she will sleep there she can occupy my luxurious bed. Yes, that will be best, because you will be near enough to keep an eye on her."

"You think she's in danger?"

"I don't know. But she was in a position to have learned too much for her own good, don't you think? As for Sapphira— Well, we'd better talk to her."

As they entered the room Pope said gravely: "Mrs. Barlow, who would inherit your money . . . if David did not?"

Sapphira said: "O-oh." She straightened her red turban mechanically, fingering the pin that fastened it; then: "No one," she said. "Of course I see your idea, but I haven't another living relative that I know of. If there were any they wouldn't know they were. If David died before Saul it went to him. That was another of his bright ideas. But with Saul out of the way—"

"I see. But you don't want to spend the rest of the night here, do you? I don't know where you can go. Perhaps Mrs. Cheney—"

"God, no! That woman is just a lump of dough; she gets on my nerves. Aren't you taking your time about breaking the news to the widow?"

Pope ignored Sapphira's jeering smile. "Will she regret Cheney's death?" he asked.

"You wouldn't think she could and probably she won't, but she'll never realize that she doesn't. He should leave a pretty fair bank account and she's certainly earned whatever money he leaves her," Sapphira said, more charitably than was to be expected. "I don't know why she stuck to him for so long. Maybe she never really knew anything about him. She was trained to be a meek and long-suffering wife and her people were missionaries, so maybe that explains it. But she wouldn't kill him, if that's what you've got in mind."

"It isn't. But if you won't go to Mrs. Cheney—"

"I don't want her coming here either. And I'm not going to move. I'm warm and comfortable here; I'm not timid and I'm not imaginative. David can do as he likes, if you can find some place else for him to sleep—stay here or go with you."

David yawned. "Oh, I guess I'll stay here. I'm getting a little sleepy now. This isn't so exciting after all, is it? Detecting, I mean. And Grandma ought to have somebody here with her."

"She will." Rocky could tell by the way Pope's lips tightened that he was irritated.

"Rocky, we'll have to call Doyle in. There aren't enough of us to go around without him and he seems the best one to use. Suppose you bring him here. Tell Eleanor what has happened first, if you like."

Rocky said: "O.K.," and left the house with a feeling of relief. He cut across the corner of the clearing with long strides; reached their camp and the tent.

He said softly, stooping down to the tent flap: "Eleanor! Are you awake?" There was no answer, and when he directed the rays of his flashlight over the bed Eleanor was not there.

CHAPTER EIGHT
"YOU KNOW I'VE BEEN OUTSIDE"

When an hour had passed and she was more wide-awake than when she had gone to bed, Eleanor got up and found a bottle of allonal tablets in the small medicine chest they carried.

"I might as well," she told herself, getting back into bed, "take two and get some sleep. I can always wake up." She looked at her watch before she put out the light and pulled the covers up to her nose. "It will be at least two hours before Mr. Pope goes on duty. This," she declared presently, "is a ridiculous business anyway," and went to sleep.

She woke suddenly, feeling that someone had spoken to her, but when she said: "Is anyone there?" no one answered. She switched the light on again, saw that it was fifteen minutes past twelve and lay back, trying to decide if she had really heard someone speak. Or had it been some noise that had lingered in her consciousness long enough finally to wake her? What had she been dreaming just before she woke?

The dream, if there had been one, refused to materialize. She found that she was lying rigid, listening to every slight sound of the forest at night. Should she call to Pope? No, if he was sleeping she did not want to cut short what little rest he would get that night. She would get up and dress, build a fire and make coffee for him.

She was putting on her sweater when stumbling footsteps approached the tent, paused uncertainly and a girl's voice said: "Where—oh damn! I can't see anything! Where did that light roll to? Mr. Pope! Mrs. Allan!"

Eleanor threw back the tent flap and stepped out into the cold night. Margaret Corwin was on her hands and knees near the tent, groping about among the pine needles. She looked up and blinked in the light from Eleanor's torch.

"I dropped my flashlight and probably broke the damn thing," she said, half sobbing. "And nearly broke my shin running into a tree. Where's Mr. Pope? Though I really came after you."

Eleanor stepped over to Pope's lean-to, finally looked in and found his bed rumpled but unoccupied. She said: "I think he must already have gone to—relieve my husband."

"Relieve? You mean they're guarding that old bitch?" The girl laughed hysterically. "That's a hot one. Oh—here's the light and busted, just as I expected. Please, Mrs. Allan, Warren said you were a nurse and I simply don't know what to do with my aunt. She's—she's had an attack and we haven't got a thing but a little aspirin. I thought perhaps you—"

Eleanor snatched the first-aid kit from the tent, stopped to scribble a note to Rocky and pin it on a pillow. She said: "Of course I'll come," wondering if Pope was with Rocky. He might be off on some expedition of his own, but she didn't think he would have left her alone in camp unless Rocky was coming back at once or something had happened. . . .

She hesitated, but the girl's hand on her arm was urgent and she asked: "What kind of attack?"

"Oh, I don't know. Her heart. . . . No, I can't fool you," Margaret Corwin said miserably. "It's nerves, pure and simple. And even if I had anything to give her I don't think I could make her take it. She hates drugs—even just sleeping tablets. She just lies there and shivers all over."

"How long has she been doing that?"

"I—I d-don't know. I was asleep. I put on the light to see what time it was. I thought," she added with a wan smile, "that the day of judgment might be at hand. Joke! Well, there she was, like she is now."

"Do you have separate beds?"

"What? Y-yes, we have cots. I expect mine to fold up with me in it some night." Margaret stopped halfway across the clearing. "Who's that?"

Henry Powell said musically: "Margie dear . . . why are you wandering around out here by yourself? Don't you— Oh, you're not alone?"

"I should think that's very evident. Mrs. Allan, this is Hank Powell. And what are *you* doing, wandering out here by yourself?"

"I couldn't sleep. Warren snores very loudly. Then he woke up and had one of his peculiar intuitions."

"It wasn't so peculiar," Doyle said. "I just thought I'd check up on Cheney, and he isn't in his tent. Ma Cheney's there. Says she can't sleep either, and that friend husband is out communing with the stars and wrestling with his soul. I wonder what he's up to? The Greers seem to be the only people in this place that are getting any sleep. What's the matter with you, Margie?"

"Minna isn't feeling well, so I thought Mrs. Allan had better take a look at her."

"That's tough. What's wrong with her? Can I help?"

"No, you can't, and I wish you wouldn't pester me with questions. Please, Mrs. Allan, let's go on."

Doyle said mildly: "I've got some pretty good whisky if you want some, Mrs. Allan," and followed them to Mrs. Leroy's tent, where a faint light showed inside. "Oh, I'm not going to bother you," he said. "But Hank and I will stick around in case you do need us."

Minna Leroy struggled to sit upright as they entered, then sank back on one elbow. She looked at Eleanor with wide, staring dark eyes; tried to smile.

"Margie, what on earth possessed you? You know I'm all right. . . ."

Eleanor said, reverting automatically to the brightly encouraging tone that she had once used professionally: "Of course you are, Mrs. Leroy, but your niece was terribly worried."

She held the woman's thin wrist with steady fingers, thinking: She's simply scared to death about something and probably a bundle of nerves anyway. She may not have been sleeping lately.

Mrs. Leroy said, as if she had guessed Eleanor's diagnosis: "I haven't been sleeping well for quite a while. I thought that a trip to the mountains—roughing it and all that—would help. But I find the nights here . . . frightening. It's ridiculous of course."

"Oh, I don't think so. I couldn't sleep tonight either." Eleanor discarded her professional tone; it was insulting to use it to this woman. "I have some tablets here, Mrs. Leroy; allonal or amytal. You know they won't hurt you."

"Why do you say that?" Mrs. Leroy began to shiver again, pushing her dark hair back from her face. Margaret said quickly:

"I told her you didn't like to take—medicine."

"Oh! No—no, I don't." She tried to laugh; stopped, as if she were afraid of what her laughter might reveal. "You wouldn't either. . . . Margie, I'm sorry I got you into this. I never thought—"

"Mrs. Leroy," Eleanor said warningly, "I don't want you to say things you'll regret before me. Mr. Pope is my friend, you know, and he's interested in this—this situation. I don't want to take advantage of you. Get that bottle of whisky from Mr. Doyle, Miss Corwin."

"Is Warren up too? And Hank? I didn't know—"

"Mr. Doyle was looking for Mr. Cheney," Eleanor began thoughtlessly.

Minna Leroy tried to sit up again; fell back, laughing. "He'll have to—to look—" She gasped. Eleanor caught her frail shoulders and shook her.

"Shut up!" she said brutally. "I can't do anything for you if you let yourself go. Here!" She

poured whisky into the glass Margaret handed her.
"Drink this—and swallow these."

She eased the woman back on her pillow. The
flannel robe she was wearing had fallen back from
her throat to show the same woven sports dress
that Eleanor had noticed that afternoon. She said
to Margaret:

"She'll be all right now. Don't you want a drink
too?"

The girl's lips trembled but she said with at-
tempted jauntiness: "Don't mind if I do." Then,
shuddering: "Well, if that's Wren's idea of good
whisky! His palate was ruined by Prohibition, I
guess." She moved over to her aunt's cot and patted her white hand. "If that doesn't knock you
out, Minna, nothing will."

"Mrs. Allan is very kind, but it won't do any
good . . . in the end.

"You know I've been outside, don't you?"

"Yes," Eleanor said honestly. "Unless you went
to bed with your clothes on for warmth. It has
been done, you know."

"Do you think anyone would believe I'd do
that?" Mrs. Leroy smiled stiffly. "No, I'll have to
admit that I was outside. . . ."

"But that isn't any crime, is it? And if it is I'll
swear you weren't," Margaret said defiantly. "I'll

swear you were here every minute and I'll make people believe me, too."

"I know you'd try. And it was really partly on your account."

"I know it, and I'd have come with you, anywhere you thought you had to go. Gosh, haven't you raised me from a pup? Only I do think Uncle Edgar isn't such a bad guy."

"I thoroughly appreciate your uncle—now. But I still think I know him better than you do."

"I'm not so sure about that. He can't talk, you know. At least, he just can't say pretty nothings, but I've seen him looking at you sometimes . . . sort of wistful and doggy-like. He can tell me how wonderful you are even if he can't say it to you. He wouldn't throw us out into the cold, cruel world. I'll bet he'd be a sweet lamb."

"I know. I don't want to hurt him." Minna Leroy closed her eyes. "And now—it's worse than if I had told him." She moved her head restlessly on the pillow, then looked up at Eleanor. "Perhaps you have some idea what we are talking about, Mrs. Allan? Some general idea.—I don't know why Mr. Pope is here and of course you can't tell me. He—he isn't—" She bit her lip and finally got the words out. "He isn't a—a narcotic squad man?"

"No, he isn't," Eleanor said quickly. "He has no official standing at all. He—well, I suppose it

must be obvious to anyone that he wants to interview Sapphira Barlow. Now, you will go to sleep,
won't you? Miss Corwin—"

"Margie to you."

"Margie will call me if you need me again. I
must get back to camp in case they've—before
they begin to wonder what has become of me."

Doyle and Henry Powell were still waiting outside. The former said:

"Anything really wrong with Minna?" He
looked at Eleanor doubtfully when she shook her
head. "Well, you wouldn't tell anyway. Better let
us take you back to your camp, Mrs. Allan." He
waited until they had walked several yards farther
before he said, lowering his voice: "I didn't want
to scare Margie, but— Were you awake when she
came over to your camp?"

"Yes, I was, but I hadn't been for very long."

"You didn't hear anything then? You couldn't
have, or— Where's your husband?"

Eleanor said: "Why? What do you mean?" in
quick alarm, but before Doyle could answer, another light came bobbing across the clearing and
Rocky called:

"Is that you, Eleanor? You gave me a hell of a
scare before I spotted your note." He shifted his
light to Doyle's face for an instant. "I started out

to wake you but you seem to be up an' about already. Something wrong?"

"I was just going to tell Mrs. Allan that I thought I heard two shots about—oh, say about forty-five minutes ago."

Rocky hesitated; then: "You did," he said. "Two shots, in Cheney's back. Where was you when you heard 'em?"

"Just going in to talk to Mrs. Cheney. You see, I was curious to know if Cheney was up to anything tonight. I was going to give some excuse to see him if he was in his tent. He wasn't. Mrs. Cheney was sitting up in bed knitting. She said she couldn't sleep."

"Didn't she hear the shots?"

"She's pretty deaf. She didn't seem to hear anything, so I kept still."

"And you think this was forty-five minutes ago?"

Doyle laughed. "Oh, I get you, Sherlock." He looked at his wrist watch. "It's one o'clock now. I left our tent about twelve, prowled around a little first. So I don't know just what time it was when I was talking to Mrs. Cheney."

"If you heard the shots then, it was a minute or two after twelve," Rocky said. "What were you doing, Powell?"

"I thought Warren was foolish, losing sleep over Cheney. So I tried to go back to sleep, but I couldn't. I heard the shots too, but I was not fool enough to investigate. Then I saw that there was a light in Minna's tent and I saw Margie going across the clearing—saw her light, that is—so I got up and dressed. I thought something might be wrong. Warren came back before Margie and Mrs. Allan did and we met them together."

"What were you doin' the rest of the time, Doyle? Not just holding Mrs. Cheney's hand?"

Doyle said, with none of the resentment that had tinged Powell's answer: "Prowling around some more. I still thought I might locate Cheney. So someone plugged him?"

"Seems so. I came after you because we're short handed. That old dame won't leave the cabin and I reckon Pope wants you to stay with her."

Doyle grimaced. "That's a job I don't care for, brother. And listen— Oh well, let it go until I've talked to the Big Boss. Hank, you'd better stick around in case Margie needs you."

Powell said: "I intend to. I'll sit in the door of our tent." He added maliciously: "It appears to me that Mr. Greer sleeps very soundly."

Greer said: "I'm not asleep, young man. Haven't been for quite some time. I could hear what you were saying but I had to get my clothes on before I came out."

"Did you hear something too?" Rocky asked.

"I've been hearing things for the last half-hour. People walking around. Well, I figured it was none of my business, but finally my wife—she sleeps like the dead—woke up too, and nothing would do but for me to come out and investigate. Did I hear you saying someone shot Cheney, Mr. Doyle?" At Doyle's nod, Greer whistled thoughtfully. "Well, I guess Eva's got the sensation she came for all right."

"Well, you go back and discuss it with her," Rocky suggested. "I don't know what Pope has in mind to do first, but he's waitin' for us. Come on, Doyle."

"Me too?" Eleanor said coaxingly.

"Oh yes, I suppose you too." Rocky drew her arm through his and murmured against her hair: "Don't you scare me again like that. You want to wait an' tell me 'n Pope together about Mrs. Leroy? I figured you would."

CHAPTER NINE
SHE MUST HAVE BEEN AFRAID

Neither Pope nor Sapphira Barlow seemed to have moved since he left them, Rocky thought, and he had an idea there hadn't been much conversation between them. Sapphira gave a last thoughtful look at the crystal ball as if she had seen something in it that interested her, and turned toward Doyle.

"This is quite a reunion," she said. "An old, familiar face. Oh yes, I remembered you at once, Mr. Doyle. I was so flattered by your interest in my séances. We should have a lot to talk about if you're going to spend the night here."

"Am I?" Doyle said, ignoring Sapphira. "I know I said I'd help, but—"

"You've had more sleep than Rocky and he can't be spared for an hour or so. Miss Wood won't stay here, so we're taking her over to our camp. And Mrs. Barlow refuses to leave here," Pope said. "She shouldn't stay alone, and Cheney's body is here—"

"Oh, I can see you need help. But what about notifying the authorities? That has to be done, doesn't it? And I want to get to a telephone myself."

"I supposed you would, but that will have to wait until morning—"

"Else we'd probably have another corpse on our hands if you tried to drive out over that road tonight," Rocky said. "Anyway, where do you reckon you're going to find a phone? Manzanita won't have any."

"How do you know?" Doyle said.

Rocky shrugged. "Well, maybe I'm wrong but I don't seem to remember any telephone wires aroun' the hotel. I don't know where the nearest ranger station or fire lookout is, but I'll bet money you'll have to find one to locate a phone anywheres near Manzanita. Otherwise you'll probably have to go"— he closed his eyes for an instant—"go on down to that place called Boulder, 'bout fifteen miles down from Manzanita," he finished. "They had a telephone sign there."

"Rocky," Pope said as Doyle looked skeptical, "has a way of noticing things like that without knowing at the time that he has."

"What Pope kind of disgustedly calls phys'cal facts," Rocky said. "You get in the way of noticin' signs and rocks an' funny trees when you fire a train up and down the canyon. He's got me to noticin' what people say and how they say it. I'll bet you the nearest phone is at Boulder. I don't re-member noticing any signs about where the near-est ranger station is from here."

"That," Pope said, "more or less settles it. It will take one of us at least two or three hours to-morrow to make the trip. You can't do it tonight. Will you stay here?"

"Oh, I'll stay, as a favor to you." Doyle looked at Sapphira with unconcealed dislike. "In this room."

"The kitchen, if you don't mind. We carried Cheney into the bedroom. You can guard that back door if you stay in the kitchen and you might be able to hear anyone who might come back to that path. If anyone does you had better investigate. Have you a gun?"

"N-no. No, I haven't."

"Take this one then. I won't need it. We'd bet-ter be going."

"Just a minute, Pope. Everybody knows you've got a lot of rubies," Doyle said to Sapphira. "Did you bring them with you? Because if you did—"

"If I had I don't know what you could do about it. However, you can rest easy about that. As I've already told Mr. Pope, I left them in a safe-depos-it box."

"In L.A.?" Doyle raised his pale eyebrows. "I heard you cleared out with everything you had so you wouldn't be embarrassed by having to go back for anything."

"You know everything, don't you?" Sapphira snapped. "Well, wise guy, I stopped in San Francisco on my way here. All I brought up here are things I'd not want any snooping cop to find if someone took a notion to open a safe-deposit box. Does that satisfy your curiosity? I— Well, it's about time you got that stuff made."

Lisa Wood said: "I burned up the first lot, not thinking what I was doing. The fire wouldn't burn right off, anyway." She put a saucepan filled with steaming chocolate on the table. "Does David want to drink it now?"

"It'll be too hot for him and I think he's asleep. I'll drink some of it myself, though I'm not fond of the slop."

"I'm not asleep, Grandma," David said drowsily. "Just listening to all of you, because you told me not to talk so much. Maybe Mr. Doyle would like company in the kitchen; someone to talk to, I mean."

Doyle grinned. "Don't you worry about me, kid. You go to sleep."

"That's all anybody has said to me all night," David remarked mournfully. "Oh well . . ."

He turned his face away from the light and curled up like a kitten. Lisa Wood took an old sweater from a nail on the wall and said, not looking at Sapphira: "I guess I'm ready to go."

Sapphira glanced at her contemptuously. "Pleasant dreams."

"You'd better ask her how much she sold out for, since she says she wasn't carrying on an affair with Saul."

Rocky thought that Sapphira's suggested question would certainly have to be answered. The girl must have had some reason for opening that door. But Pope said, when they were outside:

"I think I'll have to ask you to go along with us for a few minutes, Miss Wood, before we can go to our own camp. We will have to speak to Mrs. Cheney at once. You don't mind, do you?"

Obviously it startled the girl to have her preferences consulted. She muttered: "No, of course not. Anything that suits you." Then: "I couldn't stay there! Not even with that man there, because I'd have to sit in the same room with Mrs. Barlow and she'd look at me—and look at me."

"That wasn't what you started to say. Were you going to say that she might harm you in some way?"

"She might. I'm afraid of her."

"Why?" Pope stopped and turned the light from his torch onto the girl's face. "Did you see who shot Cheney? I don't see how you could have, but if you did you can save us a great deal of trouble by telling us who it was."

"I never saw one thing—but him! How could I when he was between me and the door?"

Pope made no answer. They were approaching the line of camps now, and Eleanor said:

"Do you want me to talk to Mrs. Cheney? I know it's an unpleasant job for you. Of course I've never spoken to her—"

"I'd like to have you come with me—but I think," Pope said, "that we aren't going to have to break the news to Mrs. Cheney after all."

Rocky murmured: "Well, I'm a son of a gun!" listening to Eva Greer's high voice within Mrs. Cheney's tent. "Little Eva didn't waste any time, did she?"

"Not much. Still, it probably doesn't matter," Eleanor said. "At least we won't have to— Mr. Greer?"

"It's me. I tried to keep Eva from going in there," Greer said apologetically, sucking on his pipe. "But it just couldn't be done. She insisted Mrs. Cheney should have a woman with her and that men were brutes."

"His murderer will be punished." Mrs. Greer said oratorically. *"Vengeance is mine'*—and you must just bow to God's will and think that it is all for the best." She emerged from the tent, unrestrainedly plump in a bright Japanese kimono, smiling at them sadly.

"Poor dear, she is still just stunned by it all, but she is being very brave. I do hope you aren't going to bother her. The shock—"

Mrs. Cheney said in a flat voice that seemed to verify Doyle's statement that she was deaf: "Did someone want me?"

"If you don't mind, Mrs. Cheney—" She frowned, looking toward Pope's face, shadowy behind his flashlight; he raised his voice. "If you don't mind telling us what time your husband left here last night—before midnight, that is."

"I couldn't tell you exactly. We've got an old alarm clock but it's always stopping. It has now. But it was about ten when Saul went to bed. Not long after he got back from taking you to Madam Sapphira's, you know. He tossed and tumbled and finally said he was going out to walk around. He did that sometimes. I tried to go back to sleep but I couldn't, so I finally lighted a candle and started knitting. I can do that almost in the dark. I did think he was gone quite a while, but I guessed he and Madam Sapphira might be talking."

"Did he say he was going to see her?"

"What? Oh no, he didn't say so. But he might have decided to go in and talk to her if she was awake. She might have had some new revelation for him."

Eleanor looked at the woman's broad, curiously unlined face; thought: I don't believe she has ever known anything about Mr. Cheney. Or that she has very strong feelings, except for what she considers her duty. She doesn't pretend to be overwhelmed with grief and probably she's just used to accepting things as they come.

"Did you believe Mrs. Barlow's—and your husband's—revelations?" Pope said.

For an instant Mrs. Cheney looked at him with the expression of an amiable cow scrutinizing some strange object.

"I never felt it was my place to question what they believed," she said. "The way I felt about it—when the world ends, we can't stop it. The best way is just to be ready for it any time. Maybe Saul and Madam Sapphira could see farther than the rest of us. Saul has—had studied those things all his life and he said Madam Sapphira had the gift of prophecy."

"Indeed?" Pope said—for him, inadequately. "Had they known each other before you arrived in Los Angeles?"

"Why no. It just happened that he got interested in spiritualism and someone told him to go to Madam Sapphira. He admired her so much that he asked to meet her, and after that he was a great help to her. Knowing all he did about Scripture, he could," Mrs. Cheney said, obviously quoting, "direct her work into worthier channels."

"I see. You stayed in your tent knitting until Mrs. Greer came in to—to talk to you."

"I stayed in there, yes." Mrs. Cheney pulled her old gray bathrobe closer about her. "But that young Mr. Doyle did come in, asking where the mister—where Saul was. We talked a little bit. Mrs. Greer tells me her husband says there were some shots fired about that time. I didn't hear them;—you can see I'm deaf. But I do remember thinking I heard a kind of—of jar, and he kind of started and looked like he was listening, though he didn't say anything and left in a few minutes."

"Mr. Cheney had enemies?"

"He's been slandered a lot; people saying he did things he didn't do. But I don't know of anyone here that didn't like him."

"Someone killed him," Pope said harshly.

A look of vague disquiet crossed Mrs. Cheney's face. She said: "Yes. I can't understand it."

"If you think of anything that will help us understand it, you will tell us? He may, without your knowing it at the time, have dropped some hint that would help.”

“We didn’t talk much,” Mrs. Cheney said. “But I’ll try to think about it. You’d better go back to bed, Mrs. Greer. You’ll catch a bad cold in that thin bathrobe.”

Nearing their own camp, Rocky said: “German? Or Pennsylvania Dutch? Not that it matters any.”

“Mrs. Cheney, you mean, because she started to call Cheney ‘the mister’? Well, one never can tell what may or may not be important. How did Greer know Doyle was with Mrs. Cheney when those shots were fired?” Pope asked.

“Oh, we were all talkin’ pretty near his tent while he was dressing to come out. Let’s see if I can tell you this without takin’ too much time for it.”

Rocky knelt down by the ashes of the campfire and began to whittle small shavings of pine from a pitchy stick. “Shots fired at just about twelve-three or four. Doyle says he got up to see what Cheney might be up to about midnight. More or less verified by Powell. Prowled round a bit, asked after Cheney an’ was talkin’ to Mrs. Cheney when he heard the shooting. He says. Far as what she said was concerned, knowin’ she was deaf he could’ve put on an act for her.”

"Yes," Pope said, "thereby gaining a not-too-obvious alibi. Won't you sit down, Miss Wood? Here, on this box. What reason did he give for not calling Mrs. Cheney's attention to the shots?"

"Said she didn't seem to hear anything, so he kept still. Then he prowled aroun' some more, to fill in the time till he met Eleanor about— When was it, honey?"

Eleanor frowned. "I can't be certain. About twelve-thirty or thirty-five, I think."

"Well, meanwhile Powell can't sleep neither; hears the shots but ain't going to risk his hide investigating. But when he sees a light in Mrs. Leroy's tent and the girl comin' here after Eleanor he gets up, and him and Doyle met them together."

"Miss Corwin came after you, Eleanor?"

"Yes. Her aunt was very—nervous, and she was frightened. She— But let Rocky finish his story."

"There ain't much more. You heard Mrs. Cheney. Accordin' to Greer, he didn't wake up till about twelve-thirty and his wife slept through for about twenty minutes more. Then he dressed and came out to us. He didn't say twelve-thirty, but he said he'd woke up about half an hour ago and it was one o'clock when he said that."

The fire was blazing brightly now. Rocky laid larger pieces of wood on it and filled a blackened pot with water. "I want something to eat. How about you?" he said to Lisa Wood.

"No—no, thank you. I'm not hungry." She twisted about on the box, holding her hands to the fire as if she were very cold, looking toward Pope with uneasy, sidewise glances. "I guess I shouldn't have bothered you folks," she said uncertainly.

"We have to talk to you, child. You know that, don't you?"

"Y-yes, Mr. Pope. I—guess you do."

"How do you happen to be working for Mrs. Barlow, Lisa?"

This was not the question she dreaded; she answered it promptly. "Like she said, I'm an orphan and they couldn't keep me in the home any more. They did get me a job but the lady decided she couldn't afford two servants. I couldn't seem to get anything else. So there was this ad in the paper for a girl who didn't have any family and would be willing to go anywhere, so I answered it."

"And Mrs. Barlow chose you from all the others? I suppose there were other applicants?"

"Yes, but some of them did have some relatives. She asked me specially about that and I told her how my mother died when I was a year old and my father—my father—"

"Yes?" Pope said gently.

"He was in prison. He died there," Lisa said, looking away from the fire's circle of light. "The asylum knew all about it. There wasn't anyone at all; not even a cousin. She said she didn't mind about my father."

Pope said, "Damn!" unexpectedly. "I'll wager she didn't. Grist for her mill. Does she treat you well, Lisa?"

"Oh . . . not bad. She makes me nervous; I'm afraid of her. But I don't have to work very hard. She's dirty," the girl said scornfully. "Doesn't take baths much, or care how a place looks. They did teach us to be clean in the asylum. She doesn't eat much either, and David eats all the time, so we don't have many regular meals. I was with her about two weeks before we came up here."

"And you met Saul Cheney as soon as you went to work for her?"

"Y-yes. He was there all the time."

"You heard what she said about Cheney; that he would have liked to kill her. Do you think that is true?"

"I—I guess so. Or she'd have liked to kill him. They never talked before me but sometimes I heard things. Once I knew they'd been fighting before I came into the room. You could tell by the funny red his face was. Then she looked at him and said:

'Acts 9:4.' That's in the Bible. I looked it up and it was something about *'Saul, Saul, why persecutest thou me?'* but she didn't say it sad at all. Just very—mean."

Pope smiled with his usual air of finding the exercise painful. "So tonight was not the first time she had reminded him of what happened to another Saul on the road to Damascus. . . . Oh yes, those mumblings of hers tonight were from the ninth chapter of Acts. Can you tell us anything else, Lisa?"

"Well, once I heard her say to him that it would be nice if someone would kill him, and then she said: 'Very likely someone will someday. The hangman, if you dispose of me. But there are plenty of people who might like to be sure you won't die by hanging.' I didn't hear what he said to that. Another time she said she'd see him in—in hell first if it wasn't for David. I don't know what about. But she is good enough to David.

"Soon as we got here she told me never to let Mr. Cheney get anywhere near anything I was cooking or any of the groceries that could be poisoned. She went out and bought all the supplies herself and saw them put in the car and carried in the house, and then nailed them up in boxes to bring up here. So I guess she must really have been a little afraid of him."

CHAPTER TEN
MRS. GEORGE EATON

Rocky poured very strong coffee into two tin cups, handed one to Pope and bit into the monumental sandwich that Eleanor had just constructed for him. He said abruptly:

"Did Cheney ever get fresh with you, sister?"

Lisa flushed. "I guess so. I mean, Mrs. Barlow hasn't any right to say I was carrying on with him, but he was always—always trying to get me into a corner or patting my—arm, or something like that. I think he'd be that way with any girl he thought would look at him. He was—was—"

"On the make is the expression you're searchin' for, kid. I was just wonderin' if Doyle had it right about his reputation. An' if he might have been castin' glances at Margie Corwin."

Eleanor shook her head, smiling. "He might have been, but Margie can take care of herself."

"I imagine she can," Pope said. "Since her name has come up again, tell me about your experiences, Eleanor."

"Well, I woke up about twelve-fifteen, and finally I decided to dress and make coffee for you. I wasn't out of the tent when Margie arrived, saying her aunt had—the jitters and did I have anything to give her. If I could make her take anything, because Mrs. Leroy hates taking even harmless sedatives. By the time we'd stopped to talk to Mr. Doyle and Mr. Powell, it must have been around twelve thirty-five and I suppose I was with Mrs. Leroy about twenty minutes."

"And what happened while you were with her?"

"She is scared to death about something," Eleanor said unwillingly. "I think she has been just a bundle of nerves for some time, anyway. But she expects to have to tell you everything—I think. She admitted—well, virtually admitted—that she had been outside."

Rocky whistled. "Did you see her shoes?"

"Shoes? No, I didn't notice them, but she was fully dressed, under her bathrobe. As I didn't know then—and I'm certain Margie didn't either—that Mr. Cheney was dead, I couldn't see why it was such a serious matter."

"Did Mrs. Leroy know Cheney was dead, do you think?" Pope asked.

"I—I don't know. But I foolishly said that Mr. Doyle had been looking for him, and she began to laugh hysterically. I stopped her before she could say anything," Eleanor said defiantly.

Pope nodded. "I don't blame you, under the circumstances. Did the girl give any account of what she'd been doing before she came for you?"

"About all she did say was that she waked up to find her aunt ill. She just had on her pajamas under her coat and she didn't mention having heard any shots. She told Mrs. Leroy she would swear they had been together all the time. Then, from the way they talked, I gathered Mrs. Leroy is in a situation somewhat similar to that of the girl you told us about. She did ask if you were connected with a narcotic squad."

Pope moved suddenly to face Lisa Wood again and the girl stared back at him fearfully, twisting her hands in her lap. Pope said gently:

"You say there was nothing between you and Cheney? That you didn't like him and that you knew Mrs. Barlow was at least a little afraid of him?"

Lisa nodded uncertainly. "Yes, I did say that."

"So you opened the door to him at midnight as soon as he told you he wanted in!"

"She—she might have wanted to see him for something. He couldn't have hurt her with me right there."

"He spoke to you so that you heard him on the other side of a thick door, yet not loudly enough for Mr. Allan here to hear his voice. And he said: 'It's Mr. Cheney. I must speak to Mrs. Barlow.' Is that right?"

"Y-yes: that's what he said."

Rocky said: "The only trouble is, sister, that Cheney didn't ever call her Mrs. Barlow. He called her Madam Sapphira. An' we know that Mrs. Leroy was right outside."

"Don't cry, my dear," Eleanor said, with her arm around Lisa's thin shoulders. "You'll make yourself sick. You know you have to tell them about it, because they've already found out without your telling. And you'd rather admit you meant to let Mrs. Leroy in than say you were willing to let Mr. Cheney in, wouldn't you?"

"Y-yes. Mrs. Leroy is such a nice lady," Lisa said indistinctly from Eleanor's shoulder. "A lady—like you are. And she told me— Well, I'm not going to tell you what she did tell me about herself. But even if Mrs. Barlow wasn't doing any—any regular business after I went to work for her, I knew there was something wrong about her. Mrs. Leroy really didn't tell me very much, but she wanted to see her alone and how could she do Mrs. Barlow any harm with me there? She gave me twenty-five dollars and promised me fifty more, afterwards, and to help me find a job. . . ."

Rocky reached over and patted the girl's shoulder sympathetically. "What's the most money you ever had at one time, kid?"

"Th-thirty dollars when I was working. Mrs. Leroy said I shouldn't stay with Mrs. Barlow. Then she said she'd get to the back door as soon after twelve as she could and toss some rocks on the windowpane."

"So that was it?" Rocky muttered. "I heard that but didn't have time to think what it was."

"Only it was Mr. Cheney instead of her. He didn't say one word but he kind of started forward. I don't know if he was going to grab me to keep me from talking, but you can't realize how fast things happened. I didn't have time to say anything and neither did he, before he just fell over like you found him."

"Where'd you talk to Mrs. Leroy, Lisa?"

"Down by the river, Mr. Allan. I'd gone down for water and I wandered off a little ways, it was so pretty. I came on her sitting on a log and we got to talking. Mr. Cheney could have heard us. He could have been in the trees back of us, and he had awful sharp ears."

"I don't reckon there's any doubt he must've overheard you. Was it because you were going to open the door that you moved in the kitchen to sleep?"

"Yes, but I'd rather have slept in there anyway, for just the reasons I told Mrs. Barlow."

"She didn't mind you movin' in there?"

"She looked at me kind of sharp but she said it was—was all right with her. Maybe she thought it would be safer—with me at the back door."

"A mind like hers works in such a tortuous fashion," Pope sighed. "Did anyone manage to see Mrs. Barlow privately since we arrived here, Lisa?"

"No sir. Quite a few tried to but she wouldn't see them. Miss Corwin didn't try, or Mrs. Cheney or Mr. Greer."

"Powell?" Rocky asked. "What did he say he wanted?"

"He wouldn't say. Mrs. Leroy tried and Mr. Doyle—he said he wanted an interview. And Mr. Pope tried, and Mrs. Greer wanted a reading but Mrs. Barlow yelled: 'Tell her she's not got enough future left to be worth reading.'"

Rocky chuckled and Lisa smiled wanly. Pope looked toward Eleanor and she got to her feet.

"It's time for you to be in bed, my dear. Come along and I'll tuck you in," she said.

Rocky watched them go toward the tent and then resignedly poured himself another cup of coffee.

"Did I say Eleanor'd draw the line at puttin' the girl in her own bed? I'll learn—sometime. I guess I sleep in your lean-to, but I won't get much time for sleeping anyway, and the girl's safer with Eleanor. Christ, what that old floozie would have made out of her if she'd had the chance. I'd like to be able to say she could've killed Cheney but I know better. Coffee?"

He refilled Pope's cup, threw more wood on the fire. "But Sapphira will never get Lisa out of Eleanor's clutches after this. You know we've got to talk to Mrs. Leroy?"

"Yes," Pope said unhappily, "I know. And if I know Eleanor, she is going to defend the woman as much as possible."

"Quite right," Eleanor said, coming back to the fire. "Why not? You aren't going to talk to her now? That would be cruel."

"I'm not so sure about that. In her state of nerves it might be a relief to her to have it over. But I suppose she is sleeping, so I won't disturb her."

"I wonder," Eleanor said, "if Margie and young Powell can be trusted to—handle her. She might— just might—be more desperate than we think. You are sure she was at the back of the house tonight?"

"Reasonably certain. Of course that doesn't inevitably mean that she shot Cheney."

"You bar the idea of there bein' any little stranger hiding out in the woods?" Rocky said.

"I do," Pope said firmly. "You cannot convince me that someone drove a car in, abandoned it far enough away from this clearing so that we would not hear him and then managed to flit hither and yon among the camps and about the cabin until he had a thorough acquaintance with the geography of the place. And just managed to be waiting for Cheney at the right time and place—"

"Oh, skip it," Rocky said, grinning. "I don't b'lieve in it either, but someone will be bound to bring it up."

"I suppose so. I wonder what part Cheney had in Sapphira's activities? In the case that brought me up here he did not appear in any way, but if he were associated with her for four years he must have had some part in her—racket. Of course she said she had never told him too much. . . ."

"And I wonder," Rocky said, "if Mrs. Leroy has any idea she left her footprints on that path. Because if she did, she might try to destroy them."

"We can't be everywhere at once," Pope said rather crossly. "Do you want to camp for the rest of the night down on that trail? No? I didn't think so. And Rocky—how much authority have you?"

"I don't know. It's been eight months since we were at Dayton's Folly an' I left the county right after. When we came back to Merton this time I told Jake Thompson I didn't care to take the job back as a reg'lar thing. He'd had to appoint someone else when I was away. But he didn't unswear me, if that can be done, or take back my badge. I don't really have it with me. I just wanted to throw a scare into Sapphira. But I wasn't lyin' when I said we're just out of Butte County."

"I suppose I should have looked more carefully at a map before we left. I'm afraid I'm not very practical. However I'm glad we aren't in Butte County. We can handle these people more easily since you do have some authority to question them."

"No one but Sapphira knows that yet, but Powell's the only one that was kind of snappy, and he did answer."

"Anyone with common sense would. You and I aren't the only ones who will report suspicious evasions to the sheriff. These people are not all of one household as they were at Dayton's Folly, so they don't present as united a front."

"Jake Thompson will be plenty griped when he gets word of this. He'll probably blame me; say there's trouble anywhere I happen in."

"How will he get here?"

"Same way we came: Brookdale to Oroville, over to Chico and up. It'll take him more'n half a day. I'd like to save those footprints for him," Rocky persisted. "Can't you take casts of the things?"

"Tonight? And with what?"

"Would tallow do? We could use candles. . . ."

"We haven't any candles," Eleanor said sweetly. "Because Mr. Nathan Bedford Allan thinks it is dangerous to use candles when camping. But we have lots of extra flashlight batteries."

Pope chuckled and after an instant Rocky grinned. "All right, you two can protect Mrs. Leroy as much as you want an' you can also settle with the sheriff if evidence gets destroyed. I'm not going to set on my tail in that river mist all night. An' I reckon it'd be better to talk to Mrs. Leroy before we jump at conclusions. If that's settled, let's see what's in Cheney's pocketbook."

"Pocketbook? You're holding out on me," Eleanor said. "Bring it out, Theophilus. You aren't going to be allowed to pore over its contents in secret."

Pope shuddered at her mischievous use of his Christian name and opened Cheney's wallet. "Sapphira wanted this, you know. She offered to give me the letter in question for it. Perhaps I shouldn't have refused."

"He carried a wad of dough," Rocky said. "Jumpin' catfish—look at it!"

"Seven thousand five hundred dollars," Pope said. "He probably closed out his banking accounts in Los Angeles."

"Damn good for a guy that was on his uppers four years ago," Rocky said. "He was takin' what he had with him, I reckon. What else?"

"Nothing of importance, except for these newspaper clippings. Come closer so you can read them with me."

"They look as if they were rather old," Eleanor said, bending forward to look at the first of the clippings as Pope held it to the fire. "Why— that might be Sapphira when she was a good many years younger."

"Mrs. George Eaton," Rocky read. "Harrison, Illinois, May 13, 1902. . . ."

"It is Sapphira," Eleanor said positively, studying the picture of a woman with blonde pompadour, small, pointed face, and lips parted in an enigmatic smile. "Warren Doyle said she was credited with being good-looking, though it's hard to believe that now. But that smile and the shape of her face—"

"Yeah, but let it wait, honey. I'm tryin' to read," Rocky said. "Sara Eaton. She kept the initial on her first name."

Stripped of journalistic verbiage, the story told in the clippings was that of a familiar and ugly triangle. Mrs. George Eaton was the wife of the owner of the small town's one department store; the said George Eaton was a pillar of the First

Methodist Church and a highly respected citizen of Harrison.

Mr. and Mrs. Eaton had been married in 1895 and had one daughter, Leona, born in 1897. The Eatons had met in Chicago where Sara Eaton had "made her home." She was, the account remarked, "a woman of means."

In the spring of 1901 a certain Paul Crane, represented as a dark, sleek gentleman with a drooping mustache, had come to work in the Harrison bank. George Eaton had liked Crane; had introduced him to Sara Eaton. He was present at all their dinner parties and often invited to "drop in and take pot luck."

At the end of six months Sara Eaton's neighbors remarked on the fact that Crane often called on her when George Eaton was not at home. By May of 1902 everyone was talking about Crane and Sara Eaton. Eaton had played the part of cuckold to perfection, but his awakening was sudden. No one in Harrison would admit to having told him what the town suspected, only events proved that he had in some way stumbled on the truth.

It was eleven o'clock on the night of May twelfth that the Eaton's hired girl, raised in print to the status of maid, ran screaming out of the house. Returning late from a night out and going toward her room at the back of the house, she had found the door of Sara Eaton's bedroom open and inside, Paul Crane dead and George Eaton dying.

A train going to Chicago stopped in Harrison at ten o'clock, and Sara Eaton had been on that train. "She didn't seem upset about anything," the conductor said. "Had one suitcase; said an old friend in Chi was sick and wanted to see her."

They never traced Sara Eaton farther than that. If she stayed for any length of time in Chicago she knew where to hide. They tried to find her, for the police were very anxious to talk to her by the night of May thirteenth.

That Eaton had surprised his wife and Crane together and that he had killed Crane was not in doubt. Eaton's gun was in his hand and three shots had been fired from it; one, it was first supposed, through his own body. But all three bullets were found in Crane's body.

The hired girl remembered that "Mrs. Eaton was nervous and kept a gun in their bureau drawer but it isn't there now." And: "I thought it was funny she gave me another night off this week. But Mr. Eaton always went to the Whist Club and she said she didn't need me." George Eaton had missed the weekly meeting of the Harrison Men's Whist Club for the first time in five years.

A clipping of later date recorded the death of George Eaton "without regaining consciousness."

It mentioned the fact that Paul Crane's accounts were short by some two thousand dollars and that little Leona Eaton was being sent East to live with an aunt who was her only relative. Crane's brother had come from Chicago to take his body home for burial.

"Well," Rocky said grimly, "you'd ought to be able to bargain with the old girl now. How'd Cheney recognize her?"

"He was an itinerant evangelist. He may have conducted services in Harrison's First Methodist Church. Perhaps the fact that I have read these will help our negotiations," Pope said. "But I'd hoped to bargain for others. Cheney, I suppose, could swear that Sapphira Barlow was Sara Eaton, but we can't."

"She must have a soft spot, after all," Eleanor said.

"Yeah? What's that?" Rocky asked skeptically.

"David Leon. Evidently the Harrison authorities dropped the case quite soon. I suppose people could disappear more easily in those days, and Sapphira had changed identities once before. And the police weren't so efficiently organized then, and in a small place. It would be just another small-town story before very long."

"But Cheney could've raised an awful stink with that story."

"I know, Rocky. And she doesn't want people to find out David's grandmother was a murderess—if she did kill her husband in a fit of rage after he'd shot her lover. Of course it would have been bad for her fortunetelling business but even that probably didn't matter as much to her as David's knowing—I think. Do you suppose she would have been prosecuted, Mr. Pope, if Mr. Cheney had told?"

"I doubt it. That happened over thirty years ago. A great many witnesses would be dead by now and the whole thing forgotten, except as an old wives' tale. The State of Illinois, so we are told," Pope said with a wintry smile, "had—and has—quite enough to do along that line without arresting or trying Sapphira Barlow. But as Eleanor says, the scandal would have hurt her business and there was David to consider. Cheney might have been able to see that he was taken away from her."

"I wonder how she ever got in touch with the kid," Rocky said. "I suppose she had ways of findin' out how her daughter was getting along. Cheney must've s'lected these clippings before he made a deal with her. No sense to him carrying them aroun' except for the psych'logical effect on her. She'd have plenty on him by now but I reckon this still gave him a little advantage. They wouldn't dare to squeal on each other far's their racket was concerned."

Rocky yawned, lighted a cigarette and passed it over to Eleanor when she held out her hand. She said:

"I'll smoke this and go to bed. Do you know it's half-past two?"

"Is it? Were you hinting," Pope said, "that Mrs. Leroy is the type who might kill herself, Eleanor?"

"I wish I knew. I don't think there would be any danger of that ordinarily. If her nerves were only in better shape. . . . But I don't see how she can help sleeping the night through."

Pope picked up a stick, drew a long straight line in the loose mountain soil, added four shorter lines at right angles to the first and brooded sadly over the diagram.

"Looks like half a centipede," Rocky said. "Does it mean anything at all?"

"The long line is the row of camps and the shorter ones the four paths going to the stream," Pope said, adding another long line that presumably represented the river.

"You've made a ladder now. I s'pose the point is that you can watch the front of the camps but not the backs of all of 'em. There's quite a few trees separatin' them from each other too. Well, are you going to watch at all?" Rocky asked. "Why don't you get you some sleep? We can make up another bed beside the fire. I've slept on the ground before this."

"No," Pope said, "I'm going to take a turn around the clearing first. Then perhaps I'll come back and curl up before the fire. You need sleep as badly as I do, Rocky, and there's nothing to be gained by talking any longer."

CHAPTER ELEVEN
"STARS FELL ON MR. POPE"

Rocky finally decided that there was no use pretending to himself that he was only dreaming his feet were cold. He twisted about trying to wrap himself snugly in the blankets, but there seemed to be nothing to the things but ends that pulled loose to let the cold air in. The bed was too short anyway. Pope would resemble the letter S if he slept in it very long, for he was an indefinite two inches taller than Rocky's six feet.

He dozed off again, drowsily conscious that it was getting a little warmer, but when he finally sat up and looked at his watch he was surprised to see that it was six o'clock. He threw back the canvas that curtained Pope's bed and looked toward the ashes of last night's fire, but Pope was not there.

Rocky yawned and sat down to lace his boots. Pope probably had snatched a catnap and was gone again. He'd make up the fire and not call Eleanor until it was going good.

Walking softly toward the fireplace he looked up at the sky and whistled. Heavy, gray-black clouds were massed to the east and, early as it was, the air was damply warm. Rocky smelled rain; a violent and probably brief thunderstorm. Those clouds were going to be right over them sometime today. Rocky eyed their tent complacently and thought it would stand up under a storm, but he expected damage to the other camps if there should be very much wind or rain.

The fire was just beginning to blaze high when he saw Margie Corwin coming toward him wrapped in a loose polo coat. She said:

"Well, Watson, are we the only survivors of the judgment day?"

"I'd forgot about that. But we are," Rocky prophesied, "going to have some of the thunder and lightnin' that Sapphira talked about."

"Is that why it's so horrid and muggy? I'll bet that damned old witch conjured up the storm, if we have one. Did Wren spend the night in the cabin?"

"I s'pose. We left him there. What'd you call him?"

"Short for Warren. I couldn't manage all the syllables when we were kids."

"He did say he'd known you a long time. Did you," Rocky said casually, slinging a kettle of water over the fire, "know this brother of his? The one that died?"

"Bill? Yes, I knew him, poor kid. That is, I'd met him," Margie added hastily. "I hadn't seen him for years."

"Doyle told us about him, you know. That he got to doping and died of it. Did he go to Sapphira's joint too?"

"I don't know. Wouldn't tell you if I did, mister. Where is your side-kick?"

"Pope? He's prowling aroun' somewheres. Why?"

"Minna—my aunt—wants to see him. She's determined to talk to him." Margie's chin jerked. "I hope he falls in the river and breaks his neck," she said brightly. "Why does he have to snoop around?"

"Somebody has to unless you'd like us just to set still and let all you people run aroun' killing each other. Anyway, don't you think the county authorities are going to ask you any questions?"

"Oh, a dumb county sheriff—"

"You been readin' too many stories, sister, where the sheriffs is all dumber'n Dora. They ain't right up on the latest in crime but they usually got plenty of common sense," Rocky drawled. "You'd be surprised how far that goes even when you got nothing else."

"Meaning?"

"Write the words yourself. An' don't expect the sheriff to be all overcome with awe because you're from Los Angeles. They don't care much about L.A. anyway up here in the no'thern counties."

Margie scowled at him and then laughed. "All right, Sherlock, but I think it's a good thing your wife has red hair. Can I wait here for Mr. Pope?"

"Sure. There's a box to set on. Is your aunt all right?"

"You mean is it all right to leave her alone? Oh yes. She had a good sleep and she has a lot of backbone.—Oh, that looks like real coffee! Could I, please—"

Rocky handed her a cup. "Sorry there's nothing to go with it yet. Haven't you been having coffee lately?"

"Lukewarm water poured over this lousy powdered coffee. We've been cooking over canned heat—what cooking we've done."

Rocky said: "My God!" and refilled her cup. "It's a wonder you weren't driven to drinking the stuff—the canned heat, I mean—to put you out of your misery. Eleanor will be glad to take some coffee over to your aunt. I'll go wake— Oh, here you are. Listen, honey, Miss Corwin wants to see Pope and he ain't aroun', so I'll go find him while you get some breakfast. That all right?"

"Of course. Lisa is still asleep. The poor child is tired out. Bring Mr. Pope back to breakfast. I won't be long getting it."

Rocky nodded and walked toward the clearing, wondering where to look for Pope. He might have gone to the cabin already, or he might be outside around that trail in back. Thinking of that trail, he realized that if it did rain there would be nothing left of those footprints to show to the sheriff. Since they couldn't take casts of them it might be a good idea to lay something over them. A piece of bark might save them if there wasn't too heavy a rain.

He glanced toward the row of camps and saw Greer squatted down starting his fire; then turned toward the cabin. Skirting its left side he stopped to look in at the windows. Sapphira was still in her chair, David a small hump on the couch. He went on to the back door and found it locked. Doyle had probably gone to sleep by now, and it was just as well he shouldn't know about the marks Minna Leroy had left on that path.

He found those footprints easily enough. They had not even had time to dry out, the evening mist from the river had been gone so short a time. Again he estimated the distance of those marks from the back door of the cabin before he covered several of them with curved pieces of bark.

He turned, then, to examining the underbrush on either side of the path. If someone wanted to get rid of a gun that would be a mighty good place to throw it. About the only way you could be sure you'd searched every inch of the stuff would be to cut it down. He had no intention of getting down on his hands and knees and crawling around the prickly brush, but he looked for some telltale break in the foliage. Slowly he worked his way down the path until he had covered half the distance to the cabin; then stopped, frowning thoughtfully.

At this point, perhaps twenty-five feet from the cabin door and to the right of the path, there was a small natural gap in the underbrush not more than a foot wide. But it was not natural that several twigs of chaparral should be broken and bruised as if someone had squeezed into that small space and stood there. The ground underneath was carpeted thickly with pine needles and twigs that looked as if someone's feet might have shifted them about.

Cheney might have stepped off the path and stood there a few minutes, for some reason. But right here was the print of one of Cheney's shoes pointed straight ahead. All the imprints of Lisa Wood's shoes went straight too. You could probably manage to jump off the path and then back again into your same tracks, but then they would show that you had jumped. And what reason would there be for either of those two to do that? In itself it was no crime to have stood off the path for a while.

Rocky muttered: "Oh well," and started toward the stream, walking carefully on the extreme edge of the path. His heavy boots left no distinct tracks there, for the ground was fairly dry and littered with tiny twigs. He realized with some disgust that only on the path's center groove would footprints show up clearly. Anyone who had sense enough to walk as he was doing would leave no marks.

Now he was passing under the pine trees whose needles carpeted the entire path. Nothing to be seen here, and when he reached the stream, though the ground there was damp enough, obviously many people had been up and down the trail that ran along it.

The growth of brush and small trees that sloped down from the clearing to the river would certainly offer a good many hiding-places at night, or even in the daytime, Rocky thought. You could lie hidden there and keep an eye on all the people who used the trails down to the stream. He had heard that Coon Hollow had once been a popular camping ground for a few people who knew of it. That must be why there were still fairly distinct trails down to the water; one for each camp.

He had passed two of these when an indefinite sound in the underbrush made him stop short. In an instant the noise was repeated: it was not so much a groan as an explosively angry grunt. Before Rocky could move to investigate, Pope's head broke through the brush and Pope followed, on all fours. Rocky said:

"Well, is this the way you hunt a needle in the haystack," and then stopped as he saw the trickle of dried blood on Pope's forehead and that his tinted glasses were missing.

He would have stopped without that, for Pope sat down on the bank of the stream and began to swear. Rocky listened, at first politely and finally with the most respectful attention. To hear Pope was more than just an experience: it was an education.

"I only understand two of those languages," he said when Pope took breath. "English and most of the Spanish. Wait a minute."

He wet his handkerchief and dabbed gently at Pope's forehead. "It don't seem to be cut here."

"It isn't," Pope said. "There's a small cut and a very large bump on the top of my head."

"Oh, I see. Well, you better come back to camp and let me put some iodine on it. Uh . . . do you figure your glasses are somewheres aroun' here or did you take 'em off?"

"My glasses are in small pieces back in that brush. Thank God I brought an extra pair."

"What do you wear the things for? Looks to me like you can see all right without them."

"I was told once that my eyes sometimes give me away but that my face never does. Don't you want," Pope said smiling, "to know what happened?"

"I sure as hell do." Rocky continued squeezing cold water over the top of Pope's head. "But I thought it wouldn't be exactly tactful to ask you right off."

"What time is it? Five minutes of seven? Well, I've been lying over there, dead to the world, for about three hours. Of course I'm not at all sure what time it was that I was hit over the head—with a gun, I think. But to go back to the beginning . . ."

Pope had walked across the clearing without turning on his flashlight and had expected to find all the camps in darkness, but a light still showed in Mrs. Cheney's tent. On a sudden impulse he had stopped and, not wanting to speak loudly enough for her to hear him, had slapped at the tent flap with the palm of his hand.

After a minute or two of this, Mrs. Cheney had appeared, looking at him tranquilly. "Oh, it's you.

I thought everybody but me would be asleep. Did you want to come in?"

Pope stepped inside. A candle gave enough light so that the woman could watch his lips and he did not have to talk loudly. He produced the money he had taken from Cheney's pocketbook.

"This belongs to you, Mrs. Cheney. It was in your husband's wallet."

"I wondered about that, because I'll need what little there is."

"There are seventy-five hundred dollars here, Mrs. Cheney."

She stared at him. "I didn't hear—did you say seventy-five hundred dollars? Why—where did Saul get that much money?"

Pope said evasively: "I don't know. Does it surprise you that he had that much? Is this the only property he had?"

"We haven't had any money for years." She put her hand out; touched the bills as if to make certain they were real. "You'd better keep it for me for a while. I'd be afraid to have it around. We— we never did have any money, even when Saul used to conduct so many meetings. The churches and singers were always cheating him. Of course we got along after we went to Los Angeles, but we just had a cheap house and never spent much money. I—I can't understand it."

"Are you sure you can't, Mrs. Cheney?"

"No, unless— I've never really trusted Madam Sapphira," Mrs. Cheney said finally. "I've tried to tell myself I was all wrong. Saul said she was a good woman, but I never quite felt like she was. If he got his money in ways that weren't right, she had something to do with it."

"I hope you won't refuse to take it on that account. He may have happened to make some lucky investments. How long had you been married, Mrs. Cheney?"

"Nineteen years. We were married in 1906. Saul was fifty-six his last birthday."

"You were born in the Middle West?"

"No, I was born in Pennsylvania. That's where I met Saul, but he was from the West. Iowa, I think. He'd been all over, though. He started preaching when he was twenty."

"I see. Did you ever know a girl named Leona Eaton?"

"Leona Eaton? No, I never did." Mrs. Cheney rubbed her forehead wearily. "I do feel pretty tired, Mr. Pope. . . ."

"Of course. I'm sorry to have disturbed you. Try to get some rest and tomorrow we'll discuss what is best to do about—everything."

Pope dropped the tent flap behind him and went silently on, stopping to listen in front of the

Greers' tent. A spasmodic, gurgling snore and a steady, wood-sawing snore convinced him that the Greers were sleeping. Powell had evidently gone back to bed, and there was no light or movement in Minna Leroy's tent.

Pope walked along the line of camps, then back toward the cabin; crept up to the windows and satisfied himself that David and his grandmother were still in the front room. A light shone from the small window of the kitchen, where Doyle must be sitting in lonely state.

Pope meant to go down the path to the river, then back up to the clearing and to his own camp. Until he reached the stream he turned on his flashlight, walking carefully on the edge of the path. It was when he had turned the light off and started along the river's bank that he began to feel that someone besides himself was out in the black night.

Pope was not, he admitted casually, entirely lacking experience in the art of stalking. But on the unspecified occasions that had given him such experience he had at least been certain he had a quarry. In this case he was not even sure of that.

Small sounds in the brush might be made by animals; the stream murmured unceasingly; the wind was in the trees. He did not dare to put on his light for he might already have betrayed himself by doing so. If this hypothetical and perhaps nonexistent night wanderer would obligingly keep to the paths, Pope thought he might be able to capture him. But that idea might occur to more than one person.

He decided suddenly to inch his way back into the brush and trees off the path and wait there for a while. He squirmed cautiously in among the thick growth, still facing the path; felt solid flesh against his own for one moment and then:

"Stars fell on Mr. Pope," he said ruefully. "But he must have caught me when I fell and dragged me farther back into the brush, because I certainly would not have fallen where I found myself when I woke. I suppose my flashlight is there somewhere. Would you mind trying to find it?"

"You went into the brush right here? Because you must have dropped the light when he hit you."

Rocky went down on his hands and knees and felt about the ground, finally coming erect again with the torch in his hand.

"It still works," he said. "Well, suppose we get on back to camp. You'll feel better when you have some breakfast. Anyway, Miss Corwin is waiting for you. Her aunt wants to talk to you."

"Does she? What brought you this way? Were you looking at those footprints again?"

"I cert'nly was. I—" Rocky had dipped his hand-kerchief in the water to clean it; now he straight-ened abruptly, staring at a spot where the stream widened into a clear pool. He said:

"Wait a minute!" and waded into the water. It was icy cold and he gasped a little when it finally reached his waist, but he bent down and brought up the thing he had seen at the bottom of the pool: a .25 automatic marked with the initials M. L.

CHAPTER TWELVE
THE DAY OF JUDGMENT

Pope looked at the gun as Rocky held it out; started to speak. Then his face contorted alarmingly and he began to sneeze. When this seizure seemed to be over Rocky said sympathetically:

"Do you think you caught cold?"

"I don't think—" Another volley followed the first, then: "I don't think I have—I damn well know I have. I am," Pope said, "subject to colds. In three hours I will be sniveling and snuffling and breathing through my mouth."

Rocky tried not to laugh. He had thought of Pope as peculiarly lean and tireless, and this was very funny. He said soberly:

"Eleanor has some kind of stuff she drops down your nose. That is, when we were first married she wanted to do that every time I sneezed. But she finally found out I don't catch cold."

"Her remedy won't—Har-choo!—do any good. Nothing ever does," Pope said with melancholy finality. "What about that gun?"

"There's been three shots fired from it. That's funny, ain't it? Of course it belongs to Mrs. Leroy. But I don't know—"

"Don't know what?"

Rocky hesitated; remembered all the times Pope had returned evasive answers to his questions and decided to pay him back. Pope could see the gun and he ought to brush up on things like that. He said:

"Well, I went over that path enough to get kind of an idea that someone might've shot Cheney from about twenty-five feet out. If those were Mrs. Leroy's footprints we've been talking about, I'd swear she wasn't any closer'n fifty feet from the cabin. It looks like she whirled aroun' and ran away, an' if she did that she didn't stop to pick up any ejected shells, so where are they?"

"Where indeed? Where are the roses of yesteryear. . . ."

"Are you right certain you weren't hit harder over the head than you think? After all, you laid there three hours."

"I wasn't entirely unconscious all of that time. I simply lacked ambition. Three shots fired from that gun, you say?"

"Yeah. No one heard but two fired at Cheney."

Pope fished out a handkerchief and blew his nose. "Well, all this can be settled by an autopsy.

That will tell from what kind of gun the shots were fired. But if we can eliminate Mrs. Leroy before the sheriff arrives, hadn't we better do it and spare her what we can? Suppose we go to that breakfast you spoke of."

But when they reached the clearing, coming past Warren Doyle's tent they met Eleanor and Margie Corwin.

"Where on earth have you been? Breakfast is eaten, but I left Lisa to keep the coffee hot and cook more bacon and eggs when you did arrive," Eleanor said. "Margie didn't want to leave her aunt alone any longer and I brought her some coffee and toast."

"So I see," Pope said, looking wistfully at the coffee.

"You don't look so chipper, Mr. Fortune," Margie said. "Been out all night? I suppose you wouldn't like to wait until I've poured this down Minna?"

"I'll drink it now, dear. I don't expect to languish in bed all day," Minna Leroy said, walking up to them just then. She took the cup from Eleanor with steady fingers. "Particularly as my bed is a very uncomfortable one and the tent is too small for as tall a man as Mr. Pope.

"I thought," she said, having drunk the coffee, "that I'd seen you somewhere before, Mr. Pope, but I couldn't remember where until this morning. I was driving by John Tisdale's home in Los Angeles and I think I saw you going up the front steps."

"That's quite possible. You know Tisdale?"

"To speak to. And I know his daughter slightly—Rose Cornish. When I remembered where I had seen you and what I know of Rose, and that I had seen her at Sapphira's— Well, if you are here to help John Tisdale's daughter perhaps you can help me."

Rocky said: "Just a minute. I'd go away an' leave you with Pope, only— You think neither of us has any official standing, I reckon, but I'm a deputy in this county."

Margie stared at him; opened her mouth and then closed it tightly.

"Of course," Rocky went on, "Pope would tell the sheriff anything he thought was important. If he doesn't think your story is, I'm willin' to be guided by him and keep my mouth shut too."

"Is that the reason Mr. Pope sent for you?" Margie said nastily. "He thinks of everything, doesn't he?"

"Hush, Margie! What difference does it make?"

"It might make a lot! They got hold of that girl as soon as they could."

"I asked you to be still, Margie. You took Lisa away from the cabin? I'm glad of that," Mrs. Leroy said. "I suppose she told you—"

"She didn't want to," Eleanor said quickly. "But these two men bullied her into it. She had to admit that or let us think she was willing to let Mr. Cheney in."

"Oh, I'd have told if she hadn't." Mrs. Leroy sat down on a box that, with the tent and what was in it, appeared to be all their camping equipment. "She did agree to let me in when I tossed some stones against the kitchen window. I'd convinced myself the first night that I couldn't get in unaided. Evidently Mr. Cheney heard our arrangements. He was always prowling around, listening. But I must go back to the beginning. . ."

"Are you sure that you have to?" Pope said gently.

"I won't tell you anything more than I have to. I— You know Rose Cornish. Figure to yourself that I, also married to a safe and unexciting husband, and a great deal older than Rose, might have been that much more dissatisfied and fancied myself even more bored than she has always seemed. I was looking for sensation and one last fling. I found it at Madam Sapphira's. A romantic-looking man of thirty-five with such charming manners . . .

"I hope," Mrs. Leroy said, her lips suddenly rimmed with white, "that Rose got off more easily than I did. Perhaps she was young enough not to need to be—pepped up. I can see all of you wondering how a woman could be such a fool. It's happened before and, as usual, I hardly realized—until I found myself wanting the stuff—"

"I think you're just a plain louse!" Margie said to Pope. "She doesn't need to tell you all this and she got over it—and I guess that took guts!"

"I know it did," Pope said gravely. "And since you did, what did you have to fear from Sapphira? Did you have the—the letter-writing habit?"

"That is about the only insane thing I didn't do. I would hate to have my husband know why I'd been under a doctor's care in San Diego. The doctor is an old friend and he will never tell. But can't you guess there was a sudden difficulty about—supplies, at just the right time. I was on the ragged edge. I had sense enough to want to prevent my husband's thinking I was really ill so that he would call in a doctor who wouldn't hold his tongue. I'd already decided to go to San Diego—he thought I needed a change—but I had to have enough to tide me over for a day or two or I could never have faced the trip.

"Well, I got it, by—pawning a pendant my husband had given me. Yes, I know that sounds odd,

but the thing is a family heirloom, made of jade.
I've never seen another like it, and the Leroy men
have always given it to the oldest son and he to
his wife.

"You see how clever it was? I was in no condi-
tion to realize I would have to get that pendant
back; that someday my husband would want to
see it—want me to wear it. Later I did realize that
only too well. I couldn't replace it or have a copy
made without the original.

"When I came back to Los Angeles the organization was breaking up. I discovered that much
from this man. Until then Sapphira had never appeared in the business and I knew Cheney only as
one of the stage properties at her séances."

"You don't need to go into that," Pope said.
"The man you dealt with couldn't return the pendant and he more or less admitted who was the
power higher up? So you came here to deal with
Sapphira herself?"

"Yes. I scraped together every cent I could, but
she wouldn't see me. And my husband thinks Margie and I are in San Francisco. I left letters to be
mailed to him, but I must get back. Something
might happen. . . . But I haven't told you about
last night.

"I thought Margie never would go to sleep. I
was a little late getting to the cabin. That is, as

far as I got. I had no light, but I took a gun with me. My husband gave it to me several years ago, but I can't shoot at all," Mrs. Leroy said, smiling crookedly. "I proved that when I blazed away at a tree on our way up here. That was foolish too, wasn't it? But I didn't expect anyone to be killed, and I thought when I talked to Sapphira, having a gun might help.

"What I've already told you sounds fantastic enough, but the last is even more so. I didn't know Mr. Cheney was ahead of me until I'd turned up the path from the river. Then I did feel that someone might be in front of me, but I wasn't certain. I stopped for a minute; then I went on and finally I stopped again, because I could see Mr. Cheney standing in the doorway. That is, by his height I thought it must be he.

"Then someone fired from farther up the path. I heard the shots and knew vaguely where they were fired from, but I couldn't see anyone. Besides, I simply turned and ran. Before I got back to the trail up to our camp I threw my gun in the river. Margie must have heard me in her sleep, because she woke up almost before I could get into bed."

Rocky said "We found your gun by accident, mostly. I've got it here but I'd better keep it for a while."

"Well?" Pope said, looking at him questioningly.

"It suits me all right. Did you ever," Rocky said, "try to kill a man from fifty feet with a .25 automatic? It ain't the distance as much as the fact that a .25's a very weak load. I shot a jack rabbit with one of them an' had to kill him with a club when I caught up with him."

Pope looked at him reproachfully. "Well, I suppose I had that coming to me but you might have told me before."

"He might have told all of us before," Margie said angrily.

"Yeah, but Mrs. Leroy just might have another gun. Only I b'lieve Cheney was killed by someone farther up the path than Mrs. Leroy ever got. Her footprints—"

"Did I leave my footprints on that path? I don't seem to be very good at this sort of thing, do I?"

"I'm afraid you aren't, Mrs. Leroy. I'll do my best to bargain with Sapphira for you, though you may have to see her yourself," Pope said. "Tell me, was Cheney at all offensive toward you?"

"Yes, he was. At least I found him so, though he never got beyond insinuating and oily compliments."

"He must have used a different technique with you," Margie said. "Not that he was what you'd call up-to-date. He was the kind who gets a big kick out of trying to pinch a girl's leg. That made Hank pretty sore. I mean, he thought Cheney had an awful nerve."

"I'm curious about Powell," Rocky said. "What's his int'rest in this business?"

"Me, I guess. I don't know what else it could be."

"Then you told him you were comin' up here?"

"N-no, I didn't. But Wren probably told him why he was coming."

"But Doyle says he didn't know you were goin' to be here, so how could Powell figure from what Doyle told him that you'd be here?"

"Oh! Well, I don't know how they figured it out between them, but Hank just came— You'd better talk to Warren some more."

"I'm very fond of Warren Doyle," Mrs. Leroy said. "I'm sure he came for just the reasons he told you. And Margie may have given either Warren or Henry some hint of our plans without knowing what she did."

"Where's Powell now?" Rocky asked.

"He allowed as how there should be wood in them thar hills, which there certainly isn't any of right here any more—"

Rocky wanted to smack her right in the back of those silly shorts, though he had to admit her imitation of his mellow drawl was a good one. She might just be getting back at him for what he'd said to her earlier this morning, or she might not like his asking questions about Powell. To make things thoroughly interesting, Eleanor's shoulders had taken on a characteristic stiffness and she was looking at Margie with undisguised hostility.

"So your young man went to gather wood," Pope said quickly. "Did he stand by for an SOS from you all night?"

"Of course not. As soon as I was sure Minna was asleep I went out and told him to go to bed. He looked so silly squatted down, puffing at his cigarette like Sitting Bull."

"But who is he, Miss Corwin? Doyle admits he doesn't know a great deal about him and I haven't so far found a perfectly satisfactory reason for his being here. Do you know everything there is to know about his past life, or even all of his activities and associations in the last two or three years?"

"I know all I want to! He never has been anywhere near old Sapphira's joint!"

"I didn't hear Pope suggest he had," Rocky said. "Did it ever occur to you he might be Mexican?"

"Mex— Why, of course not! What—"

"Oh, it did to me. I've known lots of 'em and he's got a face shaped like some of them have, besides bein' so dark. I only got one real good look at him but it bothered me, tryin' to think what he reminded me of—till Pope started cussin' in Spanish this mornin'."

"Well, being a Mexican isn't anything to be ashamed of, is it? If he is one. You all make me tired."

"I never said there was anything crim'nal about it, but if he is and he's hidin' it, he's the one who's ashamed of it, isn't he? Where had he been livin' before he came to Los Angeles?"

"Arizona," Margie said through gritted teeth. "And I'll bet Wren put you up to this. You can all go to hell!"

Mrs. Leroy looked at their tent swaying unsteadily after Margie's tempestuous entrance into it, and shook her head.

"She's really a dear girl but she hasn't any manners. I don't know any more—probably less—about Hank than she does. These children are so casual about each other's backgrounds. But I never saw him at Sapphira's any time that I was there."

"Perhaps we shouldn't have questioned her, but she's rather an exasperating child. And the same questions will have to be asked Powell," Pope said. "I'll see you again, Mrs. Leroy, as soon as I've interviewed Sapphira."

Walking away, Eleanor muttered: "Brat!" Then: "You're right, Rocky: Mr. Powell does remind me of that young Gonzales I met in Texas, though he talks perfect English. But even if he is a Mexican—"

"There is supposed to be a certain amount of dope-smuggling over the border, you know. That's an interesting line of thought," Pope said. "If Powell were thoroughly familiar with Juarez, for instance. . . ."

"Yeah, a guy that knows the place can get almost anything he wants in that hell hole. Could Powell have been the guy your friend's daughter got mixed up with?"

"From her description of the man I don't think so, Rocky. And while all this is very interesting, unfortunately we aren't able thoroughly to investigate the lives of all these people—now. It will be a lengthy business for the sheriff to do it. And that brings us to the question of which one of us is to make the trip to the nearest telephone."

"I don't think you'd better do it if your driving is still as bad as I remember it. I hate to go an' leave you here alone, but is there anyone we dare to let go? Could we ask Greer to do it?"

"We don't seem to have anything against him, if we can accept his statements and Doyle's."

They had reached their own camp now and Lisa Wood sprang up to take the coffee pot from the fire. "I watched it every minute, Mrs. Allan, and

I don't think it boiled over any. Shall I cook some eggs?"

"Better let me do it," Rocky said. "Ever handle a fryin' pan over an open fire? Well, there's a knack to it. Have a good sleep?"

"Oh yes. I feel like I'd been awfully silly now. Can I go over to the cabin pretty soon, do you think? My clean clothes are there and besides, I do feel like I ought to get David something to eat. Mrs. Barlow won't ever stir herself to do it."

"I want to see Mrs. Barlow privately as soon as I've had something to eat," Pope said. "I might send David over here to get his breakfast, but after his grandmother and I have had our talk there's no reason for you to stay away."

He reached abruptly for his handkerchief and Eleanor looked at him sharply. "Mr. Pope, have you caught cold?" Pope nodded and sneezed. "Well, we'll soon stop that."

"In some ways, nurses never get over being nurses," Rocky said sympathetically as Eleanor went off to get her first-aid kit. "She carries aroun' the damnedest collection of stuff and never takes any of it herself."

"Put your head way back," Eleanor ordered, pushing Pope down onto a box. "This will get into all your little sinuses."

"It has," Pope said unhappily. "Ugh!"

"Good for you. Now take these. I guess you'd better not have a hot whisky lemonade because you can't go to bed."

Rocky grinned discreetly at the eggs he was frying and Lisa watched Eleanor with adoring admiration. "We can't have you sick, you know."

"I never ab incab— There, you see?" Pope cleared his throat and regained control of his consonants. "I never am incapacitated. I simply become an object of disgust to myself and everyone else. When I've had breakfast I'll take a shot of whisky, straight."

"But how did you catch cold? Didn't you have enough cover?"

"I didn't have any cover at all, except for the night mist from the river that no doubt wrapped itself lovingly around my recumbent form. Some kind soul hit me over the head, probably with the idea of saving me from brain fag. But if someone cares to take a very early morning stroll, who am I to forbid him?"

"Hit you over the head! Are you sure you haven't any temperature?" Eleanor said, laying her hand on his forehead. "Here's a thermometer."

"Let me continue in happy ignorance, child. If you want to do me a favor, find my other glasses in my suitcase. That does look good, Rocky. Yes, I want coffee; a great deal of coffee."

Eleanor, returning with his glasses, said: "Mr. Pope, who darns your socks?"

"What? Oh, I do, usually," Pope said calmly, beginning on his second egg. "Don't you think I do a very good job? An old Scotch shepherd taught me how; also to knit. Very soothing to the nerves, knitting."

Eleanor giggled and Lisa looked from one to the other of them doubtfully. "I'm afraid you're a little lightheaded," Eleanor suggested.

"On the contrary, my head feels as if it were filled with the best grade of cement. Are you finished, Rocky? Then we'd better go to the cabin and you can bring David back with you if he wants to come, or keep him in the kitchen where he won't interrupt."

"He likes to talk, all right. An' for that reason I'll bet the old lady won't let him out of the cabin. A kid notices things even if he doesn't always understand 'em. We might be able to get some useful information, pumping him."

"Yes: useful as a club to hold over Sapphira's head."

"Of course, I'd as leave not work that way. I was thinking that maybe the best thing to do would be for someone to drive to Manzanita and hire the fellow that owns the place to drive to the nearest phone with a message to Jake Thompson. If you want to let Greer go—or I could do it in pretty quick time myself. We're going to have some trouble with Doyle, though."

"Yes, he will want to get to a telephone. It's very sultry. Let's hurry," Pope said, looking up at the sky. "Aren't those clouds growing darker and coming nearer to us?"

"They certainly are. Listen! I guess you brought that on," Rocky said of the low growl of thunder in the distance. "It's still somewheres across the canyon. That's another thing, though. If it rains very hard I ain't crazy about going over that road while it's doin' it. S'pose Sapphira will let us in the front door?"

"We can knock. She may still be asleep, but it's close to nine o'clock. I didn't realize—I wonder that Doyle has stayed here so long."

"Look! This door's not locked."

"So I see," Pope said tonelessly. "We'd better go in."

The fire was dead, and the trees grew so closely to the windows that the room was nearly as dark as it had been the night before. The stale sweetness of incense still hung in the room; the fat spider worked industriously at its web in the corner.

Pope went straight to Sapphira's chair and stood staring down at her, but in an instant Rocky glanced away. She hadn't been pleasant to look at when she was alive, and he thought it would be a long time before he forgot her face as it looked now.

He walked over to the couch and laid his hand on David's shoulder, relieved to find it warm and relaxed. But the boy did not stir at his touch; he slept heavily, his face half hidden in a dirty pillow. Pope said:

"She was strangled with one of her own scarves by someone standing behind her. Rocky, did you see this?"

Rocky turned reluctantly; then bent forward and stared at the small card that lay on the old woman's lap. Words cut from some newspaper had been pasted on it to form a black sentence:

THE DAY OF JUDGMENT HAS COME!

CHAPTER THIRTEEN
"NO CUFF LINKS?"

At last Pope said practically: "Have you a clean—and dry—handkerchief, Rocky? Thank you." He lifted the card carefully, wrapped it in the handkerchief and put it in his pocket.

"That more or less proves premeditation, don't it?" Rocky said. "No one was going to set down here last night an' cut those words out and paste 'em on that card. Why didn't David wake up?"

Pope walked over to the couch and shook the boy gently. He stirred, muttered indistinctly and burrowed more deeply into the pillows.

"An' why didn't Doyle wake up?" Rocky added. "Where is he? We left him here to keep an eye on things. I'll go see."

The kitchen door opened with a scraping sound and Doyle stood looking at them, running his fingers through his disordered pale hair.

"You took your time about getting here. Do you know what time it is? I admit I was asleep. I feel lousy," Doyle said, running his tongue around the inside of his mouth. "Could hardly get awake. I— Jesus Christ!"

Rocky had suddenly stepped aside so that Doyle could see Sapphira in her chair. "You must have slept right well," he said.

"I— Then the old— Then she did dope me! And the kid too."

"He certainly appears to be sleeping more soundly than is natural," Pope admitted. "But if she did give you something to make you sleep— why didn't it occur to you that she might try just such a trick as that?"

"It should have. I guess I was just a plain damned fool. But I still don't see how she did it. I didn't think— Can't we talk in the other room? I'm just a sports writer, not a police reporter. I'm not so hard-boiled that I like looking at—that. What about the kid?"

"I s'pose he's got to be waked up, and it's just as well for him not to do it here." Rocky lifted the boy out of his litter of covers, carried him into the kitchen and put him in a chair.

"Cold water, maybe," Doyle suggested uncertainly.

"He's wakin' up. . . ."

David whimpered sleepily and dug at his eyes with hands that badly needed washing. He mumbled:

"I don' wan' get up," then gasped as Rocky flung the end of a towel wet with icy water over his face.

"You don't need to do that," he said indignantly, throwing the towel to the floor. "I'm getting up. Oh! I thought it was Grandma or Lisa and that it was very early in the morning, because I was dreaming about it. I know Grandma said we didn't have to go out on the hill after all, but Wh-what's the matter with all of you? Is—is there something wrong? You look so funny. . . ."

Pope said: "Your grandmother is dead, David. No, I'd rather you didn't go into the other room. You can't do anything for her now. And we want to talk to you."

David's chin quivered and he swallowed painfully. "Do you mean she was killed, like Saul?"

"Not like Saul, but someone did kill her. Do you always sleep so soundly, David?"

"I guess I'm always pretty hard to wake up. But I do feel queer this morning," David complained. "My head is sort of tight and my mouth tastes bad. And I don't remember even dreaming until just a little while ago. Grandma and Mr. Doyle were quarreling—"

"I wouldn't call it quarreling," Doyle said hastily. "We— Oh well, I suppose the kid would call it that. She was plain disagreeable: kept making nasty remarks about reporters and stool pigeons until I got sore. That was right after you left. I'd intended coming in here right away. I didn't want to talk to her. But she kept me quite a while . . ."

"And the chocolate was getting cold," David said plaintively. "I knew it was but I was afraid to interrupt, so I pretended to be asleep but I wasn't. And Mr. Doyle said it was too bad they ex-exterminated insects and let people like Grandma live."

"Oh, for God's sake! Are you going to take his word for everything that happened?"

"Why not?" Rocky said. "Sometimes kids repeat things like that more acc'rately than someone wflo's influenced by the—the interpr'tation he wants to give what's said or done. Did you say that?"

"Well, something like it. I don't know why she started riding me, except that she didn't seem to want me here."

"I agree with that," Pope said. "She didn't want you or anyone else here except David, and she must have been certain she could see to it that he slept very soundly. The front door was open, you see, and it seems offhand, from her determination not to leave the cabin, that she must have opened the door herself to someone she expected. I said 'offhand' because we can't by any means leave you out of this, Mr. Doyle."

"What? I don't know what you mean. I was dead to the world."

"We'll go into that at the proper time. Let's get back to the chocolate. You said you saw that it was getting cold, David?"

"Oh yes: all scummy, you know. So when Grandma and Mr. Doyle stopped talking I asked Grandma if I couldn't have some of it because I didn't feel a bit sleepy. Then she looked at it and said it wasn't fit to drink, and asked Mr. Doyle if he'd see if there was still enough fire in the kitchen to heat it by."

"So, like a sap—because the kid wanted it—I took the pan out to the kitchen and set it on the coals long enough to heat it. There's the pan: you can see how black it is. I took it back to the old lady and she poured out two cups of it." Doyle scowled at the blackened pan. "I saw her do it, so how could she dope what the kid drank?"

"She stirred it," David said. "Anyway, Grandma could do card tricks and make eggs come out of your sleeves. Sometimes when I was sick she would entertain me that way."

"The hand is quicker'n the eye," Rocky said. "If she stirred the stuff in the cup she must've used something that needed to be dissolved. Did that choc'late taste all right to you, kid?"

"Oh yes. We never liked sugar in it and liked it strong, so it always had a little bitter taste."

"That's right. Because, like a fool, I drank the rest of it," Doyle said. "I took David's cup to him and she could have fixed the rest of it while my back was to her. She handed me the pan and told me to bring it back in here. She was slick enough not to suggest I drink it: that might have made me suspicious. Well, there the stuff was and while I'm not fond of it I was feeling pretty empty, and when it had cooled off I swallowed it down. I remember feeling awfully sleepy, and I tried walking around and took a look in at her. I don't know what time. The last I remember is sitting down here by the table and I woke up this morning with my head on it."

Rocky found an empty gin bottle thrust behind some canned beans in the crude cupboard on one wall of the kitchen, poured the dregs of the chocolate into the bottle and corked it.

"Not," he said, "that analyzin' this stuff would prove anything more than that it had some drug in it. We still couldn't say for certain who drugged it."

"Why—you—" Doyle's face grew red. "Are you saying I doped myself?"

"Well, you certainly could have done that. No one but you knows when you drank this choc'late, if you ever drank it at all. I reckon you did, from the way you look now. But when you heated it you could have flavored it to suit yourself so that the old lady an' David would both sleep."

"You said the front door was open.—Oh, I get it! I opened it to throw suspicion on someone else? Well, why did I kill her? To make a good story for my paper?"

"You oughtn't to jump at conclusions so quick. We didn't say we think you killed her," Rocky said pleasantly. "Just that you could've done it. If we don't point that out to you someone else will. Did you bring any newspapers with you?"

"N-newspapers? Yes, we had some but they're all gone now. Minna and Margie haven't any either. We used 'em to light fires. I think Greer has a bunch left."

"Got any paste or glue with you?" Rocky grinned briefly at Doyle's harried look. If he was only acting he was pretty good at it.

"No, I haven't. Are you going screwy or are you thinking of starting a scrapbook?"

"I like to paste pictures," David said. "But we didn't bring any paste with us and the flour-and-water kind doesn't stick very good. Saul said he had some glue he'd let me have but I never thought about it again."

"That's interestin'. Ain't you pretty hungry, David? S'pose I take you aroun' to the front of the cabin an' point out where our camp is— No, I reckon I'll ask Doyle to take you over there."

"Mr. Doyle will take a bow! Well, come along, kid."

David began to cry, shaking his head. "I'm awful hungry but I guess I hadn't ought to be. Grandma was good to me, even if I did want some regular clothes and to go to school instead of just having tutors once in a while."

Rocky patted his shoulder. "She was a pretty old lady, anyway. You want to remember that. You go along with Doyle and Eleanor will look after you for a while."

"Is that the lady with the pretty hair?" David gulped violently; then: "Well, I guess I will. My, it's cloudy over that way, isn't it? Will it thunder? I don't like thunder and lightning much, do you?"

Doyle looked at the sky; said: "Hell! No, I don't. Come around this way."

"Now what?" Rocky asked. "I s'pose you want to look aroun' in the other room?"

"Yes," Pope replied, "and I think you had better help me move the—chair into the bedroom."

"In with Cheney? Why? I'm not exactly what you'd call imag'native but the idea of leavin' her set there alongside of him gives me the creeps."

"It isn't nice," Pope agreed, "but if we are going to have a storm some of us may be forced to take shelter in here for a while."

"That's right. I wish the next time you send me an invitation to an affair of this kind you'd pick a civ'lized location where the cops dispose of the bodies," Rocky said with forced humor. "An' I think we'd ought to— What's that?"

They had just raised Sapphira's heavy chair and some small object dropped from among the gay scarves and shawls and rolled along the floor. Pope went after it; held up an empty bottle that bore the label of a Los Angeles pharmacy and had "veronal tablets" scrawled on it in a crabbed hand.

"So that's what she gave them—if she did dope the chocolate. Though I s'pose the bottle could've been planted on her. All these people come from L.A."

Pope nodded and dropped the bottle into an already bulging coat pocket. Then with a look of repugnance he felt among the scarves; found a half-empty bottle of gin and set it on the floor. Finally he unfastened the old woman's gay robe to show that she was wearing underneath it full, baggy trousers, a thin waist and embroidered velvet jacket.

"Do you think she carried her valuables on her?"

"No," Pope said at last. "Her clothing is too thin and flimsy."

"Except for that jacket. What about her turban?" Pope said: "I'd as soon touch a snake, but there's no help for it."

"She kept her hair dyed black—what she had. It was light-colored in that picture." Rocky mechanically wiped sweat from his forehead. "There ain't anything in the turban?"

"No. And this jacket," Pope said, touching it with sensitive fingers, "is just what it seems to be. All right now, Rocky—easy!"

"Do you want to look through these suitcases?" Rocky said in the bedroom. "I don't see how she'd dare to hide anything in the mattresses with people sleepin' on them."

"We'll look at them later if we don't find what we want somewhere else. I hope she didn't leave Mrs. Leroy's pendant in that safe-deposit box. We might as well take these suitcases into the other room and look them over. What," Pope said, shutting the bedroom door behind him, "did you start to say we should do—just before you found that empty veronal bottle?"

"I don't— Oh, get word to Jake as soon as we can. For one thing, this is awful hot, damp weather, though it'll cool off if it storms. More thunder over there. . . . Anyway, we'd better settle who goes to Manzanita. I will, but—"

"You don't want to and I don't think you should."

"There's too much for you to look after, the way you're feelin', even though I wouldn't leave

Eleanor here for you to take care of. If Greer'll do it, I think we'd better send him."

"Yes, I think we had. Do you want to write a note for him to give the hotelkeeper at Manzanita?"

"If I've got a pencil." Rocky rummaged through his pockets and produced a forlorn-looking stub. "Best I can do. Here, you write it—if you've got any paper handy. You'd better sign both our names. I'm certain Jake ain't forgot you."

"He'll say that I am always leading you into trouble." He wrote a terse statement of the situation at Coon Hollow; signed his name and Rocky's. "I think that will do, and here is the money to pay the hotel-keeper. Do you think it is safe for Greer to start off immediately?"

"Damned if I know. He may have skid chains, in which case he ought to get back if it rains. It'll probably take him an hour to Manzanita, but if he gets on the main road before the storm he'll be all right. I'll go find him in a minute. Is there anything in the suitcases?"

"I don't expect there will be. This must be Lisa's," Pope said, looking at the shabby but neatly mended and folded cotton underwear and dresses. "She can have this whenever she wants it. David's and his grandmother's things seem to be mixed in together."

Rocky looked disgustedly at the array of soiled silks and sang softly: *"Mam'oselle from Armentière: she ain't even heard of underwear* . . . Lord, what a mess. Gingersnaps in with the rest of it. Is that jew'lry real?"

"Genuine Woolworth."

"Scented soap—shame they didn't use more of it. Face powder, rouge an' hair remover. Incense, box of candy, red nail polish, two more bottles of gin, perfumed cigarettes, two— Ain't those books the kind you get out of a suitcase library?"

"Yes. Would you like to glance over them?"

"No thanks. I wouldn't deprive you." Rocky glanced speculatively around the room. "I wonder how many—would you call 'em documents?—the old lady brought with her. Do you think she didn't intend to go entirely out of business?"

"Very likely she was waiting to see if she could ever realize on the documents that she still had. I wouldn't be surprised if she didn't hope that it would be safe for her to go back to Los Angeles sometime, if only for a short while."

"Well, I don't know where she'd hide the things, but from the way she talked to you she must've thought she had them well hid. But I don't imagine she went outside at all, so they must be in here." Rocky picked up the crystal and balanced it in the palm of his hand. "She couldn't put any-thing in here and these walls don't offer any hid-ing-places that I can see. Or the floor, unless she took up a board. But you'll need more light than you got now to examine that. I take it your first interest is to do what you came here for?"

"Naturally, though with Sapphira dead it per-haps isn't quite so urgent. The only thing is that if one of these people was once connected with her, he might carry on Sapphira's activities if he happened on her hoard before we do. If— What is it, Rocky?"

"Something kind of funny. This blue-velvet pad she set the crystal on has been slit at one end."

Pope studied the pad, made of a piece of blue velvet doubled over and stitched together. "You're right," he said, the always-deep furrow between his brows growing more pronounced. "And from the looks of it—because the threads aren't much frayed—it was slit recently."

"Well, she couldn't have put anything much in there or someone would have noticed it," Rocky said comfortingly. "Just some one paper, probably. Maybe it had nothing to do with what you want."

"I hope not. I wonder— Well, you might as well find Greer, Rocky. This is going to be a tedious business. Oh damn!" Pope sneezed and reached for his handkerchief.

"I was thinkin' that you was getting better and that maybe it was just all in your mind."

"Well, I will admit that when I have other things to think of I don't notice each separate step of a cold's progression as I do when I can give the matter my full attention. When you come back here I wish you would bring me some whisky. I don't care to drink Sapphira's gin."

"I'll be right back and . . . I seem to be findin' lots of things." Rocky held out a green Eversharp that had been lying on the floor near the door. "Any idea who this belongs to?"

"What—no cuff links? That might belong to Doyle. He carries one like it but I do seem to remember that it was still clipped onto his pocket this morning."

"And I'm pretty sure you're right. This clip is kind of sprung so it wouldn't grip the cloth very well. Of course there's thousands of pencils just like this."

"I'll leave you to find out whom it belongs to," Pope said. "You can make sure that Doyle still has his. It might have belonged to Cheney."

"He carried it on an inside pocket if it did."

"You mean you never noticed that he had one clipped on an outside pocket? That's good enough for me. When you have Greer started on his trip— if he will go—suppose you see if there are any newspapers left in camp. But"—Pope brought out his handkerchief again—"bring me that whisky first and about half-a-dozen fresh handkerchiefs."

CHAPTER FOURTEEN
"IT MAKES A MEXICAN SEE RED"

David Leon sniffed gently, drew his sleeve across his nose and continued eating scrambled eggs and toast.

"These are awful good," he said rather timidly for, having provided him with breakfast, Eleanor had been sitting under a tree thinking over what Doyle had told them before he went on to his own camp.

"I'm glad you like them," she said absently; then: "David, haven't you a handkerchief? Would you mind getting him one of mine, Lisa?"

"Well, I can't help crying a little," David said defensively.

"Of course you can't, but it's time you learned to blow your nose when you do cry. Thank you, Lisa. Here you are, David—and use it."

David blew his nose vigorously and Lisa pushed her hair back from her forehead. "Isn't it awful hot? I thought it was going to rain and here the sun is out. It makes those clouds look blacker than ever. You'd better get out of the sun, David. You aren't used to it and I'll bet your skin is the kind that burns awful easy. Give me your plate if you're all through."

"The sun feels good. So does the fresh air," David said, but he moved into the shade beside Eleanor. "I haven't enjoyed very much of either during my life."

"Haven't you ever played with any children your own age? From your way of talking you must always have been around older people."

"I did play with children back in Pennsylvania. At least, a little bit. You see, I was only six years old when they sent me out to Grandma."

"Who were 'they,' David?"

"It was really just Mrs. White. You see, my mamma died when I was just three years old and I can't hardly remember her at all. And my father died just before I was born. So then I lived with a great-aunt. Her name was Martha Eaton. But she died too, before I was six. It seems," David said shakily, "like everybody died. I didn't know about all this until Mrs. White told me. She said I must remember it, to tell to Grandma, so I did."

"Do you know what your real name is? It isn't Barlow?"

"No, it's King. Grandma said I wasn't to tell that, but I don't see why not. Mrs. White wasn't any relation to me, but when Aunt Martha died she took care of me. Aunt Martha left just a little money and she told Mrs. White that she was to send an advertisement to be put in the Los Angeles papers, about me. I don't know what the ad said but it was something Grandma would understand if she read it."

"Then your Aunt Martha knew where your grandmother was living?"

"Grandma said she must have guessed. Grandma told me about it two or three years ago when I was curious about how she found me. She said she used to send money for my mother to Aunt Martha and that finally she got careless—that's what she said—and thought it didn't matter if the letters were postmarked Los Angeles. She said she figured Aunt Martha wouldn't give her away for my mother's sake. What do you suppose she meant by that?"

"I haven't any idea," Eleanor said brazenly. "Didn't your aunt Martha have any money?"

"She'd lost it all. I don't know how. Grandma just sent money once a year and she'd sent some not long before Aunt Martha died. But Mrs. White said she might not go on doing it and she couldn't take care of me very long because she wanted to go live with her daughter in Havana, Cuba. She said Aunt Martha hated to have me go to Grandma but there wasn't anyone else."

"Poor child. And your grandmother happened to read the advertisement?"

"That's what she said. Not right away but finally she did. So she sent some more money and said for Mrs. White to put me on the train and send me out. She gave me a big envelope with things in it; a birth certificate and some pictures, I think, but Grandma put them away. So Grandma said so long as I was not very big it would make a hit with her clients for me to be dressed up and open the door for them and stand behind her chair with my arms folded and that's how I came to help her even when I got older."

"I see," Eleanor said grimly. "David, did your grandmother bring very much baggage up here?"

"Just suitcases and the boxes of things to eat and to cook with. The couch and chair had been left here."

Eleanor hesitated, wondering how to state the situation so that the boy would understand. "We think your grandmother had some letters that—that Mr. Pope wants to see," she said finally. "She was going to sell them to him today, but she had hidden them."

David looked as if he were going to cry again. "Grandma told me Saul wasn't a nice man and wanted to kill her, but Saul was always telling me Grandma was wicked and that she oughtn't to have the raising of me. Maybe—maybe they were both right. I don't understand it all, but I know sometimes women used to come to see Grandma at night and cry."

"How do you know that?"

"Whenever I'd wake up I'd always want a drink. I slept on the first floor, so I'd go out to the kitchen and sometimes someone would be talking to Grandma and I'd listen. I never saw any of the ladies; just heard their voices. One time I did dodge into a corner and I saw a man go out kind of stumbling. I remembered his face and after that I saw a newspaper with his picture in it because he'd killed himself. Grandma grabbed the paper away from me. She didn't let me read them very often."

"Did you ever see Mr. Powell before you came here?"

"N-no, I don't think so. So many people came to the séances, you see. I'd seen Mr. Doyle and Mrs. Greer and I think I noticed Mrs. Leroy. But sometimes people look a lot alike. When Mr. Doyle first began coming so often I thought he was another man that used to come there quite a while ago, but he just looked a lot like that man.”

“Oh! I see.” Eleanor frowned, sifting pine needles through her fingers.

Lisa said suddenly: “Mrs. Barlow had a brief case with her that she kept right in her lap till we got to San Francisco. She went out with it there and brought it back empty. I think she left it in the car that went back after it brought us here. I never saw it again, anyway. Couldn’t she have had all those—things in it?”

“I suppose so.”

“But Grandma told Mr. Doyle and Mr. Pope last night that she’d put a lot of papers in a safe-deposit box in San Francisco, only not any papers that she’d want a policeman to find if he happened to get into the box,” David said. “She did keep that brief case in her lap, and don’t you remember, Lisa, how she kept one suitcase kind of under her legs all the time? But afterwards there wasn’t anything in it but my things and hers.”

“She sent David out in the kitchen to stay with me when we’d been here just a little while,” Lisa recalled. “No one else was there and I could hear her moving around. There was kind of a funny sound too. I’d forgotten it till now. Don’t you remember, David?”

"Yes, and it was a funny noise. Kind of . . . knocking or maybe squeaking."

"I thought it was more like a creaking noise."

"Not all the time," David said, his forehead puckered up in concentration. "It was— Gee, I don't know."

"Never mind. I'll tell Mr. Pope what you do remember. He may— Oh! Rocky, that pantherlike tread of yours is a menace to people's nerves."

"You all seem kind of jittery," Rocky said, watching Lisa's brown fingers twist together. "Pope wants some whisky and a lot of handkerchiefs. He's determined he's going to have that cold, spite of all your dosing. I got to find Greer, but I thought maybe Lisa would take the things over."

"Let me. I want to talk to him."

"Well . . ." Rocky glanced toward Lisa and David. "You two stick together and you'll be all right. Though I'd prefer you, Eleanor, to walk to the clearing with us and set out there. You'd better take a flashlight with you, honey. Pope's examinin' that room an' the light is pretty poor."

They left Lisa and David sitting on a fallen log at the edge of the clearing. "Are you sending Mr. Greer to Boulder, or wherever he will have to go to telephone?"

"Just to Manzanita, to see if someone there can't take a message to Boulder. They ought to be willing to. I'll come back to the cabin soon as I can."

The black clouds to the east were momentarily barred with lightning, and thunder echoed across the canyon as Rocky walked toward the nearest camp, where Mrs. Cheney and Eva Greer were sitting in front of the tent. Mrs. Greer looked piously resigned: more like Mrs. Cheney should than Mrs. Cheney does, Rocky thought.

He watched the latter's broad, blunt fingers manipulating her knitting needles. Strong hands she had. Suppose she'd been convinced, after Pope left her, that Sapphira had— Well, damned Cheney's immortal soul! You couldn't tell how she might feel about that, but Sapphira would probably have let her in even if she hadn't been expecting her.

Mrs. Greer said brightly: "Good morning, Mr. Allan. Isn't it perfectly dreadful? Who would have thought—" Then her face cracked badly. "I want to get out of here! I was a fool to ever come."

"I kind of agree with you on that, ma'am. We all want to get out but none of us can go unless we'd like to have the police hunting for us. I wanted to ask your husband to go to Manzanita to phone, to get the sheriff here as soon as we can."

"I could go with him and stay at that hotel," Mrs. Greer said eagerly. "It's near enough that you could talk to me when you wanted to. Besides, what do I know? I was asleep before Mr. Cheney was killed and afterward I just went to sleep again."

"You're to be congratulated, managin' to get in all that sleep. Where is Greer?"

"He went fishing. I tried to keep him here but he said we had to go on eating. He's so provoking. No sense of fitness."

"Well, where did he go? I'd like to get him started before it storms."

"Oh, I never thought about that! Then that awful road would get wet and I thought we'd never reach here alive when we came in. I don't see how that Corwin girl managed to drive over it. Oh dear! What would be the best thing to do. . . ."

"The best thing for me to do is to find Greer. Did he go up or down stream?"

"Oh, Mr. Allan, I'm so sorry but I don't know. I've never been with him. He went down to the stream like he was going to get water but I don't know. . . . He said something about a favorite hole he fishes. He's been talking about some big fish that's there and there's a log and a deep pool . . ."

"That's swell," Rocky said. "Maybe the fish can tell me if he's been there—pr'viding I find the right pool."

"Well, I'm sure you don't need to be rude about it! I can't tell you anything more or I certainly would!"

"Oh, I know that. I didn't mean to be impatient," Rocky apologized, "but I hadn't figured on havin' to comb the woods to find him."

"Perhaps Mr. Doyle— He seems to want to speak to you."

Doyle had been talking to Margie and Henry Powell, but now he had left them and was waiting for Rocky. He said, when Rocky walked over to meet him:

"Look here, Allan, I don't want to start trouble, but you and Pope really haven't any authority.—Oh, I know you're a deputy. At least, Margie says you are but I'm not so sure that— While it's a good thing for you to take charge, I don't see what right you have to keep me from getting to a phone. Someone's got to go."

"We were goin' to send Greer."

"Yes, and he's off fishing. And by the time you find him it may be raining. His going won't do my paper any good. This is important to me and I'm not fool enough to figure on not coming back here. But I'm going—right now. Whose business is this anyway, yours or Pope's?"

Rocky eyed him speculatively, but he wasn't bluffing. He turned and started toward his car.

Rocky took a long step after him and his fingers settled around the back of Doyle's coat collar.

"I wouldn't be so hasty," he advised. "Think it over."

For an instant Doyle presented the peculiar spectacle of a man who is walking very fast but not getting anywhere. Then he twisted about and glared at Rocky, his face very red.

"Damn you! If you were anywhere near my size—"

"You'd paste me one. I don't know as I'd blame you." Rocky let him go and brought out a package of cigarettes. "I got enough authority to say you ain't going to a phone till I talk to Pope about it. An' while this started out to be his business, I'm not in the habit of sittin' on the sidelines when two murders have been committed. You never know who'll be next. Someone who'd be a real loss to the world, maybe—and you might remember, no matter what you say, I'm still a deputy sheriff in this county."

Margie strolled up to them, followed by Powell. "Won't the big bad man let you go places? I think he's got a hell of a nerve, but you couldn't go anyway—in your own car."

"What do you mean?" Doyle asked.

"I knew you'd be wanting to get to a telephone so we'd all be spread over the front pages of your filthy paper, so I took the spark plugs out of your car early this morning."

"You—" Doyle's round face looked like a red balloon inflated to the bursting point; then, suddenly, he turned rather white. "What did you do with them?"

"Don't you wish you knew? You might go fishing. And you can't use our car because I've got the only key to it and it's where you won't find it."

Rocky blew smoke through his nostrils; drawled: "Well, *she's* somewheres near your size, Doyle, and while she's undoubtedly a female, I wouldn't say she was a lady."

Margie flushed: there was no doubt that she'd heard their previous conversation. "You just dare hit me, Wren Doyle, and I'll scratch your eyes out! As for you, Mr. Allan—"

"Margie," Powell said softly, putting his hand on her arm, "we know that your nerves are unstrung, but don't you think you are acting unwisely? We can't avoid calling in the police, you know."

"Well, we can keep Wren from letting all the newspapers know about it. I don't mind telling you I'd try to make a break and get out of here if Minna would just come with me."

"Minna's got some sense and that's a damned sight more than you have," Doyle said bitterly.

"Who said I was going to tell the newspaper you two are here?"

"No one needed to tell me."

"Well, I wasn't and you can believe it or not, just as you like! I'd probably lose my job for it, but I thought I'd give Minna a chance to talk to Leroy before he sees it for himself in the papers. He could at least pretend he'd always known where you were, then. I can't keep you out of the papers unless you can buy off everyone else here."

Minna Leroy had walked up to them very quietly. She said: "Thank you, Warren. Margaret, I'm ashamed of you. Suppose you go into the tent and stay there until you can be more sensible. And if Warren is allowed to use a car he can have the key to ours."

"I—I think you're all—all—" Margie burst into tears, put her head down and ran for the tent.

Doyle thought: *Minna speaks that way about once a year, but when she does, Margie toes the mark.* And aloud: "I guess you can see my position, Minna. I can't protect you from the newspapers. But you can tell Margie she needn't worry about me getting in touch with my filthy rag, because it looks like I'm one of the chief suspects."

"Oh, surely not—"

"He takes it too serious, ma'am. I ain't suspecting anybody—much—and no one but Pope knows what he thinks. But I don't really think he b'lieves Doyle killed Sapphira and Cheney."

"I see. And if he knew Warren as well as I do, Mr. Allan— Well, I'm going to talk to Margie. She'll apologize to you, Warren, and not just because I want her to."

When Mrs. Leroy was out of hearing, Doyle wheeled abruptly to face Powell. "Look here, was that your idea, taking the spark plugs out of my car? Did you put Margie up to doing it without coming right out and telling her to?"

"I did not! Margie knows as much about cars as I do. What's wrong with you, Warren?"

"I'm willing to stand aside and play fair as far as Margie's concerned as long as she seems to like you best, but I'm damned if I'm going to be the fall guy for this business! What did you come up here for anyway? She never told me they were coming and so I couldn't have told you. And Margie says she didn't tell you anything, so how did you know she was going to be here?"

"I never said I knew that they would be here. For heaven's sake, Warren, can't we talk this over privately?"

"You 'n me can, if you like," Rocky said. "But it happens that Doyle's asked you the very questions I was aimin' to."

Powell fitted a long brown cigarette into a carved holder. "I think I would prefer to talk to your sheriff."

"Just as you like," Rocky said cheerfully. "Only thing is, that if you satisfy me and Pope you're all right we won't pass our suspicions on to the sheriff. Otherwise—"

"Suspicions? You two gentlemen have suspicions of me? Why, may I ask?"

"We're suspicious of ever'body. Why did you come up here?"

Powell shrugged elaborately. "Warren is making a mountain out of a little hill. He— Why do you look at me that way?"

"Never mind. Go on."

"I came because he was coming and I wanted a trip to the mountains. He's told you that he told me he was coming, hasn't he? And that he told me enough about Sapphira that it promised to be interesting? Well—"

"You never even heard of Sapphira before, I suppose?"

"Except for what he told me, you mean? Certainly, in the newspapers. I had never seen her before."

"And you don't mind sayin' where you came from before you landed in Los Angeles?"

"My father had a ranch in Arizona. He died five years ago. I worked: what I could get, mostly in the oil fields. Then I came to Los Angeles. I'd always sung and I liked to act. I wanted to break into the movies. You can imagine how much success I had, though I'm getting a foothold slowly. I like to write and I've sold a few articles to papers and magazines. That's all."

"I don't think you ever saw an oil field," Rocky said, looking at Powell's white, carefully cared-for hands. "I'll bet strummin' a guitar is the hardest work you ever did." He reached out and pulled Powell's half-smoked cigarette from its holder. "Did you get in the habit of smokin' these up in the oil fields?"

"You—you clumsy fool! How dare you—"

Rocky said: "Chinga! Cabrón!" and Powell's face reddened dangerously: then he relaxed consciously.

"I don't understand you."

"The hell you don't! You can't insult an American by yellin' cabrón at him, but it makes a Mexican see red every time."

"I—I knew you meant it for an insult," Powell stammered. "I've been with Mexicans enough to know that."

"I'll bet you have. An' that you did your singin' in some joint across the border. You talk good

English but once in a while you make a little slip. The sayin' is: 'to make a mountain out of a mole-hill,' not a little hill. An' you smoke Mexican cigarettes."

"I've told you.—I will not talk any more."

"O.K. Got a pencil I can borrow for a minute?"

"Pencil? No, Warren has my pencil."

"I have not," Doyle said flatly. "This is my own. The clip on yours is sprung, you know. I borrowed it from you last night but I gave it back to you and put new lead in mine."

"Oh yes, I remember. Give him yours," Powell said. "I don't know—"

"This is it, isn't it?" Rocky said as Powell stopped, staring at the green Eversharp in his hand. "You wouldn't know where I found it, would you? Well, for your info'mation, right near the front door of the cabin. How you goin' to explain that away?"

For an instant Powell said nothing. Then he muttered: "Jesus!" and turned and walked away. Rocky called after him:

"When you get ready to talk to us we'll be glad to hear what you've got to say," but without turning his head Powell went on toward the river.

CHAPTER FIFTEEN
"THERE GO THE DOCUMENTS"

Doyle said inadequately: "Well, what do you know about that!"

"Yes: what do you?"

"Oh, nothing. I mean— Let me have a cigarette, will you?" Doyle smoked in silence for a few minutes, then: "He sort of gave himself away as being Spanish or Mexican or something like that, didn't he? It's no crime, but he never admitted he was anything but an American. He did say he knew a little Spanish. So do I—classroom Spanish. I guess yours is more colloquial."

"If you mean largely profane. I wonder what his real name is?"

"It wouldn't be easy to turn Powell into Spanish. But I remember one time I saw Hank with a foreign-looking fellow who said: 'Adiós, Enrique.' He said the other guy was an extra he'd just happened to be talking to and there's lots of foreign extras. I suppose I ought to be chivalrous, but I've got kind of fed-up with seeing him sitting around at Margie's feet crooning to her. Not that she deserves to have anyone worry about her," Doyle said belligerently. "But hell! I've known her since she was a kid."

Rocky grinned. "I know just how it is, fella, no matter how long you've known 'em. You can't alibi Powell, can you?"

"Not for Sapphira's death and not for Cheney's either, I suppose, any more than he can me. He was there when I left our tent and when I got back, but that's all I can say."

"But if you're telling the truth, Mrs. Cheney couldn't have killed her husband and neither could you. We've never found the gun he was shot with. I suppose we might comb the brush 'longside that path. Well, are you going to talk to Pope? If he'll let you go we won't have to ask Greer to."

"Oh, let it go," Doyle said wearily. "I suppose I can still get the story to my paper before it's common knowledge, after the sheriff gets here. He'll probably let me.—Here comes Greer."

Greer threw his wicker fishing basket to the ground and looked mournfully at his trout pole.

"By golly, I'm going to get that big fellow if I have to stay here a month. I've hooked him twice and I'll bet he's eighteen inches long. He likes a gray hackle: swallowed one whole this morning and took my leader with it. Lies down there under that log—" He broke off with a sheepish smile; asked: "Did you want me for anything, Allan?"

Rocky explained, ending apologetically: "I can go but I kind of hate to leave Pope here by himself."

"Sure you do. I'll start right now, son. The way I look at it, it's a vote of confidence, you sending me." Greer took off his hat to wipe his forehead, pushed back his toupee and scrubbed at a pink bald spot on top of his head. "I wouldn't wear this thing if it wasn't for Eva," he said, settling the toupee in its proper place again. "Is it on straight? Well, I'll be off. There's eight or ten trout in the basket. You'd better take them. Eva can't fry fish."

"Thanks. Have you got any skid chains?"

"Always carry them. I'm a pretty good driver so don't you worry about me. I ought to make it out in an hour, and maybe quicker coming back. But if it starts to storm I'll just wait in that place— what's its name? Manzanita?—I'll just wait there till it stops."

"I don't know when the storm'll break," Rocky said, looking up at the sky. "I'd expected it before this but it might blow over since it's held off this long. Here's the money to pay that fellow and the note Pope wrote so's he'll get things straight. By the way, have you got any newspapers?"

"A whole stack of them. Want some?" Greer led the way to his car. "They're in back here. Help yourself."

"Pope would like to look them all over. We'll return 'em when we're through."

Greer looked at him curiously but asked no questions, for his wife had come over to them and was saying: "Thomas, I just don't know what to do. What do you think? If I go with you it might storm and we might skid on that road and get killed, but I don't want to stay here."

"Well, Toots, I don't want to be unsympathetic but you were the one that got us here, so I guess you'll have to be patient about staying for a while. I don't think you'd better come with me. It's going to storm."

"But then I might be able to help you," Mrs. Greer said nobly.

Greer was unimpressed and undiplomatic. "I'd a darned sight rather you'd stay right here. I want to make good time and with a back-seat driver—"

"Thomas Gre-er!"

"Well, you are. And I can't stop to argue with you either," Greer said firmly. "You stay right here. It's the safest thing for you to do. I'll be back as soon as I can."

He leaned out from the driver's seat for an instant, beckoning to Rocky. "I don't know why

Pope wants to look over those papers, son, but you might tell him we've given away a lot of them. I seem to be the only one who thought about bringing a bunch of old ones."

Mrs. Greer said: "Well! Of all the—" and Rocky hastily picked up the basket of fish and started away. Lisa and David came running to meet him, plainly glad of any excuse for activity.

"You take care of these fish till I get a chance to clean them," Rocky said. He hesitated, shifting the bundle of newspapers on his arm. He might follow Powell, but it would probably be better to give him time to think things over and let Pope talk to him later on.

"I'm going over to the cabin now. Then— No, wait. Lisa, would you mind puttin' the fish in a pan of water an' then goin' over and askin' Mrs. Cheney if she has any glue? And any newspapers. If she has, bring them to the cabin. Dave can come with me."

"I like to be called Dave. It sounds like—like a real boy's name," David said, trotting along beside Rocky. "Do you suppose now I can go to school?"

"I don't see why not. What kind of school?"

"I'd like to go to a military one because my father was a soldier in the war. Saul wouldn't have let me but maybe Mr. Jacobs will. He's the other trustee or whatever you call him. I heard Grandma say he'd be all right by himself. He's fat and keeps rubbing his hands all the time. He's a lawyer. I heard Grandma call him a shy—shy something."

"Shyster? I wouldn't be surprised. Only I have an idea Pope might go back down to L.A. an' put the fear of God in Mr. Jacobs. Here we are, kid— and see if you can't keep that tongue of yours still for a little bit."

Eleanor had found Pope shivering forlornly on the couch and was rather alarmed by the size of the drink he poured out and gulped down. He said reassuringly:

"Liquor has very little effect on a person who has a cold. Besides—I say it with pride—no man has ever made me drunk. A good many have tried," he added with something resembling a smile. "Of course, I do turn pale at the sight of a glass of beer. Did you bring the handkerchiefs? Thank you, child."

Eleanor glanced toward the bedroom, saw that the door was securely closed and sat down beside him. "What have you been doing? Wasn't there anything important in those suitcases?"

"No. I see you brought a flashlight. I suppose that was Rocky's suggestion: he said we should examine the floor."

"Well, I've been talking to David and Lisa. They say Sapphira was in here for quite a while with the door to the kitchen closed."

"When they first arrived?"

"Yes. She had one suitcase she kept under her feet but her brief case was empty when they got here. They heard some noise—they can't agree when it comes to describing it. A knocking, squeaking, creaking noise seems to be about the best they can do."

"That's not very helpful, is it? Sapphira probably had something sewed into that velvet pad over there. Rocky noticed that it had been slit, but I don't think she could have put everything in that. I'm sure it was flat enough when we were here last night."

"If it had been at all bulky the crystal wouldn't have set straight on it. I don't see how she could have taken up the floor boards, and the walls are made of such big logs that she couldn't hide anything there. Her table—"

"I've examined that. It's nothing but a table, and there is nothing in those pillows on the floor. I've looked over the kitchen too, though I believe she was hardly ever in that room or the bedroom. No, her possessions are here, unless someone has already found and taken them away."

"Then I don't see anything left but the fire-place."

Pope groaned. "Exactly. And I have been trying to put off the evil moment. Even before you told me what those children said, I knew I would have to go into the thing."

"Turn chimney sweep, do you mean? She had a fire in it almost constantly, you said. But there would be a few hours early in the morning when the fire was out, I suppose."

"Yes, and we don't know how soon the fire was started after they arrived. But there should have been soot on some of her clothes if she put any-thing inside that chimney."

"How would she dare put anything inside?" Eleanor was already examining the hearth and fireplace, which were made out of large, irregular pieces of rough stone. "I don't see how she pos-sibly could have taken up one of these. They are very solidly cemented together and if she chipped away the cement how could she put it back again so that we wouldn't notice?"

"Perhaps," Pope said with unusual flippancy, "she carried a sack of cement and a trowel with her. I'm sure—Damn!—I'm sure I couldn't remove one of those stones without leaving traces of my work. Well"—he poured out more whisky—"let's sit quietly and think things over until Rocky comes. You might open that door: let some air in."

"The place certainly needs it. Rocky has David with him," Eleanor reported presently. "I suppose he didn't want to leave him alone. Also a large stack of newspapers on his arm."

"Oh yes. I forgot that Doyle couldn't have told you about this. It was on Sapphira's lap."

Eleanor looked at the card and shivered. "That's horrible, though she had it coming to her." She said, as Rocky had: "And it proves premeditation, doesn't it? And—hadn't Sapphira set fifteen minutes of four as the day of judgment? I wonder—"

"So do I. It's as reasonable a time for her death to have occurred as any. Well, Rocky?"

Rocky threw the newspapers on the couch. "There you are. I sent Lisa over to ask Mrs. Cheney if she had that glue and any newspapers. Doyle said none of the rest of 'em had any left, though we can look, to be sure. I don't see what good it does, particularly, to check up on that."

"None, probably—but no harm. I thought I heard Greer driving out. Did he?"

"He just left. I also had an int'resting talk with Doyle; likewise Powell. Doyle was goin' to start off to a telephone right away. I stopped him an' then Margie Corwin said she'd took the spark plugs out of his car."

"Why, the little—beast," Eleanor said.

"Yeah. So her aunt sent her off to her tent and Doyle began askin' Powell to account for why he came up here. Powell says he just loves the mountains. Tried to tell me he'd worked in the oil fields and him with hands like a woman's. He lighted one of those sweet Mex cigarettes and got pretty mad when I fired a term of insult commonly used by Mex'cans at him."

"What was that?" David said interestedly.

"Never you mind. So then I showed him that pencil after Doyle had let it out that Powell still had it last night an' that it was one with a sprung clip. Powell said he did not choose to talk, reverted to Spanish more or less and went wanderin' off down to the crick."

"So, all in all, you've had quite an interesting time of it," Eleanor said. "Why did you let him go?"

"To think it over. He'll be coming back before long, ready to talk."

"He was alone after Mr. Doyle came over here. Did someone— Someone did knock you out last night, didn't they, Mr. Pope?"

Pope touched the top of his head tenderly. "Oh yes, I was certainly knocked cold and it might have been Powell who did it."

"Greer gave me some nice fish for dinner," Rocky said irrelevantly. "Look, Pope—why don't you just leave things be for the sheriff when he gets here an' go lie down and have just as bad a cold as you want to?"

"Because I didn't come up here to have a cold."

"Haven't you located anything? If you're goin' to be stubborn I'll tear the place up for you," Rocky said, glancing about the room. "There certainly ain't much furniture here. Did you sit on the floor or the couch all the time, Dave?"

"Yes. We always sat on the floor at home—in Los Angeles, I mean. On pillows, of course. It's comfortable when you get used to it."

"And your grandma set in that big chair all the time. . . ."

Pope said disgustedly: "This gold certainly bust have seddled in by head—Oh grin, Rocky!—must have settled in my head, I mean. I did examine that litter she sat in, but— Have you a strong pocket knife?"

"Sure. What— Oh, I get you. Is there a hammer aroun' here, kid?"

"I don't think so," David said, all wide-eyed interest. "Why? There's a great big butcher knife that Grandma borrowed, because she was in here and had it when Lisa wanted to cut some bread."

"Woman's favorite all-purpose tool—a butcher knife," Eleanor said.

"Or the heel of her shoe or her husband's razor blades. I'll go," Rocky said, moving toward the bedroom. "You've done enough of the dirty work already."

"That's the same kind of funny noise there was when Grandma was in here alone," David said presently. "It's more a kind of . . . screeching noise, isn't it?"

"Nails being pulled out of wood," Pope said. "I should have examined the seat of that chair at once. My brains are as congested as by dose."

It was some time before Rocky came back, his tan looking a little faded, and handed Pope a bundle wrapped in brown paper.

"The chair had a thin piece of wood tacked under the bottom with quite a space between that and the real seat. I s'pose you heard me taking the nails out? You would, when I was usin' a knife to do it. It was easy enough to tap them right back into the same holes. I don't think the sheriff'll know we disturbed the body except as carryin' in the chair would do it."

"Thank you, Rocky." Pope opened the bundle; looked toward David. "I suppose this is really your property, young man, but I'm going to destroy it just the same."

"Oh—are you? Not that it looks very interesting. It's just a lot of letters, isn't it? And that pretty green thing—"

"Thank heaven that is here. Letters, the page from a hotel register, two canceled checks and two thousand dollars in twenty-dollar bills. Do you want to look at these, Rocky? Eleanor? I thought you wouldn't."

Pope found a match; turned to David again. "I give you my word there is nothing here but the money that concerns you in any way. This pendant did not belong to your grandmother. She was . . . keeping it for someone. These papers are other people's secrets and she had no right to them. Neither have you."

"I know what you mean," David said. "I've heard about—about blackmail. I read a story where a lady kept trying to get some letters she'd written. I'd like for you to burn them, please. And keep the money for me."

Eleanor watched the edge of a sheet of pale-violet notepaper flare up as Pope threw the papers into the fireplace and touched a match to them.

"Well, there go the documents. I never could really believe in incriminating documents, you know. But now if you produce the formula for a death-dealing gas, I'll accept it without protest. Do you think you can manage not to mention this little episode, David?"

"I'll try. You mean, 'specially not to the sheriff who's coming? I won't tell him. Here comes Lisa."

"Mrs. Cheney found this glue in Mr. Cheney's suitcase," Lisa said, holding out a half-emptied tube. "She knew she had some around but she had to hunt for it. And the only newspaper she had was this religious one. She'd like to have it back."

"Was it glue that was used?" Rocky asked, purposely vague.

"Yes. There was a little smeared around some of the letters."

"Smeared? Well, what about fingerprints?"

"There might be some but they probably would not help us. Will you see if the back door is bolted?" Pope said quickly. "I don't think anyone would try to come in the front way in broad daylight. We might as well go back to camp and wait for the sheriff."

"We'll probably have to wait till tomorrow mornin'," Rocky said. "Depends on how soon he can start, whether it storms an' if he happens to be in town to get our message. There's your suitcase, Lisa, if you want to take it."

"Well, my work—our work—is done," Pope said. Then he picked up the newspapers and tucked them under his arm. "I can look at these while Rocky fries fish. I wonder where Powell is?"

"Incurable!" Eleanor said. "And I'm not referring to that cold."

CHAPTER SIXTEEN
"ARE YOU GOING BY THE CABIN?"

Rocky had gone up on the hill above their camp "to lay in enough wood to last for a while and get enough more pine boughs for a good bed—though God knows if I'll ever be let sleep in it." Eleanor could hear the sound of his ax as she swooped down on Theophilus Pope and took away the newspapers he had been examining.

"Yes, I know you think you feel a great deal better, but that's because you've had a very large lunch and three cups of coffee. You are going into our tent, out of any possible drafts, and lie down for two or three hours. And take these aspirin first."

"Well—I've looked over these papers anyway."

Eleanor hesitated, then asked, laughing at herself: "Did you find any words cut out of them?"

"A small scrap had been torn from one of them."

"But you don't think Mr. Greer—"

"No. Rocky said these papers were in the back of his car where anyone had access to them. Besides, it's not possible to tell if any of the words that appeared on the card were on the scrap that was torn out. It might only be a hole that was jabbed in the paper. Apparently everyone else here has burned his supply of newspapers."

"Why did you say that if there were any fingerprints on that card they probably wouldn't help you?"

"On thinking it over I doubt if anyone would be careless enough to leave his prints on that card. I thought," Pope said slyly, "that I was to lie down."

"You are. Come along and I'll tuck you in. As much as possible," Eleanor added. "Would it be better for your feet or your shoulders not to be covered, I wonder?"

"My shoulders. I'm warmly dressed. In very cold weather," Pope explained, "I am forced—in most beds and with most blankets—to sleep with my knees in the neighborhood of my chin. I will not distress you by describing my sufferings when I have to sleep in a Pullman berth. Run along, child, and wake me in an hour or two."

Eleanor stopped to find a copy of *Short Stories,* which she offered to David with the hopeful question: "Do you like to read?" being rather weary of his incessant chatter. "I don't know if you can read that. Perhaps it's too difficult for you."

"Oh no, I can read anything. I mean, I don't have to spell out words and I can understand most of them. You see, I read a lot when there wasn't anything else to do."

"Not your grandmother's pet books, I hope?" Eleanor said, remembering Rocky's description of the contents of Sapphira's suitcases.

"No: she kept those in her own room and told me not to touch them. She hid them, anyway. Saul used to give me Bible stories but I'd get the chauffeur—we used to have one—to buy me magazines."

"You can lie down on Mr. Pope's bed if you like. It's not very comfortable, sitting on a box."

"I'd like that," David said. "It's a nice little—little cubbyhole, isn't it? Will Mr. Allan fix one like it for me tonight?"

"He probably will. Run along. I'll be around here if you want me for anything."

Eleanor walked over to the fireplace where Lisa was still scrubbing stubbornly at a blackened pan. "There's no use your doing that, Lisa: it will just get black again. You can't keep a camp clean, you know. Why don't you sit down for a while?"

"Well, maybe I will. I guess— Here's Miss Corwin coming, Mrs. Allan."

Eleanor said, deliberately formal: "How is your aunt this afternoon, Miss Corwin?"

The girl grimaced. "It looks like I'm in the doghouse. Minna is all right. Mrs. Greer came over 'to set a spell' and I couldn't stand her chatter. Come talk to me, will you?" She looked significantly at Lisa. "There's a good place to sit over at the beginning of the clearing. Please!

"I'll bet," she went on, when they were sitting under a stubby red pine at the clearing's edge, "that your husband thinks I'm an awful wet smack."

"Do you care? Somehow I thought you didn't have a very good opinion of—what would you call them? Country hicks?"

"Now you're making me out just a plain snob and I'm not! It's true I don't know anything about people outside of cities. But I thought," Margie said with a little-boy grin, "that your husband was beautiful and dumb. My mistake!"

"He'd probably say he is—dumb. He doesn't realize half how good-looking he is and I'd just as leave he didn't. As soon as we were married he developed the most charming paternal manner toward pretty young ladies.—Is this to be a social conversation or did you want to talk to me about something important?"

"I guess it's important. I don't want to bother Minna any more. She spent fifteen minutes telling me, in her ladylike way, what kind of skunk I was and then chased me out to apologize to Wren. Which I'd have done anyway. And I gave him his precious spark plugs. I hadn't really thrown them in the river.

"I asked Wren where Hank was and wormed out of him what Mr. Allan had had to say to him and how he took it. He hasn't come back yet," Margie said, digging at the pine needles with her painted toenails. "Wren went down to the stream to see if he was anywhere near but he seems to have wandered of completely."

"Are you worried about him? That is—are you in love with him?"

"I don't know. I guess I thought I was, a little. I don't care what nationality he is," Margie said unhappily, "so long as he's white. But why did he have to lie about it? He told me his mother was part Spanish. Well, I'm not curious but I'm honest. Why couldn't he be?"

"There's only one reason that one thinks of."

"I know: that he had some good reason for not telling. I can't get Wren to say what he thinks. I don't guess he ever did really say what his opinion of Hank is—or was. I remember that now, and that Hank has always laughed at Wren a little when he could do it without it seeming at all pointed. Well, that's all right, I suppose. But he did tell me—and then pretended he hadn't meant to and maybe he didn't—that Wren thought his brother got started doping through going to Sapphira's."

"Oh! You didn't know that?"

"Sapphira was just a name I'd seen once or twice in the papers when Bill Doyle died. I didn't know anything about her dope racket until Minna— Well, Wren never talked to me very much about Bill. That was probably mostly my fault. I knew he was crazy about Bill but somehow I just can't be all womanly and sympathetic. I just didn't know what to say to him.

"Bill was older than Wren but the kind of brilliant literary person someone else always has to look out for. He wrote perfectly putrid poetry but he had a newspaper job and wrote for the magazines too. Like as not he went to Sapphira's to write a story about her."

"And you really didn't— Is that Mr. Greer back already? I believe it is."

"Well, it's one-thirty," Margie said. "Do you want to go talk to him?"

"I suppose I'd better. He's coming over here anyway. You made good time, Mr. Greer."

"Over two hours to do less than twenty miles. It's a wonder," Greer said, wiping his hot face, "that I got the car back at all, the way I drove."

"Which reminds me that we have a broken spring Rocky must manage to tie together. Did you find the hotelkeeper at home?"

"He was there, and twenty-five dollars looked big to him. I promised him the rest of it when we leave here, if he does the job. He said he'd drive to that place—Boulder? Of course he wanted everything explained, couldn't believe it and all that, but I didn't stop to talk to him. I wanted to make it back before it storms—if it does."

"The air smells damper. It's been very sultry."

"Don't I know it? Well, you tell your husband or Mr. Pope that it's all right. I'm going down and wash up and eat a sandwich and take a nap. I'm kind of tired."

"He's a nice old thing," Margie said, watching Greer cross the clearing and stop to speak to his wife and Mrs. Leroy. "How he ever came to marry that dumb cluck— What were you going to ask me when he drove up?"

"I don't— Oh yes. You really didn't tell Mr. Powell you were coming up here?"

"I didn't even hint at it. And I didn't tell Wren. As a matter of fact I hadn't seen him—Wren— for about a week, so I didn't know he was going to be on hand. Of course I told Hank we were driving up to San Francisco: that's where we're supposed to be. But how could he guess we were coming here? He'd know enough about Sapphira from what Wren told him to know that it wouldn't be any pleasure jaunt if we did come. But there's still a big gap that I can't fill in. O-oh! Listen to that thunder!"

"It's coming closer: storming again on the other side of the canyon. Mr. Greer got back just in time. Where are you going, Lisa?"

"We're all out of water," Lisa said, showing a canvas water bag. "I thought I'd get some."

"You don't have to do that. Let it go until Rocky gets back. It's too heavy for you to carry."

"Oh, I don't mind. I'm tired setting still and I like it down at the stream. I won't fill this very full."

"Well, if you want to go. But hurry back if it starts to rain."

"I will." Lisa walked a few steps, then turned and came back. "Would you keep this for me, Mrs. Allan? The catch is loose and I don't want to lose it. It belonged to my mother."

Eleanor took the old-fashioned, gold-plated locket and put it in a pocket of her riding trousers. "Remind me to give it back to you. Are you going by the cabin, Lisa? I guess that's as short a way to the stream as any from here."

"Yes'm, I'll go that way. What time is it, please?"

"Twenty minutes to two," Margie said and, as Lisa went on: "Well, I guess I'd better go. Say, how is Sister Cheney taking this?"

"Why, she hasn't said very much."

"Acts kind of numb? From what Mrs. Greer was saying to Minna, she seems to still think that Cheney was a real preacher. A—well, a good man."

"Yes, she spoke of him as if she believed that."

"Well, don't let her kid you. I told you how he kept sidling up to Minna and me—not that it was important, but I don't see how Mrs. Cheney could miss it. I walked by their tent after dark the first night we were here. I could hear her talking—she speaks rather loudly. She said: 'You're a wicked man, Saul.'"

"Nothing more?"

"Well, isn't that somethin'? But he answered her in a low voice and she said she couldn't hear him. Then, before he could answer that, she said: 'No, don't talk to me. I've believed you for too many years. I think I hate you. Maybe I have for a long time.' I haven't an awfully good memory but that's pretty close to what she said. Before I could get in our tent he charged out and started for the cabin."

"That's interesting. From what she said they didn't talk to each other very much. By the way, Mr. Pope stopped to give your aunt that pendant, didn't he?"

"Yes. He's not a bad guy, at that. What I want Minna to do," Margie said, "is to tell Uncle Edgar that this was just one of my girlish pranks; that I got the idea from Wren and thought it would be nice to see a real day of judgment. Wren says that's all right with him. Uncle Edgar is fond of me but he thinks all the younger generation are all kind of insane, so he'd probably believe the story."

"What does Mrs. Leroy say?"

"That is might seem rather peculiar to Uncle Edgar that she'd give in to an idea like that. After going to all this trouble it would be just like her to tell him everything."

"You advised that last night."

"Oh, I was too scared to have time to think it over. Besides, it didn't look like we were going to get that pendant and I knew she'd been outside, though I didn't know Cheney was dead. If Mr. Pope and Mr. Allan keep her out of it as far as they can and she's clever enough to keep the sheriff from being suspicious, I don't see why we can't pose as being thrill chasers, like Little Eva. Of course we'll get in the papers.

"People do do crazy things. If Minna hadn't been a bundle of nerves and kind of—obsessed from thinking so long about this, she'd have had more sense than to come up here. I don't claim to be very sensible. I was with her in San Diego and she couldn't keep me from finding out—about her—or she'd never have told me anything. I was afraid it mightn't be best to stop her coming even if she was—cured. But we may get out of it safely."

"And you?"

"I guess I won't break my heart, whatever happens. I'd like to talk to Hank. He—he has a nasty temper when he gets mad," Margie said reluctantly. "I thought that was kind of fascinating. As for Wren—marrying a man you've known since you both wore diapers isn't awfully romantic, is it?"

"Are you romantic?" Eleanor said, smiling.

"I guess you wouldn't think so. I don't suppose I'll ever look at any man like you do that husband of yours," Margie said defiantly. "I guess I just won't get married at all. Say, I've got a skirt that goes with these shorts. Do you think I'd better put it on before the sheriff gets here?"

"Shorts have penetrated even to the remote fastnesses of the mountains," Eleanor said. "The sheriff's granddaughters—he has two—sometimes wear them. But to be on the safe side I'd put on the skirt and take that red polish off my toenails."

"Okey-doke. I must say short pants are more suitable for beaches than mountains. Every time I seek seclusion in the brush I get half a dozen new scratches. Well, thanks for letting me talk to you," Margie said. "I'll go back and see if I can't chase Eva away. She's easy to shock, even if she does think she's so 'modren.'"

Eleanor went back through the trees to their camp as Rocky came down the hill with his arms full of pine boughs. He said, throwing them to the ground:

"It's going to rain any minute. I got to hurry with this. Is Pope asleep?"

"I hope so. Let me help you, Rocky. I can carry quite a lot of wood."

"Well, a few sticks if you want to. I got it all piled up on the hill. I wanted some big pieces that would last awhile even if I can't bring them all down here right now." As they went up the hill together he stooped to kiss her. "Seems like I've hardly seen you for hours. Chasin' me out of my own bed last night—"

"The poor child was so nervous. She jerked and muttered all night long. Where on earth are we going to put everyone tonight?"

"It'd be simplest to spread a row of beds out in the cabin. But I like the smell of that place less than ever now. Hold out your arms an' I'll pile the wood in 'em. There—that's plenty. Where had you been just before I got back to camp?"

"Margie wanted to talk to me—privately. Oh yes, and Mr. Greer is back and he delivered the message to the hotelkeeper, who promised to go on to Boulder with it. I'll tell you later what Margie said: that is, what I can tell. Rocky, don't go so fast with that enormous load of wood! You might stumble—"

"We need to hurry. Hear that?"

"How can I help it?" Eleanor said, wincing. "I don't mind rumbling thunder, but those terrible booming sounds—"

"Just plain noise won't hurt you." Rocky looked up at the sky, where only one blue patch remained and that far to the west. A shaft of lightning split the clouds, seeming to strike so near them that Eleanor flinched involuntarily. "You stay here, honey. Get David and Pope—"

"I'm right here," David said drowsily, peering out from Pope's lean-to. "I guess I was almost asleep. Goodness, that thunder is loud, isn't it? Do you think—"

"I think you'd better help Eleanor drag those pine boughs under cover while I go up the hill again. We may want 'em to sleep on tonight."

Pope, coming out just then, helped them carry his bedding, sweaters, the freshly cut pine boughs and all their perishable supplies into the tent. Though now rather hoarse, he looked better for his nap. When Eleanor protested that he "must not get wet," he produced a long yellow slicker and an old tweed cap from his suitcase.

"One never knows when or where it may rain," he said. "I think this tent will withstand any moderate storm."

"The wind is coming up," Eleanor said, pulling on her sweater. "David, you should be wearing something besides those thin silk things. Put on this old sweater of mine. No, that's Lisa's—" She stopped and her hand went slowly to her mouth. "Lisa! She should be back by now. She went down to the river to get water—"

"How long ago?"

"It was twenty minutes of two. She asked what time it was."

"And it is almost fifteen minutes after, now."

"She shouldn't have been gone so long. Surely she'll come back now. Oh!" Eleanor said desperately, "why did I let her go? I could have stopped her—"

"Hush, child! Don't worry." But Pope's tone was not convincing and David stared at them.

"I don't know why Lisa went after water," he said. "There was quite a lot in the bag and she went and poured it on the ground."

With artillery roll of thunder and powder flash of lightning, the storm broke over them. The canvas above their heads sagged as the rain struck at it savagely. Rocky stumbled into the tent and cast an armload of wood at the foot of the bed.

"So's we'll have some dry when this is over. I wonder— What's the matter?"

Pope said: "You'd better come with me, Rocky. Did she go down by the cabin, Eleanor? Very well. I think you'd better go to the cabin: not stay cooped up in here. Tell the others, if they don't have sense enough to take shelter there."

He and Rocky were gone. Eleanor stared blindly at the walls of the tent, reached out and caught David's hand in hers.

"We'll have to run for it, David. Hold tight."

Coming out on the clearing, she staggered when the rain struck her full in the face. David had lost one slipper and was whimpering a little as lightning dazzled his eyes. Across the clearing Warren Doyle was struggling vainly to anchor his tent against the wind. Greer's stood more firmly but Minna Leroy's was swaying precariously.

Eleanor shouted: "You'd better let it go!" but Doyle did not hear her. She clutched David's hand more tightly, put her head down and ran toward the line of tents as Doyle's fell slowly sidewise. Thomas Greer was hauling a box of food into their tent. Eleanor heard him shout:

"For God's sake stop yelping, Eva! Come out of there and beat it to the cabin. You'd better get Mrs. Cheney."

Eva Greer stumbled out into the storm, her plump face pasty white. She made small moaning noises as she ran mincingly toward the cabin. Eleanor thought: *this is really funny. I'll see that it is, later on.*

She turned toward Margie and Mrs. Leroy. "There goes our tent," Margie said composedly. "Look at Eva run, will you? Just like a duck. Are we to leg it to the cabin? All right."

"Where is Mr. Powell?"

"Don't know. He hasn't come back yet. Well, to hell with him," Margie said, a half-sob in her throat. "Come on, Minna. The last one there is a cross-eyed kangaroo."

"Go with them, David," Eleanor said, letting go his hand. "Go on! I have to stop to get Mrs. Cheney."

Doyle, a carton of cigarettes under one arm, gave a last resentful look at his tent; said: "I'll see to her, Mrs. Allan. You go on. You're wet through already." As she ran after the other three Eleanor heard him calling:

"Mrs. Cheney! Mrs. Cheney! You'd better get out of there while the getting's good!" and Greer's deeper voice.

"I don't know how long your tent will stand up, Mrs. Cheney. We're all going to the cabin till this is over."

In the cabin Margie was standing rigidly in the center of the front room, clinging to her aunt's hand.

"God, this is the most awful place! Mrs. Allan—Eleanor—can't we have a fire or some kind of light? That'd help."

"Yes, it would. There isn't any wood in here. There may be some in the kitchen and some matches. I'll see."

She lifted the heavy wooden bar from across the back door; tried to see through the rain down the path. After an instant she made out two figures coming up it toward the cabin. Pope and—no, not Rocky, but Pope and Henry Powell.

She started to call out to them before she saw that Pope's long, steel-strong fingers were clamped around Powell's wrist. She stood staring while Pope entered and flung the younger man into a chair. He said:

"Go back into the other room, Eleanor. Rocky is coming."

"Coming? With—"

"With Lisa. We couldn't leave her lying out there in the rain."

CHAPTER SEVENTEEN
"EVERYTHING . . . IS GOOD FOR SOMETHING"

Rocky didn't particularly care for third-degree methods but he felt as if it would be a relief to use them right now. He had had to carry Lisa Wood's frail body up the slippery path, to place her on the blankets in the kitchen and gently cover her face. She looked like she was sleeping. That should have made him mind it less but it didn't.

If Powell didn't like sitting there he wasn't the only one who didn't. What did he expect? You didn't handle a man with kid gloves after you'd found him standing over a girl who had been stabbed to the heart. Of course there was one thing that Rocky didn't know until later—but that could wait. It would be just as well if they put the fear of God in the fellow first.

"Is that your knife?" Pope said, nodding toward a dagger with heavily ornate handle that he had put on the table.

"No to creas! I beg your pardon. If you will believe me, it is not," Powell said. "I am more or less familiar with knives but that is an ornament, though sharp enough. I don't carry one. Because—because I have a hot temper and Americans do not admire people who use knives in a fight. You—will you listen to me or do you accuse me—"

Rocky hesitated but he decided again to let Powell talk. He lighted a cigarette, feeling this was a lapse from what Mrs. Greer would call "the fitness of things," but he had to smoke. Powell looked with unconscious desire at the cigarettes, but Rocky did not offer him one, and he said slowly:

"I don't care to tell you my real name. But I am not any mestizo! My grandfather was a Madrileño and my father a well-educated man, but he could not keep out of Mexican politics so he died in front of a stone wall when I was fourteen. That was thirteen years ago: I am older than most people think.

"My mother was half French. She was dead when my father was executed and his friends smuggled me out of the country to an American who had been my father's friend; a man who owned a ranch in Arizona. I was four years there and went to high school—I'd already known some English. But he was an old man. He died and his sons hadn't

liked me and I was— kicked out. I drifted down
to the border.

"It was starve or live as you might. I lived,"
Powell said, his thin nostrils dinted with white. "I
was, finally, a singer. As Mr. Allan suggested, in
Juarez and other places. Well, I worked up from
the Calle Ugarte to la Avenida Juarez. It was in
the former district that I met a man who spoke
English and was well educated. I knew he dealt in
drugs: marihuana—"

"Did he supply you?" Pope asked.

"Ni lo permita Dios! I am not quite a fool, Mr.
Pope. I never permitted myself that habit. I managed to save a fair sum of money and wished to
make a new start. This acquaintance knew what I
was going to do and was not too encouraging. He
said that if I were ever—up against it, to go to
a certain Sapphira in Los Angeles and she might
have work for me to do. He gave me a card that
would give me a hearing with her. Though he was
very discreet I guessed that he helped to supply
her with the black drugs.

"Well, I shaved off my mustache and went to
Los Angeles. My life there was just what you've
been told except that I often met one of my coun-
trymen in mob scenes and he was in Sapphira's
employ. He never said in what capacity."

"How'd he happen to tell you that at all?" Rocky asked. "If you'd have us believe you never got to be one of Sapphira's mob?"

"Y dale! I had met Margie and her aunt. Mrs. Leroy was always very kind to me. When she first went to Sapphira's, merely from curiosity, she talked of it. Then when things went wrong with her— Well, don't you see that I know, or was fairly certain, of Sapphira's underneath activities? When Mrs. Leroy went off to San Diego I guessed what might have happened. I showed this card I'd been given, to my acquaintance, the extra—"

"Why'd he stay an extra if he got paid by Sapphira?"

"I believe the woman who dealt with these— subordinates preferred to have him there to help work the moving-picture crowd. I asked him if he thought there was any chance for me. That was to make him talk, you see? He said that the police were dangerously interested in Sapphira, so that things were at a standstill. I mentioned Mrs. Leroy's name as if by accident and he winked and looked very knowing. That was all I wished to know."

"Do you still have that card with you?" Pope said.

"Certainly." Powell brought out a billfold, found a small piece of green pasteboard the size

of a calling card and handed it to Pope. "I think
the Spanish quotation on the card is some sort of
password—'Everything in the world is good for
something.'"

"The old girl had a right nice sense of humor,
didn't she?" Rocky said. "And it's signed Pablo."

"I kept the card because I might still need it.
When Margie and Mrs. Leroy came back I could
see that things were not going well with them.
Then Warren told me he was coming up here and
Margie said she and her aunt were driving to San
Francisco. She is not a good liar, Margie. I could
guess that they were coming here and asked War-
ren to allow me to come with him."

"An' what did you intend to do when you got
here, Don Quijote?" Rocky said. "Here: have a
cigarette?"

"Thank you. Why, with this card I meant to
see Sapphira and to—to bluff. To make her think
that Pablo and the extra had told me more than
they had. I tried to see her when we first arrived
and failed. You will remember that we all attended
a—a séance here about the time you arrived, Mr.
Allan? I managed to sit near her, to attract her
attention and show her the card in the palm of my
hand.

"She saw it, though she gave no sign anyone
else would notice. As we left she dropped one of

those many scarves to the floor and I picked it up. She whispered for me to come to the cabin as near to half-past two in the morning as I could."

"I wonder," Rocky said, "if she had any idea what you wanted?"

"She probably thought that I was one of her own kind," Powell said bitterly. "Perhaps she had work for me. Perhaps she was afraid to risk not seeing me. I don't know. But as things turned out I had difficulty getting there. Cheney was killed and it would have seemed suspicious for me to be caught prowling about here, and at two-thirty I could still see your campfire burning."

"Wait a minute. What did you know about Cheney?"

"Nothing. Anyone would guess the man was a hypocrite from the way he looked at women, and his being connected with Sapphira was not in his favor. But his name had never been mentioned to me as being connected with her really lucrative activities. I'd heard of him only as—as the translator of her prophecies."

"O.K. Go on."

"I heard you, Mr. Pope, stop to talk to Mrs. Cheney, then come by our tent. I waited until I thought you must have gone back to your camp. By that time it was nearly half-past three. I was kept in the tent that long because at one time I imagined that I heard someone on the clearing.

"I hesitated to go at all, because Warren was here, but then I thought: what did it matter if he did see me here? I thought he wouldn't talk if I told him the truth, though I did hope I would not have to. I took our path down to the stream and there, Mr. Pope, you and I began to play hide-and-seek with each other."

For the first time during the conversation Pope's coldly impersonal tone thawed slightly. "What did you hit me with?" he said curiously.

"With this." Powell put a short length of lead pipe on the table. "I wanted a weapon and I found this in Warren's tool box, where he seems to keep a little of all things. I'm sorry I hit you but I was frightened. You blocked my way to the cabin and when I tried to go back the way I had come I knew you were following me. I thought you might be Cheney's murderer. I stepped into the bushes and when you unfortunately stepped back into my arms, I am sure I was the more frightened of the two. I struck instinctively. Then—I had a flash-light—I saw who it was and dragged you back from the path."

"Thank you," Pope said dryly. "The bump on my head was not to be compared with the cold I caught from lying there. So then you continued on here, saw Sapphira and—"

"*Cállese!*" Powell said sharply. "I saw her but I did not talk to her or kill her, because she was already dead. That was at five minutes of four. It was— That boy sleeping like the dead, while those eyes seemed to stare at him!"

"We know. And Doyle?"

"Yes, I looked at him, Mr. Pope. At first I had some idea that he might be gone. He was sleeping with his head down on the table as soundly as the boy. I turned and went out and I must have dropped that pencil from off my pocket during the time I was here. I saw or heard no one, going back to our tent."

"Well, it did seem like she must've been expecting someone," Rocky said. "Though she was a fool to leave that door open. It was, wasn't it?"

"Yes, it was, though I knocked before I tried it. This afternoon," Powell said, "I walked far upstream, thinking. I decided Margie would have to know everything there is to tell. I'd been promised a small part in a picture next month—" He shrugged. "I suppose that isn't important—to you. When I saw we were to have a storm I started back. I walked some time in the rain, however, and when I reached the path up to this cabin I

thought that probably everyone would take ref-
uge here. So I came up the path and halfway here
stumbled on the girl. I don't think I had had time
to move when you found me there."

Rocky turned to Pope. "The trouble is that she
was killed before it started to storm. You know
how wet the path was when we got there? But she
fell or was laid down on her back, and underneath
her was as dry as that path ever is. It started raining about two-fifteen and it was about two twenty-
five when we got there. I somehow can't believe
that Powell stood there admirin' his handiwork
for more than ten minutes."

"No, I can't believe that myself. I admit that I've
been rather venting my anger at my own stupidity
on Mr. Powell. Of course I wanted you to talk and
for an instant it did seem that we had caught you
red-handed. I didn't very greatly care who killed
Sapphira or Cheney, but that poor child—"

"And why should she be killed?" Powell asked.
"I understood that she had not been long with
Sapphira."

"Two or three weeks. Of course," Rocky said,
"with her gone and all footprints being washed
away and nothing left but a gun that almost
couldn't have been used to kill Cheney, no one can
prove Mrs. Leroy came to the cabin right when

Cheney was killed. Lisa could have told that she planned to come—"

"Even in three weeks she might have heard a good deal and suspected more," Pope said. "She was not stupid, though I don't believe she thought very quickly. She must have been, since Cheney was killed, turning something over in her mind, trying to decide what she should do—"

"What makes you think that? Maybe she didn't know she knew anything to make someone want to get rid of her," Rocky suggested.

"I believe she did know. She told Eleanor there was no water in camp, but David saw her empty your water bag. She must have done that to have an excuse for coming down here. Also, Eleanor says that Lisa asked the time. It was twenty minutes of two. From what you tell us, Rocky, she must have been killed within the thirty-five minutes that passed from the time she left camp until the storm began."

"And when it did begin, everybody was runnin' wildly aroun'.' If whoever she went to meet was at the place when she got there an' killed her right off, he had a good twenty-five minutes to spare. He'd get wet and muddy but so did ever'body else."

"Yes. Did you know Warren Doyle's brother, Mr. Powell?"

"I? No, he died before I knew Warren. I'm afraid," Powell said, flushing, "that I said some things to Margie that I should not have said."

"That Doyle's brother may have become addicted to drugs through visiting Sapphira's? Yes," Pope said shamelessly, "we talked to him about that."

Rocky looked at him thoughtfully, lighting another cigarette. Pope would never lie to you just to be polite or to save himself: you were sure of that as soon as you knew him. But he certainly could stretch the truth when he thought he needed to. Powell reacted just as people always did.

"Warren felt his brother's death very deeply though other acquaintances of his told me more about William Doyle than Warren did. He never said to me that he suspected his brother obtained cocaine through Sapphira's organization. But he used to talk to me about Sapphira and the investigations of this policeman. Blake was his name, I think.

"He said: 'She may never be convicted, but if she can be scared out of business she won't be the means of any more youngsters dying in hell.' He said the largeness of Sapphira's organization was its weakness. He thought she could be frightened away because there were too many people who knew too much, if not enough to convict her."

When Pope made no comment Powell added nervously: "I hope you don't think that Warren— I don't believe he has the—the temperament to kill for revenge. He's not even quick tempered. It's true he was angry today, but we're all on edge. I can swear he was in a drugged sleep—"

"Can you?" Rocky said. "How do you know he was drugged?"

"He told me. But even at the time I thought he did not seem to be sleeping naturally. I wondered—and since Sapphira must have been expecting me, it occurred to me that she might have taken steps so that we could talk privately."

"Well, I suppose you would think of that," Rocky conceded. "Didn't you know he liked Margie Corwin?"

"I suppose I'm very stupid. But he doesn't even talk to her politely. More like a brother. No doubt I should know by now that people like Margie and Warren do not conduct a courtship according to my ideas. They appear to understand each other but"—Powell shrugged again—"one prefers a little—romance."

Rocky looked at Pope but he was shivering as if he were in the grip of a sudden chill. Being out in the storm probably hadn't made him feel any better. He certainly didn't look like he was much interested in Margie Corwin's love affairs. Rocky turned back to Powell.

"Were you surprised when the Greers turned up?"

"If I had known Mrs. Greer I would not have been," Powell said with a little grimace. "Es ella de to que no hay!"

Rocky grinned. "No, I never saw anyone just like her myself. You hadn't known them before?"

"I had never even heard of them. Not surprising, is that?"

"Not considerin' the size of the fair city of Los Angeles it ain't. When you get to thinking about Sapphira's racket you can't help wonderin' a little about Mrs. Greer. You'd certainly think she was just like Doyle says—goes in for a new fad every year. But she also seems silly enough to have got in trouble."

"I don't agree with you there, Rocky," Pope said from the depths of his latest handkerchief. "She is silly enough but she is shrewd and selfish so far as her own well-being is concerned. I'll wager she would be a very poor subject for blackmail. I have an idea she knows the value of money, and Sapphira didn't carry on her business without being able to judge who could be victimized and who could not."

"Yeah, she must've known that, judgin' from the cases we've heard about. Come to think of it, I can't imagine Little Eva getting reckless and riskin' her skin in any way.—Christ! That was too near for comfort."

Powell sank back into his chair trembling a little. "It sounded as if it had struck this building. How long will it last?"

"God knows," Rocky said cheerfully. "The sun might be out in an hour and it might last all night. What are we going to do now, Pope?"

"Do? What would you suggest?"

"Hell! I've got no suggestions. But that gang in yonder can't be any too cheerful an' Eleanor's probably bearing the brunt of it all. It's a wonder to me Mrs. Greer ain't yellin' her head off every time it thunders."

Powell put his hands over his ears. "I wouldn't blame her," he muttered when the thunder had grumbled itself into silence again. "It's like a hungry beast. . . ." He looked white and nervously exhausted. Too much imagination, Rocky thought. Pope said:

"Go in to the others if you like, Rocky. You too, Powell. I'll stay here for a while."

Powell half rose, then shook his head. "No, I'll— I'll stay here. I can't talk to any of those people or to Margie, before them.—Jesús! Who— Is that Margie?"

CHAPTER EIGHTEEN
SHE ASKED TO BORROW MY BIBLE

Eleanor had been, and still was very thankful that
Thomas Greer was in the cabin with them. He had
not only told his wife curtly to "hush up and don't
start working yourself into hysterics!" but he had
built a roaring fire, lighted half-a-dozen candles
and then invited everyone to "draw up your chairs
and get in the circle."

There were no chairs in the room, but Greer
dragged the couch in front of the fireplace and
Eleanor collected the dirty pillows that were
heaped in one corner. Mrs. Cheney took part of
the couch and went on with her interminable
knitting. She hadn't, Doyle whispered to Eleanor,
wanted to come with them.

"She said she guessed the tent would stand up
and she wasn't afraid of the storm, but we dragged
her out, bedroom slippers and all."

Eva Greer sat beside Mrs. Cheney, automatically and unsuccessfully trying to push the wave

back into her damp hair. Rain had washed away
her powder and rouge stood out in harsh spots on
her cheekbones. Finally she buried her face in her
hands, flinching at every crash of thunder. "I—I
don't like it," she whimpered.

"I know you don't, Eva," Greer said sympathetically. "You never did. But you've seen some bad
ones in Illinois and Indiana, and it don't even begin to compare with just a small artillery battle."

"I never was in a war or Illinois, either, and I
don't see how anything could be worse. This place
may burn down over our heads if the lightning
strikes it. Besides, it isn't just the storm. . . ."

"I guess we'd get out of here before the place
could burn," Greer said hastily. "It couldn't burn
very fast in this rain. Listen to it, will you?"

"We can't very well help ourselves," Doyle said
irritably. But he followed Greer's lead. "Do you
think your tent will stay up?"

"I hope so. What about yours, Mrs. Allan?"

"It will stand if any tent can."

Eleanor was sharing the cushions on the floor
with Margie and Mrs. Leroy. As Mrs. Cheney and
Mrs. Greer together took up more than a fair two-
thirds of the couch, David was perched on its extreme end.

He had been unusually quiet, staring wide-eyed
at the fire, holding his feet out to its warmth.

Now he defeated their efforts to confine the talk to commonplaces.

"I liked Lisa," he said, drawing his sleeve across his eyes. "She was awful nice to me."

Eleanor tried desperately to produce some safe and sane remark but she could think of nothing, see nothing but Lisa walking away toward the cabin and the path beyond it. And herself, standing there, letting the girl go, never thinking to call her back. . . . Margie reached for her hand and clasped it tightly.

"Don't feel badly about it," she said awkwardly. "How were you to know? I wish I'd paid some attention to her when I had a chance. Poor kid: she never did have anything, I guess. That old necklace— Oh, I always say the wrong things! I shouldn't—"

"She knows you don't mean to," Mrs. Leroy said. "If—if I only knew that it wasn't because of me that—that—"

"But how could it be, Mrs. Leroy?" Eleanor asked.

"I don't know. But I was responsible for keeping her up last night; for her being on the scene . . ." Mrs. Leroy glanced toward Naomi Cheney; ended her sentence rather vaguely: "she might have seen or heard more than she told you."

"Well, since we don't seem to be able to ignore the subject, just what time did the girl come down here?" Doyle asked.

"It was twenty minutes of two. We know that because she asked the time and Margie told her. It was getting ready to storm and Mr. Pope and David and I had all our things dragged into the tent before I thought about Lisa, just before the rain began. Well, about five minutes later—if you want to face it squarely—I got to the clearing and know that all of you were there at about two twenty-five. . . ."

"Except for Hank." Margie lighted a cigarette with unsteady fingers. "Don't forget him. He wasn't there and they're giving him the third degree now, I suppose."

Eva Greer said indistinctly: "Utterly heartless!" and Margie scowled at her.

"I don't guess you'd say I should stick up for that kind of murderer if Hank happens to be it. Personally, I think whoever disposed of Sapphira and—of Sapphira, deserves a medal. This is different."

"Well, I don't think Hank did it," Doyle said without looking at Margie. "For one thing, it seems to me the girl must have been going to meet someone if she asked the time. If Hank had to be there to meet her, when did he arrange that and why would he wander away all morning? I looked for him while Margie was talking to you, Mrs. Allan, and I didn't find him anywhere around. I can't even alibi myself because I was down at the river just before the rain started. I did think I might have heard someone in that brush between the camps and the river—"

"I was there," Mrs. Greer said with great dignity. "I was gathering ferns."

Her husband suppressed a grin. "Well, I went down to the creek myself and washed up right after I talked to you girls. Then I came back and laid down, but I don't know that Eva saw me in the tent all the time. When this hullabaloo began she came dashing in to get out of the rain. You know," he added thoughtfully, "a person can crawl out of the back of a tent if they want to."

Mrs. Leroy smiled. "Well, your wife and I parted soon after you got back and I went into our tent."

"Oh, I wasn't thinking about you, Mrs. Leroy."

"Imagine Minna crawling out of a tent on her hands and knees," Margie said scornfully. "Still, I suppose stranger things have happened, and our camps are more or less screened from each other on the sides by trees. I guess Eleanor and I must have talked about ten minutes more after Lisa—left us. Minna was in our tent when I got back to it."

"Trouble is, there's so many places to hide down there at the river," Doyle said. "All that growth between it and the camps, and in a pinch you could dodge into those willows that grow along the stream all around the places where we get water."

"And you can't even see straight along the stream," Greer said, fingering the trout flies thrust into his coat lapel. "That path along the stream curves a lot and there's all those trails leading down to it."

"Well, we really don't know anything about all these forests around us, do we?" Mrs. Greer said, forgetting to listen to the noises of the storm. "Why, there might be almost anyone living in some little cabin farther back in the woods. Some hermit who's been watching all of us. The—the years of solitude may have preyed on his mind."

"The Mad Hermit of Coon Hollow. Swell!" Margie said. "Now we're getting somewhere. Why didn't we think of that before? Call your husband in, Eleanor. He shouldn't miss this."

"I think," Mrs. Greer said, the rest of her face momentarily matching her rouge, "that you are the rudest little snip I ever saw in my life!"

"And I think you're just a silly old—"

"Margaret! You will just have to excuse her, Mrs. Greer. Henry Powell is a friend of hers, you see. I'm sure," Minna Leroy said flatteringly, "that you can understand how she feels."

"I'd thought someone might have sneaked in here last night," Greer said. "Not from the forest but someone who parked his car a mile or two away on the road. But he'd have had to get away before I went to Manzanita. I never saw a soul. I can't imagine anyone tramping all the way in here. I'd swear no one had a car parked anywhere near here when I came back, and that girl was killed too quick after I got back— But it seems downright impossible that any of us killed her. Not Sapphira or—"

"Thomas!"

Greer glanced guiltily toward Mrs. Cheney. She said, without looking away from her knitting:

"You needn't be careful of my feelings if Mrs. Greer thought you were going to say something to hurt them. I doubt if I have any left. Not for anything but my duty, and perhaps I was mistaken when I thought I knew what that was. God is our judge and—" she looked briefly about the circle of faces; ended without expression: "Vengeance is His."

Margie said through set teeth: "Anyone know any good stories? Something fit for the parlor? I'm afraid my collection wouldn't pass muster in this polite society."

"Nor mine," Eleanor said lightly. "Not only was I a nurse but I've been married some time to a railroader."

Greer chuckled. "Well, you've both got spunk, anyway. Say Doyle, what kind of team do you think we're going to have this fall?"

"Oh, not so bad," Doyle said unenthusiastically, but Eleanor's exasperating smile and: "It really couldn't be worse than it was last year, could it?" roused him, as she knew it would, to a lengthy defense of southern California's football teams.

"I guess you're right," Greer said, when Doyle had finished his impassioned recital of statistics. "We just aren't getting the material. I've always thought I'd like to know all the inside dope on the games, like you fellows do. I suppose there's a lot of things you can't print. I've always wondered about something that happened in the Stanford game. Maybe you remember it. . . ."

Eleanor hoped she looked as if she were listening with some interest. She had an idea that Doyle was being rather entertaining. Greer chuckled now and then and asked a question, or Minna Leroy made some comment in her low, clear voice. Eva Greer was unhappily engrossed with the storm again and Mrs. Cheney probably heard very little of what was being said, for she looked at her knitting and not at the lips of those about her. David said:

"I never saw a football game. I'd like to, sometime. I've read about them," and listened raptly to Doyle's account of a nameless halfback who went Hollywood and didn't like to risk his unusually handsome features in scrimmage.

If someone kept talking so that they could pretend to listen, they might manage to get through the time until the storm was over and they did not have to sit here so hatefully close. If Rocky and Theophilus Pope would only come in to keep them company—

There was something ominous about that closed door into the kitchen. And Lisa should have some woman near here. It was hardly decent to question Powell there. Yet what could they do? Lisa couldn't be locked away with Sapphira Barlow and Saul Cheney: it was really they—or Sapphira, at least—who had killed her. Suppose that Powell were making a confession. . . .

The same thought must have come to Margie Corwin. She muttered: "Why can't they get it over? They might come in and tell us something. Maybe they think it will be good for us, just sitting here. . . ."

Doyle had stopped to light a cigarette and Mrs. Cheney looked up as if conscious of a deeper silence than that imposed by her deafness.

"I have been wondering—did Madam Sapphira predict any disaster of any kind during your meetings here?"

"Not if you don't consider the end of the world a disaster," Doyle said.

"I meant, aside from that. You see, I very seldom could hear what she said. She spoke indistinctly and in a low voice. I was wondering," Mrs. Cheney said slowly, "if that poor child—Lisa Wood—was afraid that something would happen to her."

"Didn't you hear us say that she must have gone to meet someone on the path?" Eleanor said. "Surely she'd know it was dangerous, though she did go."

"I'm afraid I haven't heard a lot that you've said since we've been here. I thought perhaps Madam Sapphira had said something to frighten her. After all, she was young. I was remembering that when she came to ask me for that glue she also asked to borrow my Bible."

"Your Bible? Why did she want that?"

"I don't know, Mrs. Allan. She didn't ask to take it from the tent. She said she wanted to look at it and she did; then gave it back to me. It's in the tent, still."

"But—why did you think she wanted to look at it?"

"It didn't seem queer to me," Mrs. Cheney said seriously. "I have read the Bible every day of my life for forty years. I thought perhaps she needed guidance."

"I've heard of people who open the Bible and put their finger on a page and text, hit or miss, and try to decide what to do by what turns up," Margie said.

"But Lisa never read much of anything," David objected. "We've got a Bible but I never saw her read it."

"I called it mine," Mrs. Cheney said, still watching Eleanor intently, "but the one I gave her belonged to Saul. I have my own in my suitcase."

"Oh! Did she keep it very long?"

"No, it doesn't seem to me she had it more than five minutes. She leafed through it, I remember, gave it back and left."

"Did Mr. Cheney make any notations in the book?"

"I never saw any. He was not really scholarly. He said that he depended on inspiration, and when he was younger he was able to make you believe that."

"But you did— Heavens!"

Eva Greer moaned: "We're struck! I know we're struck! We'll be out in the storm without any shelter."

"The cabin's still standing, Toots, and it doesn't do any good to bury your head like an ostrich unless you want to be sure it strikes your behind. Though that certainly did hit somewhere near here," Greer admitted. "Probably blasted some tree. Maybe this is the tail end of it."

"You're an optimist," Doyle said, lighting a fresh cigarette from the stub of his last one. "The windows are rattling now."

"It is always darkest just before the dawn," Margie said flippantly.

But she was watching Mrs. Cheney who, undisturbed by the storm, had resumed her knitting. Eleanor followed the direction of Margie's eyes and found herself unable to look away. There was something she wanted to ask the woman but she was too tired to raise her voice. The long red needles slid in and out of the little loops of brown yarn—in and out, in and out. Mrs. Cheney wound fresh yarn about her strong, hard fingers: the needles began to click again and Margie struggled to her feet.

"I can't stand it! She's got to stop that damned knitting! If the guillotine falls again maybe she'll look up long enough to count—or maybe she's already got it all down in the knitting." She began to laugh, high and hysterically. Eleanor sprang up and took her by the shoulders.

"Margie! You mustn't! I'm ashamed of you, acting like this. I know your aunt is—"

Rocky said: "What's going on in here? Want some water?"

"Nerves," Mrs. Leroy said, drawing the girl to her. "Well, it's your turn, Margie, so far as I'm concerned, but think of all these other people. We've really been acting very nicely but of course we get on each other's nerves. Very likely Mrs. Cheney doesn't like your blowing smoke rings any better than you do her knitting."

Mrs. Cheney smiled faintly. She had put down her work and folded her hands over her high stomach. "She's young," she remarked of Margie.

Powell had reached the doorway and stopped there, looking, Eleanor thought, like a dog who is afraid of being kicked if he dares to come closer. She looked at Rocky questioningly.

"If she wants to talk to him it's all right with me," Rocky said. "For your info'mation, we haven't got so much against Mr. Powell that it'll contaminate any of you to touch him."

Margie looked up; scrubbed at the tears that were still running down her face. She said: "So they returned you to circulation, Hank? Don't mind me. I read a book once and I happened to remember it. Don't ever read books."

Powell started to speak; shrugged helplessly. "I am afraid," he said at last, "that I cannot answer you in the—the casual way that you would admire, Margie. If, later on, we could talk—"

"I guess that can be managed. I don't feel so awfully casual, as a matter of fact."

"I reckon we could all use a drink," Rocky said. "We've got some more whisky over in our tent."

"I've got nearly a quart right here," Doyle said, producing a bottle. "Are there any glasses?"

Pope, standing behind Powell, said: "I'll get some." Returning with three thick tumblers he looked at the group about the fire. "Perhaps we could have some coffee too."

"Coffee!" Mrs. Greer's hands fluttered disapprovingly. "How can you—"

"Why not? You don't seem to realize that there are—fortunately—limits to one's power of realization. If any of us could fully realize this situation we'd all be hysterical."

"An' while you might enjoy that, Mrs. Greer— we wouldn't," Rocky added. "Have a drink?"

"I really couldn't. I don't drink." The springs of the couch creaked as Mrs. Greer shrank back from the close crash of thunder. "Yes, I will! Perhaps it will steady my nerves."

Rocky murmured: "She don't drink: she just inhales," and Mrs. Greer remembered rather tardily to cough and say:

"My, that certainly is awful! Thomas, don't you take too much of that."

Greer said patiently: "I won't, Eva. Mrs. Allan?"

"No, thank you—"

"Yes, she will," Rocky said. "Here you are—an' drink it down. Now, let's go look at the storm while Pope puts the coffee pot on."

"You're not going to open that door! You'll kill us all."

"Closin' a door don't always keep lightning from strikin', Mrs. Greer, whatever some people seem to think. However, if you feel that way about it, I'll only open it a crack and stand where it'll hit me first," Rocky promised. "It's getting too hot in here."

"I don't think it's raining quite so hard," Eleanor said, looking out toward the clearing. "And there's less wind."

"It's slacking up." Rocky put an arm about her shoulders. "You look tired out, honey. I wanted to get you away from that gang for a while."

"I know. Oh Rocky, if I'd just not let her go!"

"Well, how could you know? It seemed safe enough. Why the hell didn't I leave you in Merton like Pope said to? You always get int'rested in folks."

"So do you. You've switched over to Mr. Powell's side now."

"Maybe I have," Rocky admitted. "If he's tellin' the truth I can sympathize with him. But I like Doyle, too. I reckon we'll just have to leave it up to the girl to decide which one she wants to marry."

"I reckon we will," Eleanor said, mimicking him. She leaned back against his shoulder. "Perhaps you and Mr. Pope will make something out of a conversation I'll repeat to you. I haven't—yet, except for one thing. My brain is numb."

Rocky shook her gently. "Didn't I say to forget it? Look! There's a little piece of blue sky. It won't be long before we can get out of here."

CHAPTER NINETEEN
THE THING THAT CREPT

By five o'clock the sky was clear and deeply blue and sunlight lay warmly on the clearing. "If that fellow at the Manzanita hotel got started by one-thirty, he may've made it to Boulder in spite of the storm," Rocky said. "I doubt if it was so bad farther down. So we can expect Jake Thompson will get here sometime tomorrow. He'll probably drive all night: he's used to that. Only I hope he won't try to make it in here in the dark."

"Surely he'll stop at Manzanita first. Where," Eleanor said, "are those men going to sleep?"

For the bedding in Doyle's tent had been thoroughly soaked. Greer's tent had withstood the storm as their own had. Mrs. Cheney's was found standing at a Tower-of-Pisa angle but her belongings were only a little damp, and though Mrs. Leroy's tent had collapsed, it had fallen so that the canvas protected the cots and blankets under it. But Pope's little lean-to had been wrecked by wind and rain, and the ground obviously would not be dry enough to sleep on even by the time the sun had set.

"They're spreading blankets to dry in the cabin now," Rocky said. "Keeping the fire up. I suppose Doyle and Powell will have to sleep in the cabin along with Pope and David. We've fixed up the other tents but there still ain't enough to go aroun'."

"Isn't Mr. Pope coming over here? I thought he'd get that Bible from Mrs. Cheney after I told you what she said."

"I reckon you'll have to send him after it if you're in a hurry. I don't b'lieve it's important." Rocky opened their car's tool chest. "He went back to the cabin with Doyle after we finished fixing those tents. He'll probably come to in time to eat."

"Come to?"

"He's taken one of those streaks when he looks right through you. Just like a hen settin' on an egg and waiting for it to hatch," Rocky said disrespectfully. "If I was you, sugar, I'd leave him be. He's got a hell of a cold so he may not be thinkin' at all. Well, I am, but I've got to see what I can do with this busted spring while there's still some light. Cheney's Bible can wait."

"Can I help you?"

"Not now. Stay away so I can cuss in peace. I might want you to hold a flashlight for me if I don't get through quick enough." Rocky picked up the wet canvas that had protected Pope's bed and threw it under the car. "This'll be better than nothing," he said, easing himself under the rear spring. "Where's David?"

"Reading, by the fire."

"No, I'm not—now," David said, coming over to them. "Can't I help you?"

"You talk to Eleanor," Rocky suggested. "An' keep the fire going."

"We'd better take that hint, David," Eleanor said, walking back to the fire. "What shall we have for supper?"

"I don't know. Most anything would taste pretty good."

"If you're hungry, you'd better eat some of these cookies. I don't know when Rocky and Mr. Pope will be ready for supper. We won't wait too long, though."

David brooded happily over the box of assorted cookies; chose a chocolate eclair and a panama cream. Eleanor investigated their supplies, opened a large can of corned beef and began to peel potatoes. Rocky swore softly from underneath the car: David ate Nabiscos.

When the potatoes were sliced and diced onion added to them, Eleanor left the fire and walked through the trees that hid their camp from the clearing. Already the forest was shadowed, but late sun still shone on the cleared spaces. Smoke curled from the cabin's chimney and Eleanor could see that the front door was open.

Thomas Greer was building a fire near the front of his tent and Eleanor wondered where he had found paper to start it with. She supposed she should return his bundle of newspapers and the one Mrs. Cheney had given Lisa, but they might possibly want to look over the collection again.

Greer, appearing to be satisfied that his fire would burn, walked toward Mrs. Leroy's tent. It was interesting to watch people when you couldn't hear them, Eleanor thought: to try to guess what they were saying by their gestures. Evidently Greer was insisting that Mrs. Leroy should let him build a fire for her, as he finally busied himself gathering stones to make a small circle and then squatted down on his heels and began to whittle at a small stick of wood. He must have camped before; the beginnings of his fires were as small and neat as those Rocky made.

Eleanor looked toward the farther end of the clearing, thinking that the black-and-white sign there was going to be a severe shock to Jake

Thompson whenever he arrived. Then she saw
that Henry Powell and Margie Corwin were sitting together on a flat rock near the sign.

She couldn't help watching them and trying to
imagine what Powell was saying. He was talking:
that was evident by the movements of his slender
hands. You couldn't see the expressions of their
faces but Margie sat very still, though now and
then she nodded or kicked at the pine needles under her feet.

"They're in love with each other, aren't they?"
David said interestedly.

Eleanor started. "Oh! Did you have all the
cookies you wanted? Yes, I suppose they are."

"So is Mr. Doyle in love with her. I don't think
she's as pretty as you are, though," David said gal-
lantly. "I wonder what they're talking about."

Eleanor laughed. "Well, so do I, David, but I
shouldn't. It's none of our business."

"Did you see that?"

Margie had just leaned over, kissed Powell lightly on the cheek and risen to her feet. She thrust
her hands boyishly into the pockets of her linen
skirt and started back toward the camps. Powell
followed, his narrow shoulders drooping dejec-
tedly though he straightened them hastily when
Margie turned and spoke to him with a quick lift
of her chin.

"I guess maybe they aren't going to get married after all," David said. "Though she did kiss him."

"We'd better put some more wood on our fire and put the potatoes on to cook. They take longer in the mountains, you know."

"Do they? I guess your husband is still swearing. He told me to go away when I went over to see what he was doing."

"And a good thing he did.—Yes? What is it, Rocky?"

"If you can hold a light for me so I can see better, I think I can get this thing braced so it will be all right," Rocky said jerkily. "It's too dark under here. Son of a—gun! That hammer acts like it has wings."

Eleanor retrieved the hammer and knelt down by the car with a flashlight. "Is the light all right now? Rocky, I was just wondering. . . . What are we going to tell the sheriff?"

"I been wondering that too. I'll have to talk it over with Pope. Hell! What can I tell him? We'll have to explain Sapphira and Cheney to him and why the rest of these people are here. Well, I told you Powell's story an' I'm willing to leave out as much of it as I can. Let him say he came up here for the trip. An' the same for Mrs. Leroy and the girl."

"But you've no case against anyone?"

"Not that I can see." Rocky reached for the pliers. "I was down at the path and the rain washed under those pieces of bark I put over Mrs. Leroy's footprints. We've got her gun with three shots fired out of it—and I'll bet none of them's in Cheney. Powell was certainly there beside Lisa when we got there and it's possible he could have killed her. I don't know what his motive would be—"

"He might have persuaded her to help him in some way."

"I suppose he could've. I meant I don't know exactly what his motive for killin' the other two would be. There's several he might have had. Doyle could've killed Sapphira and doped himself afterwards, and he's got no real alibi for either of the other two deaths. I guess Mrs. Cheney hasn't either."

"I don't see," Eleanor said, "how you can keep Mr. Thompson from suspecting that some of these people were being blackmailed by Sapphira."

"We can't. Jake's head is cut in, all right. I don't intend to try to fool him, because he can be trusted not to tell everything he knows to the newspapers, and that's the most important thing so far as whoever is innocent is concerned. However, he'll probably hold the whole bunch an' start digging up the dirt from L.A. Not that he'll want to. No one's going to care so awful much about justice bein' done because a bunch of people from the south happened to stray over the line into our county to get themselves killed."

"You care."

"On account of the people that ain't guilty. Anyway Pope's got me to doin' jigsaw puzzles with my mind an' since he isn't feeling so hot— Besides, I blame myself for not looking after that girl. And I do feel some responsibility, since it's Jake that's got to be called in."

"It's going to be—perfectly awful! I suppose anyone might be guilty. No, I don't see how Mrs. Leroy could have killed Sapphira or Lisa. And Margie couldn't have killed Lisa. Mrs. Cheney and Mr. Doyle more or less alibi each other for Mr. Cheney's death but they might be shielding each other or Mr. Doyle's story might not be true. And Mr. and Mrs. Greer are just—impossible."

"Some folks would say she was—in more ways than one. Hand me those small pliers, honey."

"This pair? Rocky, must the same person have done all three murders?"

"I've thought a little about that," Rocky admitted. "And I wouldn't think it was necessary. Three diff'rent kinds of weapon. Well, the old lady more or less invited stranglin' with all those scarfs aroun' her and having a small throat— No, that's what makes it harder to figure. Diff'rent people might've killed Sapphira and Cheney, but seems to me Lisa must have been killed because she knew something about Cheney's death."

"Yes, because she was killed after we found those papers and she couldn't have known anything about Sapphira's death—or nothing definite. I know she was with me all night."

"Well . . ." Rocky crawled out from underneath the car, shook himself and wiped grease from his forehead. "We can get along with that for quite a while, the way I fixed it. I feel dirty as a hog. As a matter of fact, I do every time I have to stay very long in that cabin. I think I'll go down to the crick and wash."

"But the water's so cold."

"I know, but there's enough of it down there. Washin' in a small pan ain't very satisfactory. I won't get in all over. You might as well go on with supper. I'm plenty hungry and if Pope don't come by the time I'm back, I'll take him over a can of soup afterward."

Eleanor brought soap, towels and clean clothing; went back to the fire to stir the potatoes and put water to heat. The sun had slid behind the hills half an hour ago and its pale afterglow was fading rapidly. Darkness was slowly possessing the trees that surrounded their camp. Eleanor found

herself wishing that the growth were not quite so
thick or that it were not so close to them.

She started nervously at every rustling sound
in the underbrush and thought of getting her gun
from the tent. But Rocky wouldn't have left her if
there had been any danger. While she still stood
indecisively by the fire she saw a light come bobbing toward her.

"Oh, you and David are alone," Mrs. Greer
said. "Well, it doesn't matter. I suppose I didn't
need this light but I'm kind of nervous."

Eleanor said: "So am I," thinking that the
storm—or perhaps something else—had caused
Mrs. Greer to discard a good deal of artificial gen-
tility.

"Thomas says I'm foolish. He left me alone,
too, to try to find some dry wood. I'm sure I don't
know how he dares go wandering around that way.
But it would be a good idea to keep a fire going
all night, I think. He said I could tell you this."

"Do you want me to go away while you talk?"
David asked as she hesitated.

"N-no. Perhaps you happened to notice— Were
you ever in Mr. Cheney's tent?"

"The day we got here. He let me see what it
looked like when it was up."

"Well, Thomas says I probably am mistaken but
I'm sure— You see, Mrs. Allan, after it stopped

raining and we were leaving the cabin I—well, I just happened to glance into the kitchen because the door had swung open a little. There was a knife on the table. And Mr. Pope did finally tell us, you know, that it was a knife that—that—"

"Yes, I understand. You think that you'd seen that knife before?"

"It was a dagger really, I guess. I wouldn't have remembered just a plain knife so well. It had a fancy handle and I'm sure Mr. Cheney had one just like it. I saw it in their tent."

"I didn't see the knife in the kitchen but Saul did have one with a handle that was all carved," David said. "I think he used it for a paper cutter. Someone gave it to him: some man who'd traveled a lot. I saw it in their house in Los Angeles when he took me there one time."

"I don't like to say anything against Mrs. Cheney," Mrs. Greer said. "I'm sure she's a—a good woman. As Thomas says, someone could have gotten in her tent to take the knife. But just the same, I think you'd better tell your husband and he can ask her—not mentioning my name—if she still has a dagger like that one."

"I'll tell him when he comes back, or Mr. Pope, if he gets here first." Eleanor looked undecidedly at the potatoes and then moved them farther back from the flames. "I think I'll speak to Mrs. Cheney myself. She has something we want to borrow and perhaps we had better not wait too long to get it from her. I'll return this newspaper too. She wanted it back."

"Oh yes. Mr. Cheney gave me that paper to read. That's how I happened to be in their tent. You aren't going to leave the boy alone here?"

"Of course not. You'll have to come with me, David." But when they had reached the clearing, Eleanor made another sudden decision. "Suppose you run along to the cabin and tell Mr. Pope that supper will be ready in about thirty minutes and that I'll be very provoked if he keeps us waiting. I see a light in the front room and we'll wait here until you get there. Don't come back without Mr. Pope or someone else with you."

David said: "All right. Thirty minutes and you will be very provoked."

They watched him until he reached the cabin; then walked on toward Mrs. Cheney's tent. Mrs. Greer said:

"Did you want me to come in with you? No, maybe I'd better not. She'll probably know, when she thinks about it, that I'm about the only one who could have seen that knife. Oh, Mr. Doyle could have. I forgot about that."

"So did I. But I think I'd better talk to her alone, if you don't mind."

"N-no. No, I don't. I think I'll go sit with Mrs. Leroy until Thomas gets back. There seems to be a light in their tent so I guess she's there."

Eleanor said: "Mrs. Cheney!" in what seemed to her a subdued shriek, but she had to call again and more loudly before the woman looked out of the tent.

"Oh—Mrs. Allan. Did you want something?"

"You remember telling us that Lisa looked through Mr. Cheney's Bible this morning? Well, I don't suppose it's important but we'd like to examine it and the men have both been so busy—"

"You can take it. I looked through it myself but I didn't find any writing in it. I forgot to tell you that the girl asked me for a pencil but I couldn't find one to loan her."

"Oh—did she?" Eleanor took the Bible: an old one with dog-eared black covers. "Thank you for letting me take this. And here is the paper that Lisa got from you." She hesitated; decided that direct attack might be best. "Did Mr. Cheney use any of that glue while he was here? Or cut out anything from newspapers?"

Mrs. Cheney was knitting again; almost without looking at her work, for she watched Eleanor's lips closely. She frowned briefly at her needles; then said with her usual placidity:

"Not that I remember. I don't know why you ask me. . . ."

"Because—well, because someone put a card on Mrs. Barlow's lap after she was killed. It said: 'The day of judgment has come—' Oh! How did you do that?"

One of Mrs. Cheney's knitting needles had snapped suddenly. It might have been because her fingers had tightened on them—Eleanor searched the woman's face for any sign of definite emotion, but it was difficult as always to read. She went on:

"The words had been cut out of a newspaper and glued on the card. Did anyone ever borrow the glue you had?"

"No. No one borrowed it—that I know of."

"I've another question to ask, too. Lisa was killed with a dagger with a carved handle . . ."

"I know. I guess it must have been Saul's. Not that Mr. Pope said anything excepting she was stabbed, but I came back here and looked for Saul's dagger and it's not here. Now you say this other one had a carved handle so it seems it must have been his."

"But you've been out of your tent."

"Oh yes. Not very often, but I really don't remember seeing the thing after the day we got here. I suppose you wonder why on earth he brought it. Well, it was a keepsake from a friend, and besides, our butcher knife was dull and I forgot to have it sharpened before I left."

"Is that— Are you sure that's the only reason he brought it with him?"

Mrs. Cheney found a new knitting needle in her workbag; knit one and purled two before she answered.

"I can't imagine Saul using a knife on anyone. He didn't like the sight of blood."

"I suppose you'll think I'm just a busybody, Mrs. Cheney, but my husband will ask you the same question sometime. Why did you tell Mr. Cheney he was a wicked man and that you'd believed him too long? And that perhaps you hated him?"

"So someone heard me say that? Well, I did, but I don't know I've any right to call anyone else wicked when I've been lying to all of you. I thought it would be better for everyone if I did, though. It was just that I— Well, I began to doubt if he really did believe what he had been preaching to people. I made him admit he didn't. Well, if he had been lying about that—and it's a terrible thing to preach a day of judgment when you don't believe it—he might have lied about a lot of other things. Things that had bothered me when they happened but I accepted his word about."

"Oh, I see. But that's rather—indefinite."

"I guess you've managed to find out from Mr. Doyle some of the things that were said about Saul. He'd know," Mrs. Cheney said dryly. "Up here he couldn't keep his eyes off that Mrs. Leroy. That's the first chance I'd had for a long time to notice him and—women. Not that Mrs. Leroy ever gave him any encouragement. Then there was that money you found in his wallet."

"But you didn't know about that until Mr. Pope told you."

"I didn't know about that—or how much there was. I said I'd lied. I've been thinking for quite a while he seemed to have more money than he should. Not that I ever saw any of it. But he told me Madam Sapphira didn't even pay him a salary; just gave him what she thought he'd earned by drawing more people to her place. Was that money all you found in his pockets?"

"Well—no. But I'm afraid I'd better not tell you—"

"I don't want you to. Only I've figured out that he may have known something about Madam Sapphira and that's how he got his money."

"You're sure that's all you—" But Mrs. Cheney was looking steadily at her knitting again and Eleanor didn't like to shout questions at her. Besides, it was fairly evident that Mrs. Cheney didn't intend to say anything more. "Thank you for being so patient. Are you afraid to stay alone tonight?"

"What? Stay alone, did you say? No, I'm not afraid, dearie. I'm used to being alone and I don't hear things like most people do, you know. You run on."

It was not yet completely dark on the clearing but as she neared the trees that surrounded it, Eleanor stopped, hesitating. She should have brought her flashlight but she had forgotten that light faded so quickly at this time of the evening. After she left the clearing she must go perhaps fifty feet before reaching their camp, and the path was a narrow one, closely bordered by trees and underbrush.

She was on the point of turning back and going to the cabin but at last she shrugged disgustedly and went on. No one would want to hurt her and if he were not already there, Rocky would soon be coming back to camp and would be uneasy if she were gone. Besides, she didn't want to risk having those potatoes boil dry and burn. . . .

That noise in the underbrush was made by some small animal, of course. But she had reached the narrowest point of the path and she stopped, her back against a tree on the right side of the trail. The rough bark felt comfortably substantial behind her shoulders, but still her hands were shaking so that she dropped the Bible she carried and heard it thud dully on the ground somewhere in front of her.

She couldn't go away and leave it there; it might be important to them. But she wished desperately that she had never stepped from the clearing. It would have been better to take the roundabout way by which Rocky had driven the car, but that would have taken her in a circle over the hill.

She thought: If I just keep still and don't breathe for a while perhaps I can't be seen. But there is someone in that brush! If I scream—or run—

Her instinct was not to run: she remembered her father telling her when she was a child: "Never run from a dog. He'll chase you if he thinks you are afraid." Dog: mad dog; murderer—what was the difference? She couldn't have screamed if she had wanted to.

But the noise was gone now. She would run for it and let the Bible go. She sprang forward, felt her foot strike against the book and instinctively stooped for it. The thing that crept in the brush was something heavy that brought blinding blackness. . . .

CHAPTER TWENTY
"THE VOICE OF JACOB"

She must have had a nightmare because Rocky was saying, as he always did: "You're all right, honey. There's nothing to be scared of now."

But a nightmare shouldn't give you a bad head-ache and a dream bump at the back of your head wouldn't be wet and sticky when you put your fingers up to it. And Rocky's tanned face was as nearly white as it could ever be and his eyes were yellow. They only looked that way when he was angry. He said calmly enough:

"Can you set up so I can look at the back of your head?"

"Y-yes." Eleanor put her head down on her knees. "W-what do you suppose he hit me with?"

"Oh, something not too heavy. I'd be more interested in who hit you. If I find out there'll probably be a near murder in camp," Rocky said grimly. "The skin's broke a little and you'll have a nice lump there, same's Pope. Wait till I get some iodine. I—I hate to do this, darling."

Eleanor managed to smile though the iodine stung abominably. "I know you do. You're going to say I was an awful fool and I know I was. You see, I—"

"You went after that Bible you were talking about."

"You mean—you found it? But—I thought that was what they—he—wanted."

"It evidently wasn't. Where's David?"

"I sent him to the cabin to tell Mr. Pope to come to supper and to get him out of the way. I wanted to talk to Mrs. Cheney Oh, I'll let it go for a minute. Can you find me some aspirin?"

Rocky brought her a glass of water, watched her swallow the aspirin and then sat down on the bed. "I've been knocked cold in an accident or something like that," he said huskily, his arms tight about her, "but I never did know before this how a person feels when he thinks he's going to pass out. Seemed to me like all the blood was in my head, before I found out you were still—breathing."

"Did you stumble on me?"

"Almost. But I'd taken a light."

"I should have. I didn't realize how quickly it gets dark; once it does start to. I wonder how soon you found me?"

"I don't think I was down there more than half an hour. I got to thinking about something I found on the path to the cabin. Then I did practic'lly take a swim once I started, but it couldn't have taken me so long. You talked to Mrs. Cheney— not that it matters. From now on I'm leaving this business go and not letting you out of my sight."

"I'll agree to the last part of it but you know you'll see the thing through now. I wonder what Mr. Pope will think about this."

"He won't like it much," Rocky predicted.

He was quite right: Pope looked white and angry when he came into the tent after talking to Rocky. He sat down on the foot of the bed, having folded himself up like an old-fashioned collapsible drinking cup so that his head only barely touched the tent's roof.

"Child, if you'd stayed in Merton as I told you to, this wouldn't have happened."

"But I didn't suppose I was in any danger. I still can't see why anyone would want to harm me except to get that Bible, and it wasn't taken."

"Well, suppose you tell us about it. I should have come back here so that Rocky wouldn't have had to leave you alone."

"He was down on his hands and knees in the path back of the cabin," David reported. "Mrs. Allan, the potatoes are all burned down in the bottom of the pan."

Eleanor sighed and Rocky said: "Who the hell cares? Go eat something else if you're hungry."

"I'm not—very. I just thought I'd mention it."

"You'd better watch the fire," Pope said. "It's crowded in here. And you can put some water on so we can have coffee. Now, Eleanor."

"You remember you sent me out of the kitchen this afternoon? Of course I had to tell them what had happened and they all reacted just as you would expect—horror and disbelief. We all tried to be matter of fact until Margie went to pieces, though Mrs. Greer was frightened by the storm. Mr. Greer told her it wasn't any worse than being in a war—not that that matters. Only it was because Mrs. Greer came over here that I decided to go to see Mrs. Cheney. Mrs. Greer said . . ."

Eleanor repeated the woman's story; went on to describe her interview with Mrs. Cheney. "But I've forgotten something," she added. "Something that happened in the cabin—or was it before?"

"Well, don't try to remember it now," Rocky said. "You'd better go to sleep."

"Yes, she had. We shouldn't have made her talk this much."

"But it bothers me not to remember and my head doesn't ache very much now. I couldn't have been unconscious—really—for very long. I think I remember fingers at my throat." Eleanor put her

hand quickly on Rocky's clenched fist. "Not trying to choke me. And then—then going through
my pockets— Oh!" She sat up abruptly. "What an
absolute idiot I am! But it's gone!"

"What is?" Pope and Rocky said together.

"Lisa's locket. Oh damn! She didn't just ask
what time it was: she came back and gave me an
old locket to keep for her. She said the catch was
loose and I put the thing in my pocket. And Margie spoke about it in the cabin before all of them
except Mr. Powell."

Pope stood up; bumped his head against the
roof of the tent. Rocky said: "Well, I'll be damned!
You did have something someone wanted. That
must have been it."

"If so much hadn't happened to drive it out of
my head— And then Mrs. Cheney told me that
Lisa had wanted to borrow a pencil from her but
that she hadn't one to give her. But I had my hands
in my pockets when I walked across the clearing
the first time," Eleanor said, frowning. "I'm sure
I didn't feel the locket in either of them."

Rocky said: "Give me your flashlight, Pope. I'll
be back in a minute."

"Now, what do you suppose—"

Pope continued walking in a half-circle about
the bed, his head drawn down turtlelike between
his shoulders. "I don't know. He probably remembered something.—Well?"

"I expected to have to hunt a long time but it hadn't got buried under the dirt. This it?" Rocky said, holding out the tarnished locket. "When you scrambled after that hammer for me I thought I heard something drop but I was too busy to ask you about it. Your pockets ain't very deep and this fell against a rock. What's in it?"

"A picture of a woman who looks rather like Lisa—did." Pope pried the picture out with a long thumbnail; held it under the light. Leaning forward, Eleanor read the faint scrawl on its back.

"'Gen. 27: 22.' Why—what—"

"I don't know." Pope snatched Cheney's Bible from the bed. "She must have looked it up when she asked to see the book. She—" He stopped, staring at the page he had turned up. *"And Jacob went near unto Isaac his father; and he felt him, and said, The voice is Jacob's voice, but the hands are the hands of Esau.'"*

"For the love of— Does it mean anything?" Rocky said.

"It must," Eleanor said. "She meant us to make something out of it, but how can we know what it meant to her?"

"We can't. She'd been around Sapphira and Cheney long enough, perhaps, to have caught their trick of twisting Biblical phrases about to mean what they chose them to mean."

"Do you suppose the meaning of this partic'lar text has anything to do with the rest of the chapter?" Rocky took the Bible from Pope's hands. "Esau was hairy, wasn't he? An' Jacob wasn't but Esau was his father's favorite."

"I wonder," Eleanor said irrelevantly, "why men who have hair on their chests are so proud of it?"

"Neither one of us could tell you that, sugar. The old man was blind, so Jacob tricked him into givin' him the blessing he meant for Esau by putting the skin of a goat on his hands.—It don't make sense but she must've meant something by that text," Rocky said stubbornly. "It's dependin' too much on coincidence to say she just happened to want to look at a Bible; just happened to remember the catch of this locket was loose so that she gave it to Eleanor—"

"And just happened to be killed," Eleanor finished. "Besides, there is nothing wrong with the catch of this locket. I've just remembered: Margie spoke of it as a necklace in the cabin and she stopped before she could say that Lisa had given it to me. But someone might guess she had, when she wasn't wearing it."

"Well, when we've had something to eat I'm going aroun' and tell everyone that we found the locket and know what's in it."

"That's a good idea, Rocky," Pope said. "If that is common knowledge no one will dare try to get possession of the thing."

"I'll also tell 'em that if I think I hear anyone prowlin' around this place tonight, I'm going to shoot where I think they are and I don't intend to be careless how I aim."

Eleanor laughed. "You know you wouldn't think of doing that but if you look so fierce when you say you will, maybe they'll believe you."

"I suppose it is a waste of time to try to discover where everyone was when you were attacked?"

"I'm afraid it is, Mr. Pope, because I'd pretty well lost track of time. The last time I looked at my watch it was six-twenty, but that was while Rocky was still working on the car."

"I think it was a little after seven when I finished, but I'm not certain. It must have been, though, 'cording to how light it was. I didn't intend stayin' down at the crick so long but once I got over the first shock of that ice water, it felt good and I splashed around quite a while. An' then I washed out the clothes I took off— which I dropped in the dirt when I found Eleanor."

"You didn't come back the path behind the cabin?" Pope said. "I saw you go down."

"No, I walked from there to the one behind Mrs. Cheney's camp and came back up it. Thought there was less chance bein' caught in a state of nature there an' I remembered a deep pool somewheres near there."

"I don't know where Powell is," Pope said. "Doyle was with me, so he is eliminated."

"And I don't see how Mrs. Cheney could have followed me quickly enough and without my seeing her. Mrs. Greer could have. She said she was going to stay with Mrs. Leroy until Mr. Greer got back from gathering wood on the hill, but I don't know if either Margie or Mrs. Leroy were in their tent. David said you were down on your hands and knees in the path. Were you?"

Pope looked mournfully at the knees of his riding trousers. "I was, indeed. When David arrived, Doyle and I were examining the brush around the sides of the cabin as well as we could. But that was such a hopeless task that we concentrated on the path."

"Looking for what?" Rocky said. "You ain't fond enough of crawlin' around in the dirt to be just looking for haphazard clues."

"Oh, I was looking for a gun and I didn't find it. I never do find anything like that. I thought I might as well be useful—you helped me successfully to conclude my business here—and I know the sheriff would like to have an Exhibit A. But you and he will probably find the gun."

"Me 'n the sheriff! You know damned well Jake Thompson's got asthma and rheumatism! He'll never get down on his hands and knees."

"He probably— Eleanor," Pope said pathetically, "have you anything that might help to dry up this nose of mine?"

"Get him some of those tiny brown pills, Rocky. I thought you were beginning to get hoarse again."

"You can have some of my handkerchiefs too," Rocky said. "Here's your pills. Are you going to sleep in the cabin tonight?"

"Four of us will. Doyle brought his and Powell's cots over."

"What do you think of Mrs. Greer's story about the dagger?" Eleanor asked. "Are you going to talk to Mrs. Cheney, Rocky?"

"I'll talk to her when I tell her about the locket, but I don't see that there's anything more to ask about that knife than you already did. You lie here and I'll get supper."

"I'd much rather lie outside before the fire for a while and watch you cook. Couldn't we take a blanket out there?"

"Several of 'em and some pillows. Like this," Rocky said, pulling the blankets loose at the foot of the bed, picking them up and Eleanor with them. "Roll that rock out of the way, David? There! Is that too bumpy?"

"Just like a featherbed. Oh dear, the potatoes did burn, didn't they?"

"They taste burned all the way through," David said sadly. "Even the ones on top."

"We'll open a can of beans and the corned beef is already open. Look through that box and dig out some things," Rocky said. "Would you like soup, Pope?"

"Yes, I would. I wonder why soup always seems to go with a cold?"

"I wouldn't know," Rocky said rather absently. "I haven't had a cold since I was a kid. Have you any idea where Powell might've been while you were talkin' to Mrs. Cheney, Eleanor? He likes to hit people over the head."

"I didn't see him anywhere about and supposed he was in the cabin. He and Margie had been having a heart-to-heart talk a little earlier."

"We saw them talking," David said. "And she kissed him but not—not very much of a kiss."

Rocky grinned. "Trust you to notice that, Kid. Where was Greer?"

"Mrs. Greer said he was trying to find some dry wood on the hill above here. That was why she was going to stay with Mrs. Leroy: because she was afraid to be alone."

Rocky said: "Mrs. Cheney wears bedroom slippers but she's pretty hefty," and distributed cups of soup. "Watch out and don't burn your tongue on that, David."

"It's very hot, isn't it? I wonder if the blankets are dry by now. They were still sort of damp and steamy when I was in the cabin and they weren't drying out very fast."

"There will be plenty of dry cover—I hope. Sleeping in damp blankets would finish me," Pope said morosely. "Aren't you going to eat something more, Rocky?"

"Not now. Save me whatever's left over. You want to get to bed and I want you to stay with Eleanor till I get back, so I'll go on right now."

He picked up his gun and holster and buckled it around his hips. "Are you going to shoot someone?" David inquired, wide-eyed.

"I hope not. This is just to make me look like a real Wild West sheriff, kid. Only I'd ought to have a gun on each hip. Don't you," he said to Eleanor, "go wandering off after any more Bibles, no matter what anyone tells you."

Because Mrs. Cheney's tent was dark and he expected to talk longer with her than the others, Rocky walked on to Greer's campfire. Greer was sitting easily back on his heels eating canned corn while Mrs. Greer sat uncomfortably upright on a box. She turned sidewise; complained:

"A campfire scorches you in front and doesn't warm your back at all. I certainly never intend to come camping again."

"Then this will be something for you to remember the rest of your life, Toots. Hello, Allan. Have you— Say, you look kind of serious."

"So would you." Rocky looked through the darkness toward the larger fire before Mrs. Leroy's tent. "Doyle and Powell are over there, ain't they?"

"Yes: they're eating supper together. Awful wasteful with wood," Greer said disapprovingly. "Shouldn't build such a big fire when a small one does just as well. Why?"

"Would you two mind comin' over there with me? It'll save trouble to tell you all at once."

"Tell us what?" Mrs. Greer asked. "Oh dear, don't say that—that something else has happened! And what about Mrs. Cheney? She—"

"Never mind her. I'll talk to her afterwards."

The quartet in front of Mrs. Leroy's tent were eating pork and beans and drinking coffee. "First real meal we've had since we landed here," Margie said. "Are you making your rounds for the night, Bulldog Drummond?"

"You might call it that. How long you been here, Doyle?"

"Oh, I borrowed the coffee pot from the cabin, fixed this stuff up and brought it here. Hank and I didn't want to eat there."

"The place is enough to sour your food," Rocky agreed. "When did you go over there, Powell?"

"I? Why, I don't know what time it was. Mr. Pope had left when I got there."

"Well, where was you after you and Miss Corwin were talkin' down at the end of the clearing?"

"Privacy!" Margie said, reaching for the coffee pot. "All the world's a stage. What's up? Hank and I parted company here. Minna was here in the tent. I don't know what this is all about but I know the answers by now. Our fire was going out and Mr. Greer hadn't come back with the wood he said he was going to bring us, so Minna went over to see if there was any left in Wren's camp. While she was gone Mrs. Greer put her head in for a minute. She didn't stay," Margie admitted with a little grin. "Pretty soon Minna came back and then Mr. Greer and Hank. That what you want?"

"I saw Mrs. Allan and Mrs. Greer come across the clearing," Mrs. Leroy said quietly. "They didn't see me."

"Did you see Eleanor go back?"

"No, I didn't. I must either have been back in the trees around Warren's camp or have returned to our tent. Why, Mr. Allan? Is your wife—"

"She's all right. But where were you, Powell?"

"Up on the hill with Mr. Greer."

Greer stroked his drooping mustache reflectively. "I didn't see him," he said at last. "But I heard someone on the other side of me making quite a bit of noise."

Rocky looked at the pile of wood to one side of the fire. Part of it looked like the kind of stuff Powell would be apt to gather: green branches and a lot of small stuff that wouldn't burn a minute. He said:

"When did you decide to go looking for wood?"

"Why—after I left Margie. There was nothing for me to do. I knew Warren was in the cabin but I didn't want to go over there until I had to. I could see that this fire was going to go out if we didn't get some more wood."

"Oh, all right," Rocky said wearily. "This certainly is a swell place for playing hide-and-seek. The reason I asked all these questions is because someone hit Eleanor over the head when she went back to camp after talkin' to Mrs. Cheney."

Out of the babble of question and exclamation Margie's: "But why? What has she done?" emerged most clearly.

"She took Lisa Wood's locket an' put it in her pocket when Lisa gave it to her. That sounds harmless enough but Lisa had written a text on it.

I don't know if I can say it word for word. . . . I wish," he added impatiently, having done his best to repeat the text accurately, "that you wouldn't all talk at once. I don't know what she meant any more than some of you do. But we've got the locket, so there's no use for anybody else to be attacked because you think they might have it."

"Mr. Allan! I never even knew the girl wore a locket!" Mrs. Greer said shrilly. "Did you, Mrs. Leroy?"

"I don't know. I never saw the locket but I do seem to remember a chain about her neck. I don't think you could see it very plainly because her dresses had rather high necks."

"Well, I knew. I saw her give the locket to Eleanor. And like a fool I mentioned it when we were in the cabin. But how was I to know— Anyway," Margie recalled, "I didn't get far enough to say Lisa had given it to Eleanor. And I think I called it a necklace."

"You couldn't have killed Lisa," Doyle reminded her. "And whoever did it must have thought she was still wearing that locket."

Rocky shook his head. "No, it wasn't till after she was killed that Mrs. Cheney mentioned her having wanted to look at her Bible. Whoever killed her may've thought he'd silenced her that way an' didn't know about the locket till later on.

Puttin' two and two together— Only there's a gap there. I'll leave you to it. We can't narrow down the time when Eleanor was hurt very much because none of us was watchin' the clock just then."

"But to follow Mrs. Allan across the clearing," Powell began.

"Who said she was followed? Someone lay waitin' for her. Just a proposition of gettin' into the brush at most any point and then working your way to the right place. You'd make a noise, but there's always some noises in the brush if you listen for them. Anyone who saw Eleanor come over here would know she'd be goin' back—or hope she'd be foolish enough to. Whoever wanted that locket so bad was probably watchin' for just a chance like that. It was just luck that the thing had fell out of her pocket."

Rocky turned to go and Greer followed him. "Have you a place for the boy tonight? In the cabin with Pope? Oh, that's fine. I thought maybe you'd have to look after him and I was going to offer to take him off your hands, even if he is a walking question-box."

"If I was you, I'd sleep with one eye open," Rocky said. "I s'pose the women wouldn't want to sleep in the cabin, so they'll be alone here. Not that I think there's any danger—now."

CHAPTER TWENTY-ONE
"YOU CAN'T PUNISH THAT PERSON"

Mrs. Cheney was not in her tent. Rocky satisfied himself of that and then swore softly. What did she mean by wandering around by herself in the dark? Maybe she'd gone down to the creek for water but she should have more sense. Mrs. Greer hadn't mentioned seeing her leave her tent.

Rocky started down the path to the stream, swinging his flashlight from side to side. Since Cheney's camp was nearest the cabin, he wouldn't investigate those other paths unless he had to. It would be nice if they had to comb the woods at this time of night.

He started up toward the cabin without having seen Mrs. Cheney. But she might have gone over to the cabin—only why would she? The place should be dark and she should know that none of them were there.

So Pope and Doyle had looked for that gun and hadn't found it. Not that it mattered a great

deal. If it had been tossed away they would find
it somewhere near that small gap in the brush at
the right side of the path. The right side of the
path and the right side of the house where no
one would be on guard. If he had kept going last
night, straight around the house, instead of running into the kitchen—

But he couldn't stand there thinking about
that. Whatever it was that bothered him could be
ironed out later. He tried the back door of the
cabin, found it barred and passed around the left
side of the house to the front door.

Pope had left the lantern burning. Two cots
had been set up but blankets were still drying in
front of the fire. Rocky threw more wood in the
fireplace; turned the blankets. Pope needn't worry
about having to sleep between damp covers because his bedding had been in their tent, but the
others might do better to keep the fire up and do
without blankets.

He whirled, staring at the closed door to the
bedroom. It sounded as if someone had stumbled
over one of the suitcases they had put back in
that room. But what was Mrs. Cheney doing in
there? It must be Mrs. Cheney: everyone else was
accounted for. He said:

"You better come on out of there," remembered
that he must shout and did so. The door opened

slowly and Mrs. Cheney stood looking at him. She was rather paler than usual but she walked heavily over to the couch and sat down without saying anything.

There was just about as much expression on her face as a poached egg had, Rocky thought, and what did you do with a woman like that? If she didn't want to tell you anything—well, she wouldn't and that would be that.

"What were you doing in there, Mrs. Cheney?" he said mildly. "Don't you think it looks kind of suspicious? If you'd wanted to—to see your husband—"

"I didn't," Mrs. Cheney said flatly.

"Well then, what did you want in there?"

"I meant to— It doesn't matter. I didn't take anything."

Rocky believed her and he hardly felt up to the task of searching her. He tried another question. "How did you get in here without anyone seeing you?"

"I crawled out of the back of my tent." Rocky had to grin at the picture that evoked but Mrs. Cheney said seriously: "Then I came up the back path and I guess no one saw me come in. I told Mrs. Greer I was going to bed when she asked me to have supper with them. I didn't think anyone would miss me."

"I don't reckon anyone would have if it hadn't been for someone attackin' my wife to get that locket Lisa Wood wrote down a Bible verse in."

"What? Oh, I'm sorry. I hope she's all right? She's a nice little girl.—She is all right? What was the verse, Mr. Allan?"

"Genesis 27: 22."

"I'm afraid I don't know—"

"It starts out *And Jacob drew near to Isaac his father . . .*"

"I know the rest of it," Mrs. Cheney stared at her broad hands. "That's very queer. I don't— It can't have anything to do with the story. What Lisa Wood meant by that one text, I mean."

"I don't see how it can. But I thought maybe you could help us on that. Is it the kind of thing your husband would've said? That is: Would he be able to take that text an' twist a meaning for it that wouldn't ord'narily be there?"

"He was very good at that. So was Madame Sapphira. Lisa Wood must have caught the trick from them—if it was a trick. Saul used to tell David stories from the Old Testament. The girl might have heard him tell that one. But I don't know what that text meant to her."

"But you're sure you didn't have any pencil to give her when she asked for one?"

"Yes. And she left me and came straight over here."

"Did you notice she wore a locket?"

"I never notice things like that," Mrs. Cheney said indifferently. "Your wife told you what I said to her: to the questions she asked me? Well, I haven't anything to add to that. But I have been wondering. . . . Would it be possible for you to tell me what Saul knew about Madam Sapphira?"

"I don't see why not. He must've seen her before you married him. Back in 1902 she was a Mrs. George Eaton in a town by the name of Harrison in Illinois. She had a daughter, Leona, David's mother. She got mixed up with a guy named Crane and Eaton fin'lly surprised them together and shot Crane. Then she killed Eaton, near as anyone could figure. She just vanished and they never caught her. Mr. Cheney must have recognized her in L.A. He carried a bunch of clippings around with him. Does all this mean anything to you?"

"I've never been in Illinois and it happened before I ever met Saul. Mr. Pope asked me if I'd known Leona Eaton."

"She was sent East to live with an aunt."

"Well, I didn't know her. 'The sins of the fathers,'" Mrs. Cheney said abruptly.

"You mean Sapphira had to pay up for what she did? Or did you ever know this Paul Crane? He evidently had a family; a brother, anyway."

"No, I never knew anyone by that name. I think I might as well go back to my tent, Mr. Allan."

"You certainly haven't told me anything you don't want to," Rocky said frankly. "I feel like you know—or guess—a lot you won't tell. What did you want over here?"

"I don't hear you."

"I'm not like my wife," Rocky said smiling. "She hates to shout at people but I don't mind it at all. You know you hear what folks are sayin' when you want to, Mrs. Cheney. Why don't you just say you ain't goin' to answer me?"

"I'm not. Yes, I can hear all right when I watch and pay attention," Mrs. Cheney admitted. "Sometimes I simply don't want to hear."

"Well, maybe you'll tell me why you were so— upset when Eleanor told you about that card that was on Sapphira's lap?"

"It seemed—rather horrible."

"Oh, sure. Did your husband make the thing?"

The woman said: "I didn't see him if he did. Why would he? He couldn't have used it." She got up and walked slowly, flat footed in her heelless bedroom slippers, toward the door. Rocky followed her.

"I'll see you safe in your tent and I'd be greatly obliged if you'd stay there. Don't you," he asked, switching his flashlight on, "believe in revenge? Killing for revenge—or doing anything else for that reason?"

"I don't. My people were pacifists. Why?"

"I wondered if you felt like you wanted whoever killed your husband punished for it."

"You can't punish that person," Mrs. Cheney said calmly. "No one can. I mean that no human being can judge the—the case. Tell your wife I'm sorry if anything I said was the reason for her being attacked."

Rocky muttered: "Just as easy to get secrets from as the Sp'inx!" and turned toward his own campfire. He ate warmed-over beans and corned beef; told Pope and Eleanor the meager results of his inquiries.

"I don't know what the woman could have wanted in that bedroom," Pope said. "We left nothing of value there."

"Somehow I don't think she was looking for anything," Rocky said.

"Then why was she there? Is there more coffee there than you want?"

"About a cup. You won't sleep."

"Coffee never keeps me awake. That's all in your mind."

"I don't reckon it matters if it is, if your mind keeps you awake."

"Well, if I sleep I will wake up with one side of my nose hermetically sealed and when I turn over, the other side will immediately be stopped up. I wish," Pope said, "that I had some Dr. Carr's Kill-a-Cold."

"What is that?" Eleanor said, laughing.

"A very soothing patent syrup. People drank it before Repeal for the sake of the alcohol in it. It has a much more pleasant taste than whisky. Actually it's meant for women and children first. I can see that you are getting ready to tell me no one should use patent medicine, Eleanor, but you have no idea how comforting Kill-a-Cold is."

"We'll give you half-a-dozen bottles for Christmas," Rocky said.

"Don't you think," Eleanor asked, yawning, "that we might as well go to bed? There's no telling at what hour Mr. Thompson may wake us up."

"His language will be fit to wake the dead," Rocky prophesied. "Maybe we can keep him occupied an' happy lookin' for that gun.—Look here, Pope; why'd the person who killed Cheney choose to stand at the right side of the path?"

"Presumably because there was a small gap in the brush on that side."

"Not good enough. Why else?"

"Because you were on guard on the other side of the house."

"Yes; that's it." Rocky stopped, looked blankly at the fire and closed his eyes. Eleanor put her hand on David's arm to prevent his speaking and waited. . . .

Rocky was looking through the windows into the cabin's front room. Two of the windowpanes were broken. The fire lighted the room fairly well and he could see Sapphira sitting in her chair. She took a drink; at least her head tilted back like she was drinking. Nothing happened until Lisa Wood came in with coffee and sandwiches. She and Sapphira talked but he couldn't hear what they said: Lisa went back to the kitchen.

Sapphira didn't eat anything right away and after a while David came in, frightened, and she took him back to the bedroom. So he decided to see if anyone was prowling around the other side of the house.

When he came back Sapphira was in her chair again, eating sandwiches. She ate a whole plate of them.

Rocky turned suddenly and stared at David. He said:

"Mrs. Cheney said no one could punish the person that killed Cheney. I guess she was right. Stand up, kid. I want to see how tall you are!"

David stood up uncertainly, glanced toward
Pope and sat down again. His chin began to quiver
and Pope was smiling as if he were pleased. Rocky
said:

"I cert'nly have been a damned fool. You two
couldn't figure it out because you weren't there.
You had to take my word for what happened. It
didn't seem important that when David came into
the front room acting like he was frightened—"

"I was," David whispered.

"Maybe not for the same reason I thought. I
supposed the old lady took him into the bedroom
to get him settled down for the night again. So
then I decided I might as well see if everything
was all right on that side of the house. I wasn't
gone ten minutes and when I got back I could see
the top of the old lady's turban. It's been bother-
in' me like bugs crawlin' around in my brain."

"Go on," Eleanor said impatiently.

"And it also bothered me that maybe someone
knew either Pope or me would be on guard on the
other side of the house. Maybe any of the others could have known we probably would be, but
Sapphira would be a lot more apt to have known
Pope was there the first night he was here. And
if the person that killed Cheney didn't get away
down the path right after Mrs. Leroy, he'd have to
choose the right side of the house to go aroun'.
Which would bring you to the front door again.

"Sapphira was an awful small woman. David's about her height. They was dressed so much alike that if he put on her robe an' turban you might think he was Sapphira as long as you didn't see his face. All I did see was the top of a head. She was stout, but her robe was full and so's David's.

"Anyway, she wanted Lisa out of the bedroom even if she didn't admit it. An' you remember how she straightened her turban when we were talkin' to her after Cheney was killed. Like she might've put it on in a hurry. An' I thought I saw her eat a whole stack of sandwiches, but Lisa said she hardly ate anything at all but David ate all the time."

"Conclusive!" Eleanor said dryly.

"Unh-uh. Only I didn't really see her come back to her chair so I shouldn't have said I did."

Eleanor put her hand on David's shoulder. "Don't you think you should let him tell his story? You're frightening him."

"I've been frightened a long time. Will they put me in jail for what I did?"

"Good Lord, no! I suppose the old—your grandmamma made you do—whatever you did," Rocky said.

"She said she'd whip me if I didn't. She never did that but twice, but I didn't," David said, wincing, "want her to do it again. Besides, she said Saul was going to try to take me away from her.

And she didn't tell me what she was going to do, but she did have a gun."

"What kind?"

"I don't know, Mr. Allan. Only it loaded different than Mrs. Allan's does. Well, Saul and Grandma were talking yesterday and I wasn't supposed to hear them. I didn't hear all they said but Saul said something about midnight and 'we'll have the lady where we want her.'

"Grandma said he meant 'where he wanted her' and she said something that made him mad. Wasn't he ever going to quit—'catting around.' Is that the right word?"

"I don't know of any better one for his habits," Rocky muttered.

"After that I didn't hear much except Saul mentioned midnight again and something about rocks, and he said Lisa's name once. When he was gone Grandma laughed to herself like she did sometimes.

"Well, after you people were there the first time, with Saul, she told me I was to stay awake and after Lisa brought in the coffee I was to come in the front room. I was to act like I was frightened at something because she thought someone would probably be watching at the windows like she was sure Mr. Pope had the night before. It was easy to act scared, because I was, lying awake and wondering what she was going to do; and Lisa wasn't there with me. Grandma really wanted Lisa to sleep in the kitchen."

"She knew Lisa was to open the door for Mrs. Leroy but that Mr. Cheney would be there first," Pope said. "Then, I suppose, she could use both those facts to cast suspicion on Lisa and Mrs. Leroy."

"Did she?" David said doubtfully. "I didn't know for sure Mrs. Leroy would be coming there, but I guessed some lady was and I didn't think it would be Mrs. Greer or Mrs. Cheney.

"Well, I came out like Grandma said and told her I was there and what did she want. She took me back to the bedroom and grabbed off her robe and turban and stuck them on me and a scarf pulled up around my chin. She took her gun out of a suitcase and put on my shoes. I guess because I'd been outside in them.

"She told me—she wouldn't give me a chance to talk—to go back and sit in her chair and act like she would and not to turn around. She said to put a handkerchief up to my mouth like I was coughing when I went out and to kind of stoop over. But when she'd peeked out she said she didn't think Mr. Allan was at the window any more and she'd thought maybe he'd think I'd heard something at that side of the house and come to see."

"She was a smart old devil and Mr. Allan did just what she wanted him to," Rocky said disgustedly.

"Then she sneaked out the front door and I sat there a long time. I didn't think about her not eating much so I ate all the sandwiches and drank coffee because she would have. Then I heard those shots and in just a minute Grandma came in all out of breath and she didn't have the gun. She put the bar on the door again and put on her things and told me to go put on mine and come out right away. So I did."

CHAPTER TWENTY-TWO
"THE WOLF WOULD'VE SAID . . ."

"Were you surprised to find that Mr. Cheney was dead?" Pope asked.

"I don't know. I guess not. Grandma dug her fingers into my arm so it hurt and I thought I'd better act as natural as I could. I felt like I must be dreaming anyway."

"She didn't have very much time to go on," Rocky sad. "Enough, though. She got back to the front door while I was chargin' around to the kitchen and making plenty noise doing it. She wore padded shoes an' she didn't have to get in the damp part of the path at all."

"And she was very—very spry," David said. "You wouldn't know how quick she could move when she really had to unless you were around her a lot. And she could shoot good too."

"I guess she could. She took a hell of a chance, at that. S'pose I'd run right into the living room or aroun' the house. . . ."

"She was a gambler," Pope said. "And old enough that perhaps she thought it wouldn't matter a great deal if she were caught. She'd free David from Cheney. And of course you'd run to the place where you thought the shots came from, Rocky. What did she say to you after we were gone, David?"

"She never had a chance to say much. While you two were in the bedroom she looked at me—" David screwed his face into a scowl, imitating Sapphira. "She said for me to keep my mouth shut, kind of twisting her lips so I could tell what she was saying. And that I wasn't to leave her.

"Then when Mr. Doyle was heating the chocolate she told me I could go to jail for what I'd done but that if I kept still, everything would be all right and she'd tell me about it when she could, so I'd understand. After that I couldn't keep awake."

"And it was because of what she said about your being sent to jail that you didn't talk after she was dead?" Eleanor asked.

David nodded, crying a little. "I wanted to tell, Mrs. Allan, and I thought I would if anyone was 'rested for killing Saul. But she didn't ever say she did kill him."

"But you were sure she had, weren't you?" Rocky asked.

"Well—pretty sure."

"Don't you think Lisa may've had some idea what had happened?"

"Oh, I told her, Mr. Allan. I had to talk to someone and so I asked Lisa what to do. She said she'd wondered if Grandma hadn't managed to kill Saul, but for me not to talk for a while. She didn't think it was my fault because she'd been afraid of Grandma too. And then when she was killed we wondered if she had killed Saul, after all."

"Well, you two would, of course. Only she always admitted she had more reason to kill Cheney than anyone else here seems to 've had, because we probably won't ever be sure how many of her business secrets he knew. She said she never let him know too much for fear he'd squeal, so the folks she was blackmailin' didn't have to be afraid of him. What did your grandmamma keep in that blue velvet pad?"

"What pad? The one under her crystal? Gee, I don't know. I never felt anything in it. I—I feel awful tired," David said, putting his head down on his arms. "Seems to me this is the longest day in my life."

"Well, I think you'd better go over an' go to bed," Rocky said to Pope. "Eleanor's wore out and so is David—and you'd ought to be. We can save the rest of it for Jake Thompson. He ought to be right grateful he's only got two murders left to solve."

He watched Pope start off with David, then followed them; drew Pope to one side and whispered briefly. Pope stared at him for an instant, nodded and went on. Rocky came back and began raking ashes over the fire.

"Does your head still ache, honey?"

"No, I'm just tired. I— Rocky, what are you remembering now?"

Rocky opened his eyes hastily. "The old lady's suitcases," he said.

"I thought I could read you like a book but right now some of your pages are blanks—to me."

"Prob'ly they would be to anyone. Look, Eleanor—you never told me what-all Lisa and David talked to you about this mornin' when you were alone with them. Tell me now?"

"Well, about Sapphira's being alone in the front room to hide those papers. But we found them. Then I got David to tell me how his grandmother managed to find him and about the people he saw at her séances. I'll give it to you in detail while I plaster cold cream on my face. . . ."

Rocky interrupted once, as she talked: "David knew for sure his father was dead?"

"Well—he spoke as if he did. I suppose he had to take his aunt's word for it. Do you—but never mind. I won't ask you any questions—now."

Rocky said: "Thanks," when she had finished and lay staring thoughtfully up at the sloping sides of the tent. "Is that sweater over there Lisa's?"

"Yes. Why?"

"Is there a pencil in the pocket?"

"The stub of one."

"Well, come on to bed, honey. Your teeth are chatterin' and you need a good night's sleep."

She did sleep easily enough but presently she woke, trying to scream because she had dreamed that a hairy hand was fumbling at her throat. For the rest of the night Rocky kept one arm about her, instantly alert every time she stirred uneasily. When Eleanor sat up blinking at the morning sunlight, they were both glad enough to go out into the crisp morning.

They were just finishing breakfast, wondering at what time the sheriff would arrive, when Margie appeared carrying a thermos bottle.

"How's tricks, Philo Vance?" she said to Rocky. "We've used up all the canned heat and didn't eat the stuff either. I thought you might let us have some coffee."

"All you want. As long as you're here," Rocky said, "I'm going over to see how Pope is. Be right back."

"I don't blame him for not wanting to leave you alone. I couldn't sleep very well," Margie said. "Do you feel all right this morning?"

"Except for dreaming too much." Eleanor filled the coffee pot and set it on the fire. "You'd better drink your coffee here and take the full thermos to your aunt. Would you like an egg?"

"I couldn't look an egg in the face this morning. I've got that dark-brown taste in my mouth."

Margie had finished her second cup of coffee before Rocky came back with David. She took the thermos Eleanor had filled and slipped away before Rocky said:

"Pope is hoarse as a frawg an' feels lousy. I told him to stay where he was an' keep warm. Doyle got kind of a breakfast and he can keep an eye out for the sheriff and tell him where we are."

"But where are we—if not here?"

"We met Greer and he offered to take David fishing so I thought I might as well go along. You can go over to the cabin."

"I'd rather go with you but I suppose I'd better prescribe for Mr. Pope again.—Oh! Good morning, Mr. Greer."

"I'm going to have another try for that big fellow before the sheriff gets here and I promised to take this kid along," Greer said. "I might as well get some vacation out of this. Are you dressed warm enough, sonny? You ought to have some real boy's duds."

"I put on an extra robe and the sun is nice and warm," David said.

Rocky came back with his fishing tackle. "Well, you lead the way, Greer. Eleanor's going over to the cabin."

"I don't think I am," Eleanor said as they reached the clearing and saw Pope ambling dispiritedly toward them. "Not if Mr. Pope is going with us."

Rocky lifted his shoulders impatiently; began: "I thought I told you not to—"

"Fresh air is good for a cold," Pope said huskily. "I am interested in—fishing. It occurred to me— Well, you'll excuse me if I don't talk?"

"You needn't look so apprehensive, Mr. Greer," Eleanor laughed. "I've been well trained not to talk and scare the fish away."

"That's more than I've ever been able to train Eva not to do. Well, it's down this way." Greer led them down to the stream and then for some distance along its banks. "This is it," he said finally with proprietary pride. "The big one lays right in there under that log."

"It looks good, all right," Rocky said of the deep brown pool that washed gently against an enormous fallen log. "An' the sun ain't on it yet. What'll you do to me if I catch that fish, Greer?"

"Admit you're a better man than I am." Greer cast expertly. "I could probably get him with salmon eggs or caseworms, but what would be the glory in that?"

Eleanor walked a little way from them to sit on a rock at the edge of the stream. Pope sat motionless on the bank as Rocky moved down to fish the water below the pool with David standing entranced at his elbow. It was very pleasant here, Eleanor thought, running her fingers through her brilliant hair; enjoying the feel of the fine spray that dashed up into her face.

She kicked at a pebble and Rocky looked at her disapprovingly. A man ceased to be a very nice husband when he had a trout pole in his hands. But Greer was reeling in, and in spite of Pope's sudden explosive sneeze, landed his fish.

"Nice one," Rocky said, coming over to look at it.

"Fair. It's not the big one."

"How do you know? Have you and this big fellow ever met face to face?"

Greer laughed. "If you hook him you'll believe anything I've told you about him. It's going to be warm today."

He rolled up his sleeves; saw Rocky's eyes for an instant on a scar across his forearm and said: "Shrapnel."

"You was in the army durin' the war?"

"Yes, I went over with a bunch from Chicago. My wife was dead—my first wife—and I didn't care much. Well, as a matter of fact," Greer said, closing his fishing basket, "I didn't mind it so much. Everything these new writers say about the fighting is true, but just the same it's about the only—adventure some of us ever had."

"My father was in the war," David said. "I guess you never met him, though. Were you a soldier too, Mr. Pope?"

"Well, I was in the army," Pope said painfully. "Had mumps—both sides—in Camp Lewis. Measles in Norfolk. Chicken pox in Camp Kearney. Bad cold every time my feet got wet. My father was killed in the war too so I tried not to mind, but the mumps strained my sense of patriotism a good deal. Don't believe my father ever had them—both sides."

Greer chuckled as his line sang into the water. Rocky was looking intently at the stream but not as if he really saw it. The muscles about his mouth tightened briefly; then:

"I think your big fellow strayed away from that log, Greer," he said. "Or else he's got a brother."

He backed away from the edge of the bank, his supple pole bent nearly double. David squealed:

"Why don't you pull him in? He'll get away!"

"You don't just yank them in when they're this big, David." Rocky played out his line again. "Got to let him wear himself out a little."

"I saw his tail then!"

"He's a whopper, all right," Greer said, putting down his own pole. "Don't stand too close to him, youngster." He watched Rocky approvingly, his round face glistening with perspiration in the warm sunlight. "He's getting tired. . . ."

Rocky began to reel in. "I think he's pretty well hooked or he'd already have gotten away. Still quite a bit of fight left." He beckoned to David. "Want to land him? Take a good grip an' keep on winding. Easy! Let your line out a bit."

"D-did he get away?" David said, trembling with excitement.

"No. Look at your pole. Try windin' up again— that's enough! Swing your pole over . . ."

"Beauty!" Greer pronounced. "About fifteen inches, I'd say. But I think he's just a little brother."

"You would," Rocky said. "I caught him on one of those gray hackles you like so well."

"It's a good fly up here and I'm all out of them. Have you any extras?"

"Here's one. I reckon it must've belonged to you. It's been out in the rain—on the path where Lisa Wood was killed."

Greer stood still, looking at the little gray fly in the palm of Rocky's hand. "I—mislaid one—" he began.

Someone had said once that there were times when Rocky's drawl sounded like a cat's purr. It did now.

"David, did your grandmamma ever tell you that story about Red Ridin' Hood an' the wolf?"

"Grandma never did but Aunt Martha used to," David said, his smooth forehead creased into puzzled lines.

"Well, if the story had been turned aroun' so it was the wolf that said to little Red Ridin' Hood—" Rocky reached out with a movement quick as light and caught David's wrists in an unbreakable grip. "S'pose that the wolf would've said, if she'd had a chance: 'What strong hands you have, grandson!' Wouldn't you have answered: 'The better to choke you with, my dear—'"

Eleanor was never certain afterward whether or not she screamed. But she was always to feel a little sick when she remembered that sudden and terrible change in David's face. It might have been a younger Sapphira who looked at them with unbelievably vile words spilling from writhing lips.

She turned and ran blindly along the river path as Rocky said: "I'd like to see what it was you took from that pad after you killed your grandmother. It didn't happen to be a birth certif'cate with your real age in it, did it?"

CHAPTER TWENTY-THREE
"THE HAND OF ESAU"

Jake Thompson said: "Don't mind if I do," and settled his corpulence more comfortably in the one large chair in the hotel bedroom. "About half a glass. What th' hell is that stuff you're drinkin', Pope?"

"Dr Carr's Kill-a-Cold," Eleanor said, laughing as she looked at Pope, flat on his back on the bed with his feet extending stiffly over its edge. "With a dash of whisky in it. He seems to thrive on the stuff. At least he's improved a great deal since we got here."

"He looked pretty seedy, all right. Well, Rocky. . . ."

Rocky looked thoughtfully at Doyle. "How much of this you going to print, fella?"

"All of it," Doyle said. "Except about Minna and Margie. I'll keep them out of it if I can. I sent the dope to the paper when we hit Oroville but without being able to say exactly how the 'baffling mystery' was solved. You didn't seem to be in a talking humor."

"I wasn't. Well, Greer says he'll keep Eva from blabbing if he has to black her eye. Mrs. Cheney won't talk and neither will the rest of us if Jake says it's O.K."

"I never seen either of them ladies before," the sheriff said placidly. "I got a poor mem'ry for names—and faces. If we don't get any real smart reporters up here we can prob'ly pull it off all right. I understand the lady's already kind of explained a little to her husband over the phone."

Rocky put his whisky glass on the table and sat down in the open window. He looked out at the old mountain town of Brookdale, somnolent in the cool August evening. There were almost no summer visitors left in the big hotel that, except for the county courthouse, was Brookdale's one large and modern building. And the courthouse, Rocky considered, had been built for the glory of Brookdale by the rest of the county. He said:

"Say, Jake, have you got a shovel?"

"Hunh? Why sure. But—"

"Then why don't you take it an' bury this town? It's dead."

The sheriff snorted apoplectically. "You tough railroaders from Merton—"

"Please don't renew the eternal Brookdale-Merton feud," Eleanor said. "Rocky, you can't put off talking about it. How old was—he?"

"Not quite eighteen. He was born March, 1918. His father—David King—got sent to France that January an' died in Feb'uary. At least he got shot tryin' to desert. Leona Eaton only married him just before he went over. I guess Martha Eaton was kind of a conscient'ous lady because she wrote all that down for Sapphira on the back of that birth certif'cate."

"So he was really not six but about twelve when he came to Los Angeles?" Doyle said. "I saw him a year or two later and I'd have sworn—"

"So would all of us," Rocky said grimly. "It was him admittin' how he helped Sapphira out when she killed Cheney that made me begin thinking. Because she was smart as a whip. We all laughed because David talked so much but if he really couldn't hold his tongue would she ever have dared trust him on a proposition like that? An' imagine a kid that age keeping still even after she wasn't there to make him. And the act he put on after Cheney was killed.

"He might just have been—nat'rally bad, even at twelve. His father couldn't have been worth much and what we know about his mother don't sound so good. And we always did know he was

Sapphira's grandson, and he'd been with her five years. Even a kid can't touch pitch— It gave me a shock when he imitated the way she was supposed to 've scowled at him. He looked too much like her. She could act and so could he.

"Well, I couldn't quite believe a kid of twelve could murder two people. So I began playin' with the idea he might be older. I re'lized if he took after Sapphira in build his height wouldn't have anything to do with his age. He was already taller'n she was. I remember he looked across her shoulder at Cheney that first night. And—this don't seem important, you may think—he said to Pope and me that we were both very tall, weren't we. . . ."

"You are," Doyle said.

"Yes, but he said it like he envied us and thought he'd better not smoke so's he'd grow more. But if he was just twelve he was sort of tall for his age. He told Eleanor Sapphira dressed him up like she did because he wasn't very big. He just was admitting without knowing it that he knew he was undersize."

"I suppose," Pope said, "that was why Sapphira kept on employing him as she did and because people who came to her thought he was 'too cunning.' It's been done with child prodigies. Go on, Rocky."

"Well, that rig he wore kept you from havin' any real idea how well developed he might be. His hands was small and strong like Sapphira's. That's why I wanted to see him land that big fish. His voice was a lot like hers too.

"I got a friend who's thirty an' he'll always look like a pinkish baby. I wouldn't've had a beard before I was twenty-one if I hadn't scraped my face so hard with a razor that the whiskers had to grow in self defense. I guess he had that kind of first fuzz on his face he had to take off now and then with hair remover."

Pope sighed. "Yes, there was some in those suitcases."

"Well, Sapphira may've used it too. But all that stuff's got a funny smell no matter how they try to doctor it up."

"Rocky, don't give away my beauty secrets!"

Rocky grinned. "Well, I admit I learned about that from you, Eleanor. He must have got some of it on his clothes. He stunk bad enough because he needed washin', but I fin'lly picked out what that smell had been—as being diff'rent from all the rest. He'd evidently used it not long before we first saw him."

"And Lisa knew it," Eleanor cried. "Knew he had used it at other times, perhaps, but I remember now how she told him to move out of the sun so he wouldn't get sunburned."

"Did she? Well, we hardly ever saw him in a strong light and his face was smooth enough that she needn't have worried. I told Pope to take a good look at him when he was asleep and tell me the next mornin' how old he thought he might be."

"Which I did, without any definite result except that I thought his forefinger might be rather yellow. That made me think of the way Sapphira laughed when David said he wanted to smoke one cigarette before the judgment day. We thought she was laughing at Cheney but it may have been at David's little comedy. I began to think that perhaps that little act might have been too 'quaint.' Rocky certainly murdered sleep for me that night. No, Eleanor, it was not the coffee that kept me awake."

"Well, when you knew how he'd been raised I can see how you'd swallow a lot of his talk," Thompson said. "I'd have taken him for a kid who'd been around grownups too much. But Rocky says he made a slip or two."

"He did. I was the only one that happened to know both things he said. He told me his dad fought in the war. King might've lived through that and died a good deal later. And he told Eleanor his father died before he was born. I was going to work aroun' to the war somehow when we went fishin', and that scar of Greer's gave me the chance. Pope made it easier. We'd talked as much as we could at the cabin that mornin'. He went along because he thought he saw how he could catch David. So he said: 'My father was killed in the war too,' and David let it go. If King died before November 1918, David had to be around seventeen."

"And Lisa Wood's text?" Doyle asked.

"That helped when I'd started thinking about that dep—depil—hair remover, though it was mighty farfetched. She must have meant David's voice was like a child's but his hand was a hairy hand—like Esau's. She didn't mean 'hand,' of course: she meant he had the beginnings of a beard. But I reckon none of us could've done better than that if we didn't want to be too def'nite. Not as well, not having been aroun' Sapphira for two or three weeks."

"But establishing the fact that he was seventeen years old didn't make him a murderer," Eleanor said.

"No." Rocky got up and poured himself another drink. "But he certainly did benefit by Sapphira's death and had plenty of opportunity to kill her."

"But if he was doped, like I was—"

"Not till later. You were, Doyle. But I guess Sapphira didn't care if David was awake when she talked to Powell. He said she did tell him to play 'possum. If he knew how quick she was with her hands, how could she dope him without him at least suspecting she might? Did you think he drank his choc'late right off?"

"Why—yes, of course I did."

"But you said you took what was left out to the kitchen and drank it 'when it cooled off.' So his cup would've been too hot to drink while you could see him. Even Sapphira probably couldn't have been sure he drank it, with the poor light and him over on the couch, though he did drink it because it was all right.

"He said he pretended to sleep and fin'lly Sapphira dozed off, because Powell was late. So he waited awhile till he thought it was near three forty-five—her judgment day—and got up and went aroun' behind her. He—giggled when he told us that," Rocky said in a low voice. "It made me— sick."

"And unbarred the door, put that card on her lap and swallowed the rest of that veronal?" Jake Thompson said. "But you said Cheney made the card."

"Well, Pope guessed that. He said fingerprints probably wouldn't help if there was any on it."

"Yes. Though the card should inevitably have suggested the connection between David and Cheney. It was meant, of course, to suggest a murder for revenge or the work of a fanatic. It appealed to David as a dramatic gesture. But it was a peculiarly Cheney-like trick. Unfortunately I didn't think on from there."

"I didn't hear—didn't want to hear—what David told you. But it was Mr. Cheney's idea that he kill Sapphira, wasn't it?" Eleanor asked.

"If David told us the truth, and I reckon he did. Sapphira was right when she said the boy was 'impressionable' and that Cheney had too much influence over him. He had a bad heredity and bringin' up and Cheney worked on that. David must've been pretty superstitious an' ignorant in lots of ways and influenced by all those séances he helped with. Cheney worked on him two ways: told him Sapphira was a wicked woman and had ought to be removed from the earth, and he talked about what a swell time David would have with her money and Cheney in charge of him.

"Only Cheney didn't know David b'lieved just the first part an' that he also believed what Sapphira said to him about Cheney. He didn't know

David's real age. I reckon Sapphira thought he'd better not know he'd have charge of David just about three years if she died, an' not nine. So she didn't put David's birth certif'cate where Cheney could get at it an' maybe destroy it when she died. She put it in that velvet pad and told him she did. He took it and carried it pinned inside his jacket. When he thought it was safe, he was going to say he'd just happened to find it and it was all news to him when he was born.

"We knew some people wanted Sapphira's papers but they weren't disturbed. It did seem like anyone who knew what was in that pad could've found the other papers if they'd been after them. David wasn't going to risk meddlin' with them an' was afraid, anyway, to take time to get at them. But that made it seem possible that whatever was in that pad didn't have anything to do with Sapphira's blackmail business an' so she wasn't killed by anyone she'd blackmailed.

"Cheney'd meant David should poison the old lady but that didn't work out. He didn't intend to kill her till she'd got rid of Cheney for him. Cheney had dragged her up there an' then all those folks followed them. But he saw they'd be suspected if she died. The card was to help that idea along an' make David think he was a kind of holy avenger—Cheney was dumb in some ways.

He ought to 've known a message like that would sound like him. An' the kid was dumb enough to use the card after Cheney was dead, though he didn't get his fingerprints on it.

"David was as light-fingered as Sapphira, so he helped himself to Cheney's dagger the one time he was in the tent. He didn't use it the first time because the other way was easier. He'd hid it outside in the brush because he didn't dare take it in the cabin. So it was right ready and waitin' for him when he needed it."

"Did Mrs. Cheney suspect David?" Eleanor asked.

"She thought Cheney—like she said—was tryin' to corrupt the boy. He got careless an' told her David would 'make them rich.' She couldn't believe Cheney'd go as far as murder or make a child kill for him. Then Cheney an' the others was killed. She was plenty upset. She thought Cheney must've made that card and gave it to David. She was afraid David had taken the dagger.

"But she said she was fond of children and couldn't stand to speak too quick. You know what she was going to do? Hide out in that bedroom an' watch him all night because she thought it was her duty. But you couldn't get her to talk till she was sure. She suspected Sapphira'd killed Cheney even if she didn't see how. When I told her Sapphira

had prob'ly killed another man years ago I guess
she thought what David had inherited from the
old lady. That was when she said 'the sins of the
fathers . . .'"

"And Lisa?" Eleanor said as Rocky was silent
for a few minutes.

"I'm—sorry about her. It shouldn't have happened. If he hadn't killed her we wouldn't have
caught him. She was the first girl he'd ever really known. I don't know what the old lady's plans
were but he said he thought he'd like to marry her.
He told her so anyway. He told her all about how
much money they'd have and what they could do
with it. She'd never had anything much but she
must have had some—principle, I reckon you'd
call it.

"Well, she couldn't *know* who killed Sapphira—
she wasn't in the cabin then. And if Sapphira killed
Cheney, Lisa wasn't killed because of anything she
knew about his death. Mrs. Leroy had talked to
her but their stories agreed an' she'd hardly spoken to the others. So about all she could know was
something about David or something he'd told her.
Sapphira or Cheney wouldn't have trusted her.

"She didn't know David had killed his grandmother, but when she died so soon after his plans
for what they could do with her money it was
suspicious. She didn't know what to do. She did

know he wasn't what he seemed like to us. They had time to talk when I left 'em alone on the edge of the clearing. She must've began to be afraid of him and took a long chance an' wrote that text in her locket.

"Only two people could've seen her do that: Mrs. Cheney and David. Mrs. Cheney said she hadn't a pencil to give her. And even if she was lying she could hardly have attacked Eleanor. Lisa didn't get a pencil at the cabin and Mrs. Cheney said she came straight there after looking up that text. So she must have used the pencil in her sweater. None of us saw her get that or write in the locket. So she did the writing when she and David were alone in camp."

"While I was with Margie? And you were on the hill and Mr. Pope in the tent and David lying in the lean-to pretending to read," Eleanor said. "I remember now that when we gathered things up to carry into the tent before the rain began, Lisa's sweater was one of the things I picked up. I started to put it on David when it began to rain and then dropped it when it made me think of Lisa."

"Well, I guess she was restless. Maybe she wanted to think things over and she'd said she liked it down by the crick. She probably thought David was asleep or reading. So she made an excuse to go to the river. The minute he saw her leave—he could guess by the water bag where she'd go—he got into the trees an' to the cabin the way I did when I went to mount guard there. Then he went aroun' it and came out on the path after he'd got his dagger. Got back to camp just before Eleanor and I met there. She didn't go to meet him: we made a mistake there. I don't know just why she happened to ask what time it was.

"Fate—or somethin'—kind of caught up with David far as that gray hackle was concerned. Nine out of ten times the hook would've stuck tight in the pocket of his robe, but somehow it fell out when he bent over to get that locket—which she wasn't wearin'. Greer remembered giving that fly to David, but bein' a gentleman wasn't going to speak too quick when I showed it to him."

"But I still can't see how David could have hit me over the head when he was with Mr. Pope," Eleanor said.

"He wasn't with me all the time, I'm sorry to say. I sent him into the cabin because I didn't want to be bothered with him outside. I was in back of the cabin with the kitchen door closed, so I couldn't see him."

"And that gave him his chance," Rocky said. "He just had a few feet to go to get into the trees aroun' the clearing and then he worked his way over to the path to our camp an' waited with a nice heavy piece of wood from the cabin in his hand.

"He took an awful risk, but he thought he could say he was just curious—like a kid—and wanderin' around, if he got caught. When we did read what was in the locket I reckon he was relieved. He'd thought she'd be more def'nite. But there it was. Anyone else would've had to guess a lot from what Margie an' Mrs. Cheney did say in the cabin, to know there'd be a message in that locket. I never knew Lisa wore one. You couldn't see anything but a chain on her neck an' not much of that because it came down low. But David would know she had a locket even if he hadn't actually seen her write in it. He'd know what Margie meant by 'necklace.'"

"Queer, how he went to pieces," Doyle said. "You didn't have so much on him."

"He didn't have his grandmother's stamina," Pope said. "He was more inclined toward hysteria. He had her shrewdness up to a certain point but he couldn't think coolly when he thought he was defeated. The surprise of Rocky's accusation was too much for him. I imagine Sapphira was sometimes liable to fits of senseless fury."

"But aren't we," Eleanor said plaintively, "to have wedding bells as an ending to this story?"

Doyle reddened. "Margie still doesn't know if she wants to marry Hank or me. Give her time and maybe she will. Or," he added sturdily, "I might fall for someone else. Or she might marry some third guy. You can't ever tell about Margie."

Jake Thompson shifted a dead cigar to the left corner of his mouth. "I ain't very proud of my small part in this. I heard what the kid said—gettin' there when I did—an' what you felt like tellin' me. Well, I'd find myself starin' goggle-eyed at the kid in spite of that. After we fin'lly got started out of there he was so quiet an' just said Yes and No and Thank you.

"Them handcuffs bothered him and I said to him I'd take 'em off if he'd promise not to make a break for it. He said he wouldn't. We hit that real narrow cliff-road stretch ten miles past Manzanita an' I was givin' pretty strict attention to my drivin'. Well, I don't know if he intended to jump off—"

The sheriff shook his head, chewing at the ends of his tobacco-stained mustache. "I didn't re'lize he'd got the door open. He was on the outside an' he moved quick an' fast. There wasn't no place for him to go but over the edge. I got half a look at his face an' it was like he was—was in a kind of blind rage an' didn't know what he was doin'. Of course it saves us a lot of trouble—" He looked at

Rocky. "Would you have believed him an' took off them handcuffs?"

"I wouldn't have believed him," Rocky said finally, "but I'd have taken off the handcuffs."

COACHWHIP PUBLICATIONS
CoachwhipBooks.com

VIRGINIA RATH

DEATH AT
DAYTON'S FOLLY

COACHWHIP PUBLICATIONS
CoachwhipBooks.com

VIRGINIA RATH

FERRYMAN,
TAKE HIM ACROSS!

COACHWHIP PUBLICATIONS
CoachwhipBooks.com

VIRGINIA RATH

THE ANGER
OF THE BELLS

COACHWHIP PUBLICATIONS
CoachwhipBooks.com

VIRGINIA RATH

AN EXCELLENT
NIGHT FOR
MURDER

COACHWHIP PUBLICATIONS
CoachwhipBooks.com

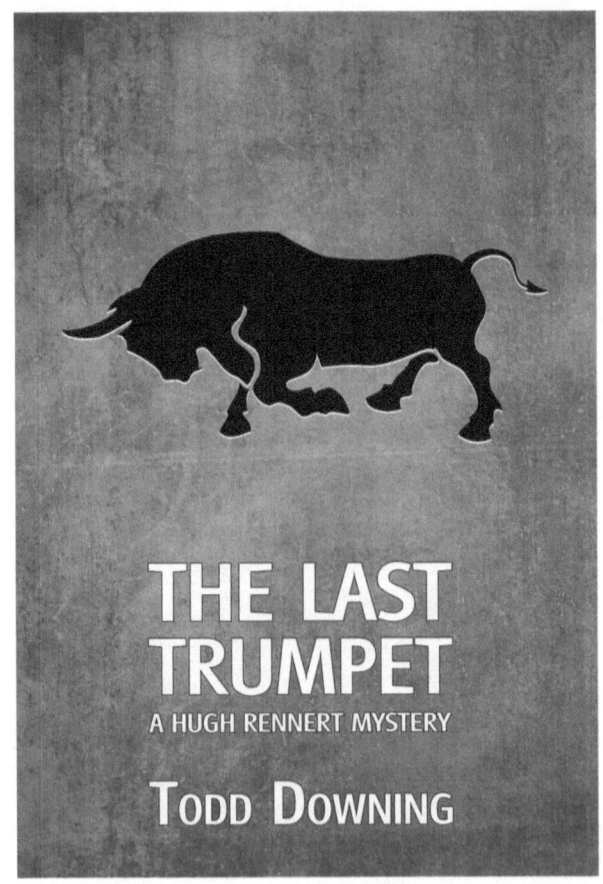

THE LAST
TRUMPET

A HUGH RENNERT MYSTERY

TODD DOWNING

COACHWHIP PUBLICATIONS
CoachwhipBooks.com

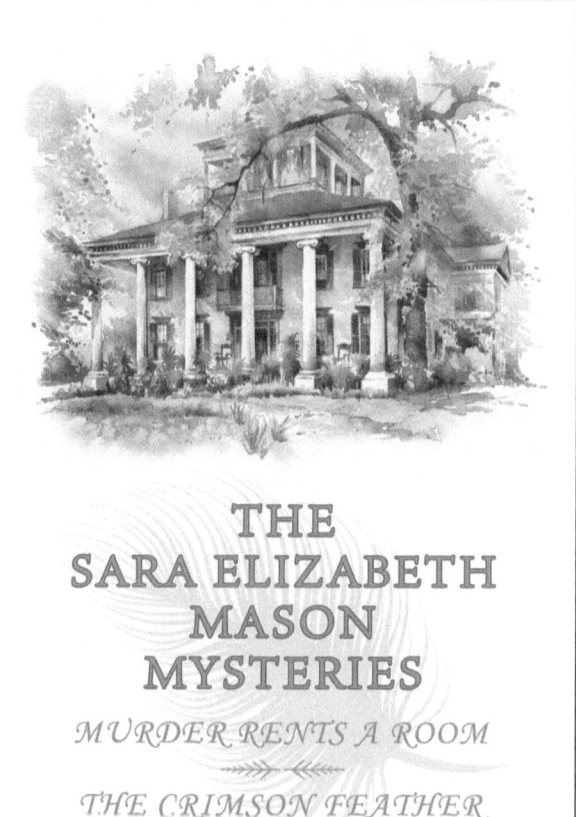

THE
SARA ELIZABETH
MASON
MYSTERIES

MURDER RENTS A ROOM

THE CRIMSON FEATHER